PANGEA

PANGEA

An Anthology of Stories from Around the Globe

Edited by
Indira Chandrasekhar and Rebecca Lloyd

THAMES RIVER PRESS

THAMES RIVER PRESS
An imprint of Wimbledon Publishing Company Limited (WPC)
Another imprint of WPC is Anthem Press (www.anthempress.com)

First published in the United Kingdom in 2012 by

THAMES RIVER PRESS
75-76 Blackfriars Road
London SE1 8HA

www.thamesriverpress.com

A CIP record for this book is available from the British Library.

ISBN 978-0-85728-463-1

Cover Artwork By Steven Brunner
Design by B2Creative, Asbury Park, NJ 07712

ACKNOWLEDGEMENTS

The World's End by Andy Charman was longlisted in Cadenza Magazine Short Story Competition 2008.

Signs of Our Redemption by Tara Conklin was first published in the Bristol Short Story Prize Anthology Volume 3 (2010).

Sofía the Beautiful by Mary Farquharson was longlisted under the title of 'The Eagle' in the Bristol Short Story Prize 2010.

Breakdown by Vanessa Gebbie was first published in Foto8—the photojournalism magazine.

LoveFM by Sarah Hilary was published online in Zygote in my Coffee.

Boston Brown Bread by Liesl Jobson was published in Diner, Volume 6, 2006.

Missy's Summer by Oonah Joslin was originally published in Every Day Fiction in 2008.

Fallout by Trilby Kent was published in The African American Review, Volume 4, and Stealing Their Churches behind Them was published in the Spring 2008 issue of Mslexia, and reprinted for Broadsheet Stories in September 2009.

Passport by Sarah Leipciger was first published in Room Magazine Vol. 30.3, 2007. Some Game was longlisted in the Fish Short Story Prize 2009/10 and shortlisted in the Bridport Prize 2010.

The Undercurrent by Clayton Lister was highly commended in the HISSAC 2008 short story competition and published in Scribble No. 46.

The River by Rebecca Lloyd won the Bristol Short Story Prize 2008 and was published in the anthology that followed.

You're Dead by Tom Remer Williams was originally published in Pen Pusher 7, and also recorded and broadcast by BBC Radio 4 as part of their 'Ones to Watch' series.

Places to Go and People to Meet by Lisa Marie Trump was originally published in Chimera Magazine and performed at the Poetry Cafe in Soho, London.

Mother's Not Home by Jennifer Walmsley was first published in Bewildering Stories in 2008.

All for just Fifty Baht by Joel Willians was first published in issue 14 of Southword. **The Fixer** was first published in the Momaya Annual Review 2008.

Shuttered Landscape by Fehmida Zakeer was shortlisted in the Open Spaces (India) 2010 competition and appears on the Open Spaces website.

CONTENTS

INTRODUCTION

The stories in this anthology were written by members of Writewords, an online writers' community whose founders live in the UK. The twenty-five writers represented come from, live in, or have connections with many countries including Canada, England, Finland, Ghana, India, Ireland, Mexico, New Zealand, Nigeria, Scotland, South Africa, The United States of America, and Wales. Naturally, the thirty-four stories reflect many different perspectives and strike a range of different tones. However, as editors of the anthology we chose the title *Pangea*, meaning all lands or all earth, because there is huge commonality in these stories as well. As readers, we can recognise the conflicts confronted and the emotions experienced by the characters in all the stories, irrespective of the cultural identities of the authors or the cultural settings of the stories themselves.

The Writewords website went live on Valentine's Day 2003. It is run by co-founders Anna Reynolds (editor), Richard Brown (directory editor) and David Bruce (webmaster). Anna Reynolds says of the site that it is 'as close as you can get to a real-world writing group but without the need to go out in the rain.' There have been over 10,000 members since it first opened, and although the actively involved members are a great deal fewer than that, it is still a very large and thriving virtual community. Despite its size and diversity however, it is a friendly environment. Anna imagines it as being like 'a big, friendly old country house where writers hang out, try different rooms and workshops, and at the end of the day, meet in the forum lounge to chat.'

As contemporary members of the Writewords Short Story Group, we—Rebecca and Indira—came to know each other and each other's work, and on recognising that there was a great strength and diversity of voice and view amongst our fellow short story writers, we decided to compile an anthology together. Our filter established itself quickly and naturally—of each story, we asked, does it evoke a world with a coherent spatial, temporal, and cultural integrity, does it transcend man-made boundaries?

If we were to try to categorise the stories, we might say that we have stories set in places the writers used to know, stories deeply steeped in places the writers live in, we have urban stories, stories set in the countryside, stories that are reflective, coming of age stories. Of the four stories contributed by us, two of them, *The River* and *Adoration* are firmly rooted in places we have lived in. The majority of the stories in the anthology examine relationships be they familial, parental, or other. Broadly, they might be classified as stories of loss, identity, entrapment, and order and chaos. Liesl Jobson is one among the nine authors who has contributed two stories, both, in her case, set in her native South Africa. In one, *Boston Brown Bread*, a boy enmeshed in the complexity of family, culture and social balance, is beginning to glimpse his own inner identity—the scene is brilliantly set in the kitchen where he helps his mother make batter for bread while his father looks on and pontificates about the world. The idea of identity arises again in Stephen Tyson's finely observed story, *Hollows*, set in the English countryside of Cumbria, where a young boy discovers the fragility of friendship when he and his friend, looking for newts in a pond that smells of 'molasses and mouldy bread' are interrupted by a girl all 'jutting and bony'. The boy in Dee Weaver's *Hunter's Quarry*, an extraordinary story of displaced roots, has already, and with tenacious insistence, established his own identity as an act of rebellion.

Stories that comment on life in a place other than the author's own often have a sense of being acutely observed. In Joel Willan's moving story, *All for just Fifty Baht*, Sinee, who must decide whether to follow her American 'farang' even further from her family than she is already, asks the fortune birds at the Wat Ratchapradit Temple in Bangkok to help her make a decision. Trilby Kent writes with clarity and honesty, in *Stealing their Churches behind Them*, in which Wilf, returning to South Africa for the first time in thirty years, is forced to confront his own behaviour as well as that of the world he grew up in. The carefully paced *The World's End* by Andy Charman takes the reader back to 1846 and the Dorset countryside where two brothers are reconciled after a long separation. This too, can be seen as a story about identity, as can Clayton Lister's *The Undercurrent*, an intriguing story in which the ghost of a child trails an old man to the river and in the process discovers the identity of her own father.

Some of our stories can be described as having the theme of order versus chaos. We have included two particularly hard-hitting stories, *The Doe* and *Some Games*. In *The Doe*, author John Bolland, examines with raw intensity, a man's confrontation and failure on the road, and in parallel, in his life. *Some Game*, a story from Sarah Leipciger, is chilling in the extreme, as it is apparent that the character of the young girl telling her story here has come directly from real life in twenty-first century London.

Each of our stories opens up a world that is intimate and all encompassing. Nigerian writer, Shola Olowu-Asante, takes us into the drama of preparations for a big birthday party in her vibrant story, *Big Sister*, where Mama Kunle has visions of re-establishing her place as a first wife. The balance of order and chaos teeters back and forth when a schoolteacher reaches out to one of her disturbed young students in the tightly paced *Manic* by Juli Klass. *You're Dead* is both the title and the school bully's terrifying threat in Tom Remer William's skilfully controlled and disturbing story, where finally the bully goes too far and chaos must return to order.

Entrapment, be it in social expectations, physical space, emotional attachment, or in chosen lifestyle is another theme we saw amongst the stories. The cultural context is transcended in Fehmida Zakeer's sensitive story, *Shuttered Landscape*, where reluctant bride-to-be Razia, who is to be married the next day, opens an old trunk containing saved bits of fabric that trigger a mental journey of her past life. *Places to Go and People to Meet* is a brave and unusual piece from Lisa Marie Trump. Set in London, this is a story of young street people surviving and operating in a drug induced swirl. In *Rabbit Cake*, Emmanuella Dekonor draws us sensitively into the inner thoughts of a Ghanaian girl trying hard to please her sister with whom she lives in a London flat, all the while pining for life in her village back home. *The Wedding Fair* is a richly described story by Sarah Hilary in which Ella dreams of escaping the cloying sweetness of the wedding fair where her parents work side by side, he in chocolate and she in shoes. *Signs of Our Redemption*, a story by Tara Conklin, takes place in pre-civil war America, and is told through the strong and quiet voice of a girl in slavery who examines the implications of freedom and what it means to her.

Loss is often one of the most powerful and fundamental human experiences, and six of our stories are directly about loss—coming to terms with it, as in *Sofía the Beautiful* and *Breakdown*, or denying it as in *Mother's not Home*.

Mary Farquharson contributed the wonderfully entitled contemporary allegory, *Sofía the Beautiful*, in which a Mexican farmer who is confronting his daughter's independence chances upon the American president's eagle, Alberta, 'a symbol of ... freedom and excellence' and must decide what to do with the animal. In the beautifully rendered story, *Breakdown* by Vanessa Gebbie, Tom, the breakdown man, keeps a list and uses randomly chosen photos to deal with personal tragedy. Caroline Robinson's *Matilda and the Missing* is a haunting tale with a powerful sense of loneliness in which Isaac, who has the ability to find lost objects, contemplates his own irreplaceable loss. Oonah Joslin's convincingly told *Missy's Summer*, is a story of loss and fragmentation set on a farm in Ireland, and seen through the eyes of a young girl when 'a crack opened up in Mammy's heart.' *Mother's not home*, Jennifer Walmsley's tender story, tells of a deeply vulnerable man who does all he can to stop the social worker from getting into the house to discover what he is hiding. Then, a story from Katie Mayes, *There's Nothing I can Do*, told with simple clarity, examines loss from the unique perspective of a ghost girl who tries in vain to bring balance back in the world she has had to leave.

All thirty-four stories collected here address important issues in human life. However, in the end, rather than highlighting the differences in our many cultures, the stories, brought together, show instead how strongly bound we all are to each other through our shared experiences and hopes. It has been a fascinating challenge for both of us to work on this project from different ends of the 'real' world—Mumbai in India, and Bristol in the south west of England. We think this collaboration between us is a perfect demonstration in itself of how small the world really is ... and how Pangea.

Rebecca Lloyd and Indira Chandrasekhar.

1. THE RIVER

by Rebecca Lloyd

I didn't know my grandfather had started fishing for eels again until the
landlord of The Ropemaker beckoned me one afternoon as I came home from
work. 'I've banned him from the walkway. You should look after him better,
Miss,' he warned me. 'He pulled up a whooping great thing and my son had
to help him with it. They lost it. The old geezer said he'd gladly have gone
down with it.'

'That sounds like him,' I said, looking towards our house. 'How big was it?'

'Girth of a drain pipe, according to my boy.'

Grandpa was on the balcony as I came in, looking down into the water
at the floating island of rubbish that docked for a short while between our
house and The Ropemaker. 'We never had rubbish like this down at Tilbury,'
he said.

'It's all the trash from the city, Grandpa.'

'Where do you think it goes?'

'Down to the sea, I expect. You were fishing again. You said you were done
with it all.'

'Tide's coming in fast, look.'

At high tide, water slapped across our balcony floor and wetted the
windows. In violent weather, you could feel its force as it struck the house
wall below in swelling waves, and pulled away and struck again. There was
a drop of some five metres between tides, and at low tide, the foreshore was
exposed for as far as we could see in either direction. We liked the sound of
the river's brown waves rolling upwards as the tide came in again, they made
the pebbles gleam, and deposited their foamy edges in a ridge of scum as they
reached out again for the river walls.

'Next door said you were fishing.'

'I was just checking that there really are big fish up here so close to the city. That kid from the pub had an eel bucket. So I was curious.'

I'd been busy with my exhibition and forgotten the long hours my grandfather spent alone, forgotten to tell him how much I cherished him. I stared at the scores of plastic milk bottles moving serenely in the white rubbish island. 'Did you eat something?'

'Couldn't open the biscuit packet. Could no more open the bloody thing than get out of my own coffin,' he muttered.

Grandpa used to dream about his death. I'd glimpse him sometimes through the patchy mirror above the stove when we got up in the morning, and terror was clear on his face. 'You can warp a persistent bad dream,' I'd told him. 'If you think about it angrily, you can take your anger with you into the dream and change the course of it.'

'I've never heard of that, Maggie.'

'Try it with the dreams you have. Tell yourself you just have to reach your hands up and push the lid off, and in a minute you'll be out again and free.'

'And tell myself I'm not on fire alone in a dark place amid horrible music?'

'Tell yourself that before the coffin slides behind that creepy curtain that doesn't even sway, you burst out and run through the crematorium laughing.'

'That'd be funny,' he said, but I could hear him thinking it would make not a jot of difference to the real thing. He made out it was working for a while to make me feel better; inventing moments in his dreams that I suspected weren't true, '... and I was flying above the library at Tilbury and I could see the river below me, all curving and glinting in the sun.'

'Yeah?'

'It was glorious, Maggie. As I flew in the vaults of the church I could see dark figures below with their hands raised up, and they were all hissing with anger. And then I flew over our old house with the concrete yard and the outside toilet.'

'I'm sure you did. But Grandpa, when you die, you're free from that very moment. You don't know anything then.'

'Maggie, it's not deadness itself I fear, it's how they fiddle and fuss, where they put you and what they do to you; they take away a man's uniqueness.'

'But you won't know.'

'Of course I'll know. I know now, unless you can do something about it for me.'

I'd had a persistent dark dream about his death as well, one I didn't tell him about for fear he'd covet it. I sing in the dream loudly, desperately, but it makes no difference, the monster he caught when I was seven, slithers off the bank with scarcely a ripple, taking him under the brown water with it.

I never did go down to the river with him again after the day he landed the creature, and a while ago he told me he'd regretted me being there too, 'It was a man to man thing, and you were only a wee girl.'

The smaller eels, bootlaces he called them, were only a few pounds in weight, and when they wrapped themselves around his wrists like living bracelets, I'd thought it funny. My job was to make a groove in the earth by the bank. 'A bed for them,' he told me, 'so they're all comfy when we get them up.'

When the big hit came, my grandfather got to his feet very quickly. I saw him brace his legs and straighten his back. He whistled low under his breath and muttered something. He gave no slack on the line, and three times the great eel headed fast for the rushes and he forced it out into the open again. 'Make the bed, make it really big,' he called to me. I could feel my heart thumping against my knee as I scraped at the soft mud with my trowel. 'Make another groove through the middle so it's like a cross. Do it quick, Maggie.'

The backs of Grandpa's legs were trembling. He had the net ready, and the eel was close to it; it rose to the surface and thrashed its pointed head about, fighting hard and foaming up the water. Five times he nearly lost it, then, when he finally had it netted and brought it to the bank, the fight between them escalated. Grandpa shouted and pleaded with the thing in turns. It thwacked violently in his grip and when he stumbled backwards, I thought he'd fall into the water with it. I backed away and looked towards the path, thinking to run home and hide.

Finally, he had it tight in both hands, holding it at arm's length, upside down. It was thicker than a lamppost, a great slimy pillar of silver-grey muscle. The creature thwacked hard a couple of times more and became still. It seemed a long while before Grandpa, his face white and set, moved again to lay it in the groove on its back. He beckoned me to crouch down beside him, and taking my trembling hand, showed me how to stroke it so it'd stay quiet. 'Talk to it gently, Maggie, stroke it softly.'

I felt like crying. 'What'll I say to it, Grandpa?'

'Sing the hymn you learnt in school last week.'

'All things bright and beautiful?'

'That's it. I've got to ease the hook out, and the man's got to stay very still so I don't harm him.'

I remember the sound of my thin voice singing the song on the wrong note, and the feel of my fingertips on the slime of the eel's belly. It wasn't deep-hooked and Grandpa was glad, although he told me if it had been, the hook would dissolve in the eel's acid juices in time. 'See, Maggie,' he said, as he watched me work the creature, 'you don't have to be strong, or a man, to do something awesome in life.'

And that was it; that was the feeling that had come upon me, if awe is a solemn quiet thing that reaches deep inside you.

'Why do you throw the big ones back, Grandpa?'

'Because they've come and gone so far against the odds. Three thousand miles from the Sargasso Sea, think of that. Mind you, no one's ever found an eel egg there.' He took the hook gently out of the animal's lip. 'This man's a toothy one, see? That means he hunts fish, and doesn't bother much with bloodworms and things.' He scooped the beast into his arms, and cradling it there for a moment, took it to the river's edge. As it slithered off the muddy bank and away into the water, I wiped my slimy fingers on my dress and Grandpa waved to it.

'I'm glad he's back, he looked all wrong out of the water.'

'Oh, you'd be surprised the places you find eels, and how far they can travel over land. They're gypsies. They're clever and free, not tied down like most people are, you know.'

#

On the night of the eclipse of the moon, I took the old armchair out of the living room and onto the balcony, and settled my grandfather in it with a blanket. 'A good night for eels,' he said.

'Grandpa, you remember when we got the big one, why did I have to make two grooves for it?'

'Oh, I just got overexcited. My own grandfather always made a cross for eels to get the devil out of them. They're not like other fish, they get anywhere where there's water, drains, ditches, ponds, the lot.'

I remembered the great wriggling mass of muscle and the way Grandpa sighed when he took the hook out of its lip. 'How big do you reckon it was?'

'He must have had a twelve inch girth, and I had him at about four foot. I've always wished I'd caught him at night. There's nothing like eel fishing in the moonlight. They go into the upper layers of water and the moon makes the small fish visible to them. You use a float then, and they're a sight to see swirling around the bait before they take it.'

'Did you do that Grandpa, fish at night?'

'Of course I did. They're nocturnal feeders, those men.'

'While I was asleep at home?'

He shrugged. 'Yes, sometimes. I used to go out with my fishing mates.'

'Did you want to be free—like an eel?'

He laughed. 'Clever and free and not tied down like most people. Who wouldn't?'

'You left me at home. How often did you go?'

'Oh, things were safe in those days, my love. It's not like now.'

'What is now like, Grandpa?'

He rocked forward for a moment and slumped back in his chair. I kept my eyes on the moon; it was brilliantly silver with grey countries all over it. 'It's meaner, Maggie, darker. When you get old, you can't be bothered with meanness and darkness because it's not your time anymore. But you don't want to mention it, because the ones you love, in my case the single one, have to go on living in it.'

My throat tightened. 'Was I a burden to you all those years after Mum and Dad died?'

'Don't be daft, Girl, you were the centre of everything for me, you and the men.'

'How often did you go out at night?'

'Well, you came with me at the weekends, didn't you? You seemed to enjoy it before I caught the big one. That day you were all queer and dreamy on the way home; I felt as if I didn't know who you were.'

'I sometimes feel as if I don't know you. How often?'

'Every night,' he whispered. 'Came back at dawn. There now.'

'Christ, Grandpa!'

'It's in my blood Maggie, eel fishing. I could never resist it.'

'Every night. I was a burden to you then.'

'It's hard bringing up a kid, Maggie. But you were no burden, not like I am to you now.'

'You're not, Grandpa. Don't think that.'

'Thank you, Maggie. But I have become a burden to myself.'

The moon was changing colour, dimming to a strange browny-red, and by the time we went inside it was hanging in the sky like a moist red grape.

#

The rubbish island came our way on the high tide at around four o'clock. The larger objects, lumps of polystyrene and wooden planks, gave the thing cohesion, between them floated plastic bottles of all kinds, and the lids from take-away cappuccinos. I never saw an island without a couple of footballs amongst the jumble, and a few shoes. The whole sad flotilla, a peculiar combination of the once cared for and the utterly irrelevant, stayed together in the calm waters, and if disrupted by a wave thrown up suddenly by a speeding boat, formed as one mass again quickly, aided by the underwater currents.

It was as if each object, disengaged from its original purpose, found a new legitimacy in the great river, where in its kinship with other floating things it formed a forlorn mosaic about the lives of careless people. And objects that once had meaning, private things—shoes, baseball caps, the occasional jacket, gave the island a curious poignancy as they floated amongst the other trash.

'Why are you taking pictures of it, Maggie?'

I'd rather Grandpa had thought my work was to do with the light and the sky; I didn't think he'd understand my fascination with ordinary things in the wrong places. 'There's interesting stuff down there, Grandpa.'

He came to stand beside me. 'I suppose there is. Are people going to buy pictures of sunglasses and rubber sandals all bobbing and floating in the water like that?'

'I don't know yet.'

'Funny business, life.'

He became ill for a couple of weeks that spring and the last of his stamina and muscle fell away from him. I stayed at home and sat with him on the balcony. We played a game of trying to name the colours on the river before they changed. There were afternoons when the tiny choppy waves that signalled the incoming tide were yellow ochre at their crests in the low sunlight, and the writhing valleys of water between them were a war of deep blue and silver. Yet, you could turn away for a second and look again to find the waves had dulled to a translucent muddy brown, and the green algae on the river wall was no longer vivid.

He was as light as a cuttlefish bone, and I could've carried him easily through the rooms of the house if he'd allowed it. Instead, he shuffled painfully from one room to the other and out onto the balcony. It was fine weather. In the early morning, a silvery-blue light lay across the metal roofs of the factories on the other side of the river so they looked like slabs of molten metal, and the detail on all the buildings was obliterated in the haze so they became no more than giant cubes.

I took him out to walk on the foreshore at low tide, along the band of white sand against the river wall. Closer to the edge of the water the sand turned to fine grey silt dotted with half bricks from houses once standing along the shore. We could smell the sea the Thames finally reaches sometimes, and in the sunlight, the old bricks cast square shadows behind them on the wet mud.

Then quite suddenly one morning, my grandfather was gone. I checked the street and the local store. I called out for him stupidly, and finally went to The Ropemaker. The landlord hadn't seen him and he looked at me distantly and hopelessly.

At four o'clock that day, the son walked in through my open door and joined me on the balcony. 'No luck yet?' I shook my head. I'd fallen into a terrible dreaming state, a state of knowing and denying at the same time. Of all the people I might've wanted with me, this ugly youth with remote eyes that slid about and never rested, was not one.

The island submerged and surfaced languidly, pale. Two tennis balls, furry and light green, bobbed amongst the rubbish and a shoe floated sole upwards nearby. I noticed the second shoe emerge from beneath a slab of polystyrene, and as if by its own effort, turn itself over to mimic its partner. The water was dark, all its facets sombre, slate-grey and rippling. A shaft of sudden sunlight flung a field of silver across its surface and blurred the island's contents. No boats mangled the pattern of currents and ripples, no birds flew overhead. A plastic paint bucket, half sunk and half floating, moved amongst the sticks and bottles. As the sun dimmed, a face appeared within the island, a face and body, hands waxen.

The boy caught hold of my arm and I didn't pull away. 'It'll go down to the sea presently,' he murmured.

Grandpa was beautiful down there; the water had softened the sharp contours of his face, and his hair floated around him like fine weed. His hands were relaxed and his fingers spread open as if in a gesture of welcome. He'd put on his navy-blue suit, and his tie lay like a strap around his chin. One of his shoes had come off, and he hadn't bothered to put on any socks. A sodden trilby floated nearby with a feather in the headband, it wasn't Grandpa's, but he would've liked it.

'There was an old geezer in the water a couple of years ago,' the boy whispered, 'in the lower pool by Wapping.' I began to cry. 'Only in his case he didn't have no family. He had a purse on him, they said, and they found a note in it written in grammar. It said I am Shaun Peters. I have no relations. To my way of thinking Jimmy was a lucky man having you.' He let go of my arm and shuffled backwards as if he'd suddenly become aware of his intimacy with me.

The island began to creep out of the recess inch by inch as the currents changed. Grandpa floated in the midst of it, elegantly. I could feel my fingers bruising on the wooden rail. 'I don't know what to do.'

'Don't do nothing, Miss.' The sun threw another blinding field of light across the rubbish island and blurred the contents once more. 'He might make it to the open sea.'

I felt a sudden twist of anger. 'You didn't know my grandfather.'

'I did too. Him and me fished together most every afternoon.' His eyes were deep and steady, and on my face. 'He's me, only old. Don't disturb him now. He wants it this way. Look at him down there; he looks like he's sleeping.'

The island swayed gently on its outward journey and Grandpa lay languid in the midst of it, and as I watched the beautiful serenity of the floating trash, I felt awe, if awe is a solemn quiet kind of thing that reaches deep inside you.

2. BOSTON BROWN BREAD

by Liesl Jobson

Renier Ahrends whisked his son's homework assignment off the fridge door. The fairy magnet that had held it in place popped off and broke as it hit the floor. Renier kicked the snapped off ballet slipper under the fridge and smacked the magnet back in place.

'Is *this* supposed to represent advancement in education?' he asked, thrusting the paper in his wife's face. His voice, which had once been a pure baritone, was now a rasping growl. She bit her lip and turned her head, continued paging through the recipe book.

The crest of the Welkom Preparatory School at the top of the page contained a stylised swallow that swooped above a curlicued scroll bearing the school's motto, like the one on Peet's new blazer. He'd been there just one term.

When a young black man had been promoted ahead of Renier at the Johannesburg head office, Renier manoeuvred a transfer to the mining town where traditional values still thrived. Just three years off retirement, he believed he might yet avoid the humiliation of answering to a black 'baas' who was also, he said, an inexperienced fool, an incompetent poephol.[1] His wife had wondered privately whether his attitude—and not simply his chain-smoking—was what had given him throat cancer in the first place. She'd said, more diplomatically, that he shouldn't speak so harshly. He roiled at that, saying he'd give up cigarettes before he kissed a kaffir's butt.

Renier flicked the homework assignment, pronouncing the school motto with punctilious clarity, 'Sa-pi-en-ti-a et Ve-ri-tas.' He scowled as his son

---

[1] asshole

adjusted the oven's temperature. 'I bet not one kid in your class even knows what language this is, let alone its meaning.'

Peet knew what it meant. He also knew it was unwise to reveal his knowledge with his father in such a mood. Pa would either repeat the ghastly tale of how he had been taught Greek *and* Latin by masters who reinforced lessons with heavy rulers on dull boys' knuckles, or he would demand the notice announcing the season's rugby fixtures.

Peet hadn't tried out for the rugby team and hadn't told Pa either. The grunting and heaving of so many bodies made him nervous. He felt claustrophobic in the scrum. He preferred the company of the gentle Mr. Bouwer, who taught him to play the recorder and conducted the senior primary choir. When the music teacher sent home notices of rehearsals and concerts, Peet lost them at the bottom of his satchel.

'Isn't that right, son? Do you know what the motto means?' asked his father.

Peet nodded. He would wait until Pa had had a brandy or two before he risked saying anything. His father's mood improved when his mother poured him a drink, but she was busy. Her hands were sticky, stirring the sludgy mixture in the bowl.

Peet wondered whether he should offer to pour one. But if his father were to say, as he did last time, 'So Mummy's little helper thinks Daddy needs a little helper, does he?' then his mother would start crying and nobody would speak to anybody for the rest of the day. At this stage of the weekend, his parents were still talking. Things usually went downhill after lunch on Saturday, although today it looked like it was starting early.

Renier read the instructions for the latest school project.

All Grade Seven learners will participate in Global Culture Month as part of the Life Orientation programme. In Week One, learners must research the dominant lifestyle of the country they have been assigned.

He sneered, 'Life Orientation, or *Lifestyle* orientation?' and gave his son a dark look.

Your child is requested to bring a typical food item from this country. Learners must prepare a five-minute speech on their topic. Your child has been assigned ...

'America' was written in Miss Smit's graceful script.

His mother levelled a cup of rye flour with the back of a knife. She'd bought the flour at the only health food store in town. She passed it to Peet, showing no sign of having heard her husband.

'I ask you with tears in my eyes, haven't we heard enough from America to last a hundred lifetimes?'

In Week Two, learners should bring music from the country they are studying. They will be taught how to download sound clips from the Internet in their Design & Technology class.

'And what's this about downloading sound clips from the Internet? Let's breed a nation of copyright pirates. Is that the way to go?'

Peet shrugged. His mother said, 'I have no idea.'

'Those educators I pay so highly haven't got a freaking clue. Don't even think of downloading anything at home unless you plan to go to jail. For a long time. That's plain and simple copyright violation.'

In Week Three, learners research the habits of the indigenous peoples of the region using periodicals like National Geographic.

'Indigenous people? Oh puh-lease. Who's studying South Africa? You're going to come home having learned to say, Eish! and Heita! and Yebo-yes!'

Peet would never speak slang like that at home. He couldn't even get it right at school. Black boys didn't want to play with him unless he took marbles to the playground, and then they beat him at the game. When he aimed at the target, his shot bounced wildly over the sandy terrain. He'd stopped buying marbles because other boys always went home with their pockets bulging with his.

At break, he would slip into the music block and practise his recorder instead. Mr. Bouwer had entered him for a Trinity College exam and there were lots of scales to memorise. He never practised at home unless his father was away.

In Week Four, learners focus on Language and Literature (details to follow.)

'Did you hear me?' asked Renier.

'Uh huh,' mumbled his wife.

Peet said nothing.

'And now Britney Spears is on the new curriculum and you're studying the poetry of 'Overprotected'?'

Peet tipped the flour into the sieve with the baking soda and salt. He wondered what Mr. Bouwer thought of Britney Spears. They'd never discussed her. Mr. Bouwer played CDs of the Amsterdam Loeki Quartet. He'd let slip that he had a lover once who played in that ensemble. Peet had looked at the CD cover when his teacher went to the gents. It seemed there were no women in the group. The picture of the players was very small though, and he couldn't be certain.

Peet flushed just thinking about Mr. Bouwer and spilled flour on the counter. His mother said nothing. If his father hadn't been there, she might have said, 'Easy now, darling,' or 'Wipe that up, my love,' but she held the sieve with hands that were starting to shake. Peet took it from her and turned the spindle. He watched the dry ingredients form a pointy mine dump in the bowl below.

'Way-way-wait. Let me guess. We ditch a Eurocentric system to fawn over American Imperialists and our son gets to study it? This is what Outcomes Based Education is all about?'

'Perhaps,' said his mother.

'And this is *acceptable* to you?'

The boy stirred the bowl with a cracked wooden spoon. He wondered why his mother kept it. She always said that germs collected in cracks. But she also said that germs were killed by heat. There were lots of other countries on Miss Smit's list: hot countries like Bolivia and Chile, cold countries, like Denmark, England, France. It was a pity his surname was Ahrends. Miss Smit had assigned the countries alphabetically.

Peet poured a slow stream of Lyle's Molasses-Flavoured Golden Syrup into the buttermilk, which had pooled in the bottom of the mixer. Pure molasses was unavailable in Welkom, his mother had said. She thought one might buy it at Thrupps in Johannesburg.

The ingredients swirled into a uniform toffee-coloured mixture. Peet wondered if it would have upset his father less if he'd come home to find them cooking Bolivian bean broth.

'Can't he just take a Big Mac to school?' asked Renier.

'No,' said his mother, closing the flour bag with a clothes peg. At the library, they had found the Betty Crocker Cookery Book. His mother said she wished they still lived in Johannesburg. Peet wished he lived in Boston.

The recipe required Graham flour. Peet had looked that up in the Oxford dictionary. 'Graham' was an adjective of North American origin, denoting un-sifted whole-wheat flour, or biscuits or bread made from this, e.g. Graham Crackers.

'He could take Barbie Pre-mix Cookies,' suggested his father.

'He could not,' replied his mother.

She had told him while they stood in the dry goods aisle that Snowflake's Nutty Wheat was similar to Graham flour and cornmeal was like mieliemeal. His mother had been to America. He very much hoped she was right.

Peet read some stuff on the Internet about Reverend Sylvester Graham:

A Presbyterian minister, Sylvester Graham was born in 1794. He believed that physical lust and masturbation were harmful to the body, causing dire maladies like pulmonary consumption, spinal diseases, epilepsy, and insanity, as well as lesser afflictions like headaches and indigestion. Too much lust could cause the early death of offspring, who would have been conceived from weakened stock. He died in 1851.

Peet wondered whether Boston Brown Bread would remedy his frequent urge to stroke himself. Perhaps it would also cure the feeling that arose when Mr. Bouwer sat beside him at the music stand, and touched his little finger, which stuck straight out. Sometimes he slouched deliberately, so that Mr. Bouwer would place his hand at the base of his spine, reminding him to sit straight.

'Is our son learning about Imperial conversion or the history of North America?' asked Renier staring at the recipe in pounds and ounces.

'Looks like it,' said his mother, handing the boy a damp cloth. First he brushed the excess flour that had fallen on the counter into his hand. Then he threw it in the bin, and wiped the counter.

'Looks like what?' asked Renier.

The boy took a few raisins from the cup and slipped them in his pocket.

'Probably both,' said his mother.

She opened the fridge and removed the folded butter wrappers stored under the freezer compartment. Peet greased the inside of the transparent pudding bowl. He held it up to the light to inspect a line running from the chipped edge to its centre. The butter formed a ridge along the line. He ran his finger along it, trying to smooth it out. If his father had not been there, he would have shown his mother the unusual feature.

'So is the Minister of Education trying to produce a city of global traders, a nation of international merchants—or what?' asked his father.

'Dunno,' said his mother, spooning the batter into the bowl.

Peet scraped the bowl clean with the floppy spatula. He licked his fingers. They tasted of cinnamon.

'We're educating our son to be a new age man?' asked his father. He curled his fingers making quotation marks in the air.

Peet wiped his greasy hands on a paper towel before rinsing them under the hot tap. Then he fixed the lid in place.

'Maybe,' said his mother re-boiling the kettle. Peet held a length of tape, which she cut in longish pieces.

'Or is this 'Restoration of Family Values 101'? Is this the wisdom and truth of the school motto?'

His mother taped down the lid with firm strokes of her thumb and placed it in the roasting pan to be steamed. 'I s'pose it is,' she said.

'I'm paying private school fees for my son to bake American teacakes at home?'

His mother poured boiling water into the roasting pan. As it touched the glassware, a sharp crack split the silence. The bowl fractured in a clear arc. The family stared at the pudding that oozed slowly through the gaping slit.

'Ja,' said Peet's mother, staring directly at her husband, 'I guess you are.'

Peet felt for the raisins in his pocket. He would have liked to throw them onto a bank of pure white snow, to watch a crow swoop down from a lofty pine tree to make spiky footprints before snatching them away.

'Get another bowl, Peet,' said his mother, 'our job's not finished yet.'

There are only dusty plains in Welkom, dusty plains and tired oleanders. No crows here, only Indian Mynahs.

3. ALL FOR JUST FIFTY BAHT

by Joel Willans

Sinee crouches down next to an old woman sitting beside cages packed with sparrows, swallows and weavers. They bounce around, chittering and flapping tiny wings, eyeing Sinee while she undoes her pink heels. Even though it's morning, the pavement outside Wat Ratchapradit is busy. In Bangkok every hour is rush hour, but inside the temple she knows it will be cool and peaceful. It's beautiful, too, and difficult to find. Maybe her foreign boyfriend, her farang, will get lost. Maybe she won't have to answer his question after all.

'Want to get rid of your sorrows, child? Only fifty baht for a swallow, seventy-five for a pair.' The old woman flaps her hands. 'They fly so high they touch the heavens.'

'First I have to think, and the quiet in Buddha's house is good for that.'

The old woman grins. 'Silence is as precious as dragon's tears in this city, but you need a bird first. One now, one after you speak with Lord Buddha. Think of all the good it will do for your karma. Give life to another being, all for just fifty baht.'

Sinee smiles, the old woman talks like a street hustler, but brings her grandmother to mind. She counts on her fingers. It's now almost a year since she left her family in Chiang Mai. It feels longer.

'If Grandmother is to get better, we need money. There is no other choice,' her mother said. 'You must go south.'

And she did, of course. What else could she do? She didn't mean to end up in Patpong, but the treatments were expensive and the cash was so much better in go-go bars. The men were mostly okay, some even friendly like her farang.

Sinee tiptoes down the steps looking at her feet. She suddenly realises with horror that she has forgotten to remove her glitzy silver nail varnish. She feels exposed but carries on in, head bowed, towards the golden Buddha sitting cross-legged inside. Kneeling in front of him, she breathes in the sandalwood and jasmine until her throat tastes sweet. Two monks, boy apprentices in mustard robes, sit at the side chanting soft words. Flowers, yellow roses and violet lotuses, lie at Buddha's feet. Some still beautiful, others wilted and old.

She tries to clear her mind but finds herself looking at the monks. Their smooth, round faces wear a frown. They know what she is. When her farang comes and speaks with his strange loud voice, the monks will smirk at each other, she is sure. Despite their glares, the temple calms her. She stares at the garlands. They make her think of herself in ten, twenty years. Only Buddha's smile comforts her and she realises that her farang often looks at her with the same expression. Feeling a little better, she lights a stick of incense.

She hears his whiny voice before she sees him. Like a cat yawning, it sounds wrong here.

'Hey Sinee, it's me! Sorry I'm late, baby, it's been a hell of a place to find. Goddamn tuk-tuk driver didn't speak a word of English. You want me to wait outside while you do your thing?'

She nearly nods, but he might touch her before he leaves and she doesn't want that. Not here. Not in front of the boy monks. She gets up, bows, and goes to him.

'This place is amazing, and you look great. You don't know how much I've missed you. You'd never think I'd just seen you yesterday.' His grin stretches his chubby, shiny features.

He dabs his head with a blue handkerchief. She tries to smile at him, feeling sorry that he has to lumber around the sopping city in his bloated body.

'I got you this.' He hands her a necklace with a jade S and beams at her. 'I hope you like it. I thought it'd go great with your eyes.'

She thanks him and slips it in her pocket.

'Have you made up your mind yet?'

'I tell you outside.'

The monks' gaze flitters around her like a startled moth. She ignores it. Her farang tries to take her hand in his damp paw but she pulls it away. Outside, the sun has cleared a path through the tin-coloured sky. There has been no monsoon today, but the world still smells like an old sponge. Sinee puts her shoes back on and listens to her farang's soft wheeze. An old man's lungs in a wobbly chest.

'I haven't been round here before. I've been to Wat Po, the big old temple. Damn impressive, too, but this is somehow nicer. I can't put my finger on it, it's like it's been grown instead of built.'

He talks too much, even more when he is nervous. She wonders if she'll ever be able to handle his constant noise.

He nods at the old woman. 'They didn't have any birds in cages at Wat Po, though.'

'They aren't for tourists,' Sinee says.

He grins and stares as Sinee walks towards the old woman and hands her a new note. 'I'll take two swallows, please.'

The old woman snatches the money and reaches inside the nearest cage. With two quick jerks she grabs the birds and hands them over. Cupped in her hands, Sinee can feel their little hearts beating faster and faster.

'What will you do with them? Careful of their beaks, baby.' He puts his arm around her and she flinches. 'Will you be happy in Chicago without all this?' he asks.

Sinee holds the birds tighter, picturing the faces of her mother and grandmother in the haze of her mind. Then she remembers the way the monks looked at her, her grandmother's sickness and the flowers around Buddha, beauty gone, wilting. She sighs, kisses the swallows, whispers a few words and throws them as high as she can into the sky. When they are nothing more than swirling specks of black, she turns to her farang and answers his question.

4. ROCK FALL

by Indira Chandrasekhar

'It is very steep climb, Madam,' Joseph Raju told Marcia as they prepared to set out. 'We must be careful, rocks are slippery.' But he was not worried. Foreign ladies like Marcia didn't fall. It seemed that they could do anything. They travelled alone from one country to the next. They trekked high and low without fear. They didn't send for the wash-woman to have their clothes washed. They always smelled fresh and soapy. And they climbed rocks. All the same he cautioned Marcia, 'We must be careful Madam.' She didn't seem to hear him. She was busy writing in a small black-bound notebook.

Marcia was always jotting something down. Even when they paused briefly in their walk across the hot, arid riverbed strewn with boulders, she bent over the page, her rough, dry hair blowing across her face. Joseph, standing discreetly to the side, was looking down at the ground, but he saw the shadow of her hand as she tucked the errant strands carelessly behind her ear.

The sight catapulted him into the past. The first time he had touched his Jeeva's hair it had been to tuck it behind her ear. They were in the church quadrangle, and a sudden gust of wind whipped Jeeva's white dupatta[1] about like a main-sail in the cross-wind. Her cotton kurta[2] clung to her body. Joseph had stood still, captivated.

Then the dupatta set sail, like the boats in his native town departing for the open seas. Jeeva giggled and Joseph ran after the piece of cotton. By the time he brought it back, Jeeva's hair was like a cyclone around her head, a heavy, black, silk cyclone, alive and seductive. Unable to resist, Joseph caught

---

[1] A long scarf for covering the head and/or upper body worn by women
[2] A loose shirt or tunic

a strand of that piece of her and tucked it behind her ear. All this time later, he could still feel its weight on his fingers, a thick, silken, fluid weight. Jeeva giggled once more and stepped back, her eyes brilliant with excitement at his boldness.

'Come, come Joseph, we must forge on. Got to get to the cave and down before dark,' Marcia declared.

'Yes Madam, finished writing madam?' he enquired as he hurried up to her, his cloth shoulder bag swinging.

'Thank you Joseph, notes for a novel. I think I'll put you in it.'

He was to be a character in a novel? Would it be one that had a thick paper cover, with a man touching his mouth to a foreign woman's under a blue sky with brightly coloured flowers in the background? Or maybe it would have a shadow picture pressed into shiny paper, a curvy lady holding a gun and leaning against a man in a hat. Marcia was not really curvy, more square and hard and tight. Joseph didn't know how to respond. He stared at Marcia and she stared back. Finally, he said, 'Thank you Madam,' and she laughed, hefting her backpack onto her shoulders. Beads of sweat stood out on her fair skin that was turning red in the sun. She didn't seem to notice as she strode purposefully ahead, her short, sturdy legs choppy and confident.

They walked for two hours, along the dry riverbed toward the dam. Washed by river water for an eternity, the rocks shone dark and intense as if layer upon layer below the surface threw the sun's brilliance back. It was hot and hypnotic. Joseph, who had been here many times, was always impressed by their beauty. Shining—like Jeeva's hair, like her eyes.

'I am a tourist guide, specialisation—Vijayanagar Empire,' he'd told Jeeva soon after he met her in her native southern city where he was studying. She had giggled and her sister and friends who stood around near her, giggled like a chorus responding. The carved granite ruins of a forgotten empire seemed remote in their grimy, urban reality. 'I will show you. It is beautiful,' he'd said to Jeeva.

From the moment he had first seen the blazing hot landscape of giant boulders he had been compelled by them. He immediately put in a request to transfer to the region. The other tourist guides were locals. They had grown up in the granite, took it for granted. They took the rocks for granted, took the sculptural extravagance of the kingdom that had flourished there three or more centuries earlier for granted. They spent their energy wheeling and dealing, seducing young travellers who, mellowed by heat, camaraderie, and cannabis, were ripe for exploration.

However golden, the tourists never interested Joseph in that way. He found them distasteful and unclean. And once he had met her, for him, there was only Jeeva.

The day Jeeva had arrived among the rocks as Joseph's bride, it was forty-five degrees Celsius. 'This is it, your famous place,' she said, looking around as they stepped down into the dusty bus stand. He nodded and started to point out various features when she interrupted to say, 'I'm so thirsty, get me a Gold Spot, Joseph.' They only had Mangola at the shop, warm Mangola. Squeezed into the rickshaw on the way to the room he rented on the main street, Joseph tried to put his arm around Jeeva but she shrugged him away.

Jeeva was afraid to step out alone. Mosquitoes swarmed and it was rumoured that there were leopards on the outskirts of town. When she eventually ventured to the riverbed, the young men didn't look at her, but made crude, leering love to scruffy sunburnt girls from foreign countries with tattered clothes and easy morals.

'My friend Kumar, also a guide, his sister is ready to befriend you,' Joseph said when Jeeva complained of boredom. 'She is training to be ladies' tailor.' But Jeeva didn't want to make friends with some local woman with a vocation.

After a few days she asked, 'Where is the movie theatre? The new Rajnikant film must be out.'

The theatre was in the district centre, a two-hour bus ride away. They were late, but despite that, Jeeva was happy, chattering excitedly through the film. By the end of it, Joseph was exhausted by the imagery and the noise and the coarseness of it.

The cinema became a fortnightly event. One that Joseph dreaded. 'Three more days before movie day,' Jeeva would say happily.

Joseph's ardour felt like the river that dammed upstream, had transformed from a wild, gushing flow to a sludgy, polluted trickle.

Often they would meet some of the young men from town on the journey. Soon Joseph stopped going to the cinema, letting Jeeva go off with the busload that departed when the new movie came out. He renewed his passion for the rocks, taking intrepid tourists to remote meditation caves far above the riverbeds, accessible only when the waters were low.

One such intrepid tourist, Marcia, lodged in a guesthouse at the bazaar. She was exacting and rejected many guides before she met Joseph. He thought she found him acceptable because he was quiet and left her alone when she was writing.

Marcia liked to talk to him as they walked—about her travels and her life. And she listened to him as well. When her face lit up with interest he forgot that he didn't like her thick body and pale hair. He felt tempted to touch her strong, muscled shape. He told her about the extraordinary hidden carvings of the goddess.

'Take me to see that sculpture you were telling me about Joseph,' Marcia said after they had walked for two hours. 'The Adi shek aara Naara devi.... Oh you know I can't say it right, will you take me?'

He had tried to take Jeeva there once. It had been difficult to persuade her to come. It had been difficult to keep going. 'I'm slipping, I'm slipping. Why do you bring me here,' she complained as he helped her. A few steps later she said, 'Oh, it's so hot. I can't go further.'

'Come Jeeva, it is beautiful,' he had responded.

'Enough beauty, Joseph, it's enough, I don't want to see another stupid rock.' He walked on quietly and Jeeva muttered, but followed behind.

Suddenly she'd shrieked, 'Look, look,' and pointed with her finger. Joseph, who was considerably higher by then, thought she'd seen a snake. He took out his precious binoculars, a gift from a grateful client, and tried to scan the rocks as he clambered down. The binoculars slipped and landed in a crevice.

Jeeva was standing with a rapt expression on her face.

'What happened Jeeva?' he asked, terrified.

'Can't you see?' She pointed emphatically.

He shook his head, confused.

'That's the place. That's the exact place they shot Rajnikant in his last hit.' She indicated the flat rock on the other side. 'The exact spot. Song sequence.' She'd hummed a filmy tune. 'I have to tell Somnath.'

Somnath was Jeeva's latest beau. He had a motorbike. She didn't have to weather the crowds on the bus anymore. The movie events seemed to happen with greater and greater frequency. Often when Joseph returned home, Somnath was just departing, a pleased smile on his face. Joseph had tried not to care.

#

Marcia was telling Joseph about her recent break up. 'He never saw the beauty I saw in nature,' she said of her partner.

Joseph nodded. 'Yes, yes, I am understanding. Always the exact same problem with Jeeva.'

Marcia continued, 'Once I was so mad I felt like pushing him off a cliff.'

'I have same feeling, Madam. In my case, not cliff but rocks. I am pushing off the rocks.' He turned and pointed, 'This is the place.'

'What am I looking for Joseph? I don't see anything, no carvings,' Marcia stepped precariously ahead and peered at the rock faces.

'No, no! No carvings, Jeeva's resting place,' he said. 'There,' he pointed again, 'there is Rajnikant song sequence rock.'

Marcia looked up, startled. 'You mean,' she said.

Joseph nodded. 'Here,' he indicated where Marcia was standing, 'here, I pushed her off the rocks.'

'Literally? It's true?'

'Yes Madam, I am never lying. When recounting mythology I am always telling clearly that it is mythological story, not fact. When describing archaeology detail I am putting in full context, not presenting story like truth. That's why I am getting such good evaluation in my tourist guide course.' Marcia stared at him. He nodded. 'Yes Madam, 97%, first rank. Same way I am always telling the truth about my life.'

Marcia scrambled backwards awkwardly. Joseph thought she was trying to imitate Jeeva. He laughed politely although he didn't think it was funny. It was no joking matter. This was a sacred spot; he had consecrated his emotion to the eternal, burning stillness of the rocks here.

He regretted showing Marcia this place. He regretted telling her about Jeeva. He thought Marcia understood, but now her eyes were not shining but afraid, like he was a strange, ugly animal. He felt a surge of anger as he stepped towards her, and thrust his arms forward with a snarl. Marcia staggered and fell.

After a moment's silence, Joseph's sense of correctness, of formality reasserted itself. He advised Marcia to be careful, just as he had advised Jeeva. Jeeva had answered, alternately begging and screeching, her voice echoing and distorted. He had covered his ears and left.

Marcia didn't respond at all. If she was going to play games, he would leave her. 'I am returning to the town now Madam,' he bent down and called into the crevice. His voice echoed back faintly, Madam, madam, mad …

5. SIGNS OF OUR REDEMPTION

by Tara Conklin

Freedom is a curious thing. Are the chickens free, running their fool heads off in the yard? Is the horse free, galloping in the pen and tossing its mane to scare off the flies? It still got to put on the harness, reins slip round its neck and that piece of iron tween its teeth. Mister say you only ever ride a horse hard when there's nothing else to be done or else next time he won't ride for you at all. Lottie tell me not to think on things like this. She say it'll end in no good, and that ain't no place to be. Sometimes I think Lottie my only friend in all the world, and if I listen to her right and tie my apron strings and bend my head to whatever task afore my eyes, then my heart will rest easy and calm.

Mister and his Pa built the big house out of wide yew beams and nails thick as your thumb. They painted it white and the paint still there more or less, though peeling now in places round the door and near the upstairs windows where the moss's eaten its way in. The front door they built wide and tall, a proud front door, and the porch come out from the house like a bottom lip stick out from a face. Mister and Missus Lu sit out there on a summer night, rocking in the big rockers Missus Lu had old Winton make for her, and I hear the sound of their rocking, just a little creak creak, regular as rain. Most days I don't think of this house as a prison, but that's what it is all the same.

Missus Lu ask me yesterday if I'd take her to town, just us two. It's always Mister who take her, sometimes with old Winton driving the coach. I never go. I just know the house here and the stream, and the old dirt road that lead over to the Stanmore's plantation house. That house there is big, big as a ship, rooms enough for everyone in the county to sleep it seems, and dance too. They've a big room and Missus Lu said sometimes they clear away all the furnishings there and roll up the rug and just use for dancing, with Mr.

Stanmore on the fiddle and his man Hal playing spoons. Missus Lu went just the once. She don't go down there much no more, don't go much a anywhere. Which is why she surprised me so with her cravin for town.

'Just you and me Josephine, we'll buy us some new hats. You need a new hat, keep the sun offa your face.' Her skin white as milk, smooth as a peach. She wear her hat all day long, sit in the shade, walk careful over the mud in the yard. She was on the porch then, in one a her rockers, creaking away. I'd just finished clearing away the breakfast things and come out to sweep.

'Missus, who'll drive the horses?' I stop my sweeping and the dust settle back down, I see it turning in the air.

'Why you and me of course. Whoever said a woman can't drive a horse. I've been holding the reins since I was six years old on my daddy's farm.'

I didn't ask her if Mister had word of her idea. She look so happy, her eyes gazing down the road towards town already, her shoulders straight like they straining against the horses and wind in her face as we set out to buy us some new hats. I didn't have the heart to say boo.

#

Missus Lu not been herself lately. Ever since, well, ever since the barn burned down? Or the old cow Maisie stopped giving milk? I can't remember when it started off. For a while now Missus Lu's days been passing her by without a nod in hello or good-bye. She laugh sometimes, sitting on her own on the porch or in the sitting room, and she cry too for no reason at all. Lottie say its cause she never had no children of her own. I remember Missus Lu used to go down to where the field hand children played, over by the tall oak with the roots that rise and twist away from the earth so there's places to hide underneath, cool and dark. She would go down there and sit on one a them roots and clap her hands with them, sing songs, play hidey seek. She don't do that no more. Now seems hard to believe was the same Missus Lu that sat down there singing Round the Rosy, the same one sitting here now on the porch, wanting to go to town but not a thought as to how rightly she might get there.

Lottie down in the flowerbeds, pulling out golden rod and lady slipper. Missus call them weeds so Lottie pull them up, fling them back cross her shoulder into a pile on the grass. Lottie stopped pulling when Missus ask about town, and look up at me as I come down the steps to find old Winton.

Lottie raise her eyebrows just a touch and smile. 'Mornin, child,' she say to me. 'Have yourself a good ol mornin now.' She knows the trouble with Missus.

Winton got halfway towards getting things ready for town, hooking up the coach and harnessing Little and Big, Mister's two swaybacked mares, before Mister notice anything untoward happening. But then a horse whinnied, the wind shifted and Mister must've sniffed something in the air. He came striding up from the fields, poplar switch in one hand, yelling: 'What in God's good earth is happening here? Who is taking these horses into town?'

Missus Lu just sat, creaking back and forth. I'd already brought out her boots and her travelling wrap ready for the journey. She waved a fan in her face to cool from the heat starting to rise as the day pass from morning to noon. She didn't look at Mister, and poor Winton not sure which way to turn, he look at Mister, then at Missus Lu and stood his hands on the horse's back, not moving any which way. Then Missus Lu start to sing, a low sad song, making sounds like the wind on a winter's night blowing through all the open spaces in the attic roof, sounds that made me shiver when I was a child til I grew customed to them. A body can grow customed to anything if the mind tell it so, Lottie always say to me. But I don't believe that to be true.

I can't make out the words of Missus Lu's song, just the tune. She don't look at Mister and he just stood there down in the yard, dirt streaked cross his face shining with sweat, his eyes dark and cloudy.

'Josephine, are you looking after your Missus?' he asks me, looking up at the porch.

'Yes'm.' I'm standing beside Missus Lu's chair. 'Yes'm, I am.'

Mister look to his right and then to his left like he looking out for someone on their way to help him outta this mess, a farm with earth too rocky to plow, a barn full of old and dying animals, a wife not right in the head.

Mister look to the right and to the left and then step up on the porch and strike me cross the face. I hear the whistling of it in my ears and the smack of skin and suddenly I'm looking back over my shoulder, down to where the fields start and the few men Mister got left are working there. I see a bare back and a hoe raised, and another man staring back up at the house, leaning on a rake.

Missus Lu don't say a word, just go on singing her song and now I hear the words:

Over the mountain, and over the moor
Hungry and weary I wander forlorn

My father is dead, and my mother is poor

And she grieves for the days that will never return

Was this the moment? Was this the first time I knew I would go? No, I knew this was coming, sure as coolness follows a rain. One slap, then another, then a thousand more, or maybe one, or maybe two. Then one day, a day like any other, this day, the last.

Mister brought his hand down and step off the porch. 'Put those horses back in the barn,' he say to old Winton. 'Rub em down good, not right for them to be waiting out here in the heat of the day.' He don't say nothing to Missus Lu. It's planting time now and they all busy. He won't be back to the house til suppertime, after the sun set and too dark to work.

My cheek smart from Mister's palm and I taste blood in my mouth. I watch the back of him go on down to the fields and I don't touch my cheek though I want to. I don't say nothing to Missus Lu and she don't say nothing to me. Just her rocking and singing, creaking of the porch floor beneath the curve of the chair, and her voice soft as cornsilk, soft as a child's skin.

#

Lottie always say Missus Lu look to me like I a daughter of sorts, but I don't see it that way. I still just like the horse, the chicken, something to be fed and housed, to do what I been born and raised to do. Lottie say Jesus know the truth. She look for signs of our redemption, signs like the two-headed frog they done found in the river last summer, or the night the sky filled with lights falling, and it be so bright that all us at the house and down by the cabins woke and stood on the front lawn, even Mister and Missus Lu, all us together side by side, eyes open to that burning sky. Lottie say these all markers along the way, promises Jesus be coming soon. She waiting for Him, she tell me. But who I waiting for?

The rest of the day pass, my cheek grows stiff like the board I use for the wash. A storm gathers in the hills, I can see it shift from grey to black but not a drop falls here, though don't we need it. Night comes and Missus says when I pull the covers to her chin, 'Josephine, watch the rain now,' as though it's pouring outside her window and not in some far off place. I nod as I do to everything she says, foolish or wise, wicked or kind. My mother is laid under a mound of earth beyond Mister's far fields, beside a sickly ash with leaves that's always yellow when they should be green. That's where my mother rests.

Mister comes back late from the fields. Upstairs I lay awake and hear the sounds of him eating the supper I laid out, then his feet on the stairs and knocks and creaks of him readying for bed. Then it's quiet for a long spell.

I pull back the blankets and put on my shoes. I know each board of this floor that Mister and his Pa laid, I know each wail and whine, each spot where the wood now growing soft and weak. I know this house like it my own body, every curve and wrinkle. Mine but never mine.

I make my slow way down these stairs, out the wide front door, the porch rockers silent now, still as the dead and gone.

There's a moon tonight, just enough to see by, a slice thin as my smallest finger and no more. The storm rages far off, I can feel it in the air, and I'm running away from those clouds though I cannot say what the sky might bring me later on. I run. The ache of my feet. The thunder of my heart.

6. YOU'RE DEAD

by Tom Remer Williams

When Peterson was sent upstairs he was meant to go and pack, but now he's out on the roof and nobody knows what to do. The teachers are all standing around on the grass looking confused, and the Head is holding a megaphone to his beard and shouting upwards. His voice bounces off the building and echoes across the field into the woods.

Then the first black square comes spinning down through the inky-blue sky. It looks like a UFO crashing out-of-control and explodes on the path, showering the lawn with stones.

Teachers murmur nervously. The Head squats down and picks up a piece of tile shrapnel. He turns it over and over in his big hand, unsure what to do next. I bet he regrets not sending someone to supervise Peterson with the packing.

Then the Head stands up and shouts again, louder, 'Matthew Peterson, you are going to be in a lot of trouble for this!'

The megaphone sings a long, high note of static, which chases after the yell into the darkness. The next tile flies right past the Head's head, and shatters on the gravel behind him.

The teachers don't know this, but from where I'm sitting I can see Peterson throwing tiles down the other side of the building, into the staff car park. He knows his punishment can't get any bigger, so it doesn't matter what he does. The Head understands this too, and has run out of ideas.

It's getting late. Kip has come up from the woods because she heard all the voices and wanted to know what was happening. Now she's lying on the grass by my feet, chewing on something she dug up. Peterson's mum is on her way.

\#

Peterson sleeps in the bed next to mine, but tonight it'll be empty. That's something I've been praying for since my first week.

Once in 3A I found some boys cutting the heads off of Peterson's soldiers with a Stanley knife. I knew straight away there'd be trouble and wanted nothing to do with it. I even said, 'I am *nothing* to do with this.' They all looked at me as if *I* was the one being stupid. I left quickly, so I wouldn't be there when Peterson found out.

But then later on in the upstairs corridor I saw Peterson marching towards me, angrier than I've ever seen him before. The birthmark on his face throbbed purple, and as he got closer he muttered, 'You're dead' through his teeth, his lips not moving. When he ran at me I couldn't move, I just stood there saying 'wait' and 'but' like questions. And when his fist hit my mouth, I crumpled to the floor and held my lips closed around my bleeding teeth. I cried not from pain but because I hadn't done anything.

Later on, Peterson and I had to stand in the Head's room for hours, waiting for Peterson to say sorry. The Head just shuffled piles of paper around on his desk and did marking. He was prepared to sit there all night, he said.

We were in there so long that I had time to memorise all the authors and titles on the Head's bookshelves, and I hadn't even heard of any of them. Peterson spent the whole time looking out of the window.

Finally, when even the Year Sixes were in bed, Peterson said sorry. He was still looking out of the window when he said it so it shouldn't've counted, but I think the Head was getting tired by then because he just nodded to himself and told us to go upstairs.

Just as I was falling asleep a fist thumped into my belly, and I lay in the dark gulping for air, blinking away hot tears, desperate not to make any sound at all.

#

The tiles are still falling when Peterson's mum arrives. One of the teachers hears the car in the drive and goes to explain where her son is. She comes around the side of the building just as another tile comes cartwheeling through the sky. This time it stabs into the lawn and stays there, upright, like a shark's fin swimming through grass.

Mrs. Peterson looks even angrier than the Head. She snatches the megaphone from his hand and tries to shout through it but nothing comes out.

'How do you work this fucking thing?' she snaps at the Head, who fumbles as he demonstrates how to pull the trigger to make your voice come out. This time her shout works.

'Matthew? Matthew do you hear me? I have driven for three bloody hours to get here. You have got one minute to get down here, before I come up there and throw you down.'

Peterson is sitting on the peak of the roof. The sky has just enough blue light left in it for him to be a silhouette. Then I see the sitting figure stand and clamber down the slope of the roof to the edge.

Do it, I think. Jump, trip, slip, fall down and die and then nobody will be sad.

I send this up to him like a prayer—you're dead Peterson—for the slippery slate or loosened tile.

I bet he's smiling. The whole world is silent, and we're all watching him standing on the edge.

#

What happened is this. Everybody else had the swimming competition today, but I was allowed to go out in the field because I had a verucca. Nobody else was off games so I was surprised when I heard shouts coming from the woods. Whoever was in there shouldn't've been.

I couldn't tell how many voices there were but one of them was definitely Peterson, which was weird since he was meant to be doing front crawl. Peterson has the record for two lengths and always wins the swimming competition.

I started walking towards the woods to investigate, but I didn't hurry. If you've got any brains, when Peterson shouts you run away. But something about this shout made me go towards it, as if I already knew.

As I walked across the field, I could see everyone up by the pool. Chlorine floated down and mixed with the smell of cut grass. I could hear the dives hitting the water and girls' screams as high as Miss P's whistle. The sun was out over the school roof and warmed one side of my face. There hadn't been clouds for days.

I walked close to the woods, where the grass is long because the branches are too low for Mr. Way's tractor. Mr. Way's job is to look after all the grass. He is always rolling it and mowing it, sometimes even talking to it. He has a page in the school magazine called 'Thoughts on Grass' where he tells us about the grass and whether or not it had a good term.

I went along the edge of the trees looking into the woods but didn't see anyone. The shouts had stopped, so I thought whoever had been there had gone away. But then from deep inside the woods I heard sobbing, and saw someone. I couldn't see who it was because her head was turned. She was tied to a tree.

I ran in, and it was Gemma. She was shaking so hard she couldn't speak. Tracks of salt had dried across her freckles. The shoelaces had burned purple lines across her wrists and ankles. The knots were tiny and tight, and got tighter as I tried to snap the laces. I had to use my teeth, even though they always tell us teeth are for eating and nothing else.

When the laces snapped Gemma ran away. I could hear she was crying again, loud and free.

I shouted after her, 'Was it him?'

She didn't answer me, but I already knew it was and ran after her across the field.

Everyone was still splashing and cheering, and nobody seemed to notice or care that we weren't up there with them. She ran into the Lecky block and I found her in the French room.

'Just go away,' she cried.

'I know it was him,' I insisted, 'I heard his voice.'

'Go away,' she screamed.

I stood around outside. After a while I opened the door again but I couldn't walk in. The door swung back closed, and my shutting reflection looked like a hologram.

I walked back up the steps towards school. Inside, the long corridor was dark and smelt of varnish. Crowd cheers bounced through the open windows and along the empty walls, down to the Head's door at the end.

I don't like telling, but rules change when it's something big.

#

In total, I have had to stand in the headmaster's study five times. But when I went in there to tell him about Gemma, that was the first time I had ever been in there on my own.

I knocked on the door. A chair squeaked, and the Head groaned.

'Come in'

He waited for me to talk but I couldn't, my tongue thick and useless like a sponge.

'Yes?' asked the Head.

And then it tripped, everything suddenly spilling out, a long line of words and gulps only half making sense—Gemma, the woods, shoelaces, shouts, she's there in the French room, it was him, Peterson, he missed his race, I heard his voice—on and on until I had to stop to breathe.

Through the open window behind the Head I could see people in the pool, but the races had finished and they were doing bombs off the diving board. The Head stroked his beard as he asked me some more questions and then said thank you, which means get out.

Back in the corridor came the voice in my head, 'You're dead.'

I went back down to Lecky. Gemma was still in the French room and would only let Matron near, who came to the door when she saw me. The upside-down clock safety-pinned to the top pocket of her shirt reflected the sun into my face. She told me I wasn't needed, then went back inside.

Matron is big and laughy and has a nickname for almost everyone. Once I called her 'Mummy' by accident but she just laughed.

I walked over to the woods again and Kip appeared with mud all over her nose. She followed me back to the tree and watched as I threw stones at the knotted bark, picturing Peterson's face. I only rested when I heard voices approaching across the field. I realised I was crying too, but the realising made me stop.

Kip ran out to investigate, and it was Miss P and Mr. Trotter. They whispered to each other and Mr. Trotter knelt down and felt the marks on the bark with his hairy fingers. He was shaking his head lots. Miss P told me to go in, but I just went out into the long grass.

They were only in the woods for a few minutes, and when Miss P came out the lenses of her glasses changed colour and became sunglasses, hiding her eyes. Mr. Trotter followed, and when he stepped into the sunlight I saw millions of tiny ginger hairs in his beard that I had never noticed before. Normally his beard is the colour of mud.

I heard the bell ring but the thought of food brought sick taste to my mouth.

Mr. Trotter and Miss P started walking back towards school. I followed them, but hid behind the tree on the lawn and looked into the Head's study. When I leaned over I could see past the curtain, and that's when I saw Peterson, smirking like he'd just farted. I've never seen *him* cry. The Head was talking into the telephone. They couldn't see me. I wished as hard as I could that Peterson would go before I became Sneak.

That's when I heard a car engine starting down by Lecky and I ran. Gemma was wrapped in a red blanket and put in the back of the white car that's always parked there. Matron got in the front. The car bumped up the hill and Gemma held up her palm at me in a wave. I waved back, slowly closing my hand as the car drove away. I didn't want to go back up to school, so I walked out across the field again.

The sun was coming down now, and made the sky behind the school look like a gigantic bruise. Kip was alone on the other side of the field, digging again. Mr. Way was by the pavilion hammering something metal, and the noises came a long time after each hit. The three of us were a triangle, and in the middle the shadows of trees were a hundred metres long.

#

When they found out that Peterson was up on the roof the teachers sent everyone to bed, even though it was still early. They've let me stay out here on the wall by the pool because I am something to do with this.

Mr. Way is now over with the teachers, who are all interrupting each other trying to explain what has happened. I'm not sure if Gemma will be back.

Peterson isn't on the roof anymore.

When he walked to the edge he looked down at the ground as if he was about to jump. We all held our breath, waiting for Peterson's fall.

It didn't happen, and now he comes out through the back door and walks across the lawn towards his mum. The teachers sigh in unison, relieved that no more people got hurt. Peterson's mum snaps at him 'now get in the car,' and he turns to walk away. He's just about to leave when he notices me on the wall. He stops, turns, and he comes this way. He's going to kill me in some unthinkably bad way 'cause he knows that I'm Sneak. My heart is in my head as I wait for his words to hit me.

He gobs on the grass between us, then turns and goes away. And just like that, the bed beside mine becomes empty.

#

Now that the excitement is over, the teachers have gone back inside school. I'm sitting on the wall in the dark, with Kip lying near my feet.

When I walk over the lawn she gets up and follows and watches as I wrestle the embedded tile out of the turf. The surface of the pool is tight like cling film; the water so still you can't even tell there is any.

The tile sluices the surface and sinks. Waves bounce off the sides, echoing and overlapping, as the dark shape sinks beneath.

7. THE DOE

by John Bolland

As he checked the nearside wing, Iain sensed Cath watching from their bedroom window. He crouched down on the gravel, his fingers probing in the shattered headlamp. Rain was falling. He felt dizzy in the light. He drew his hand back and there was red on his knuckle.

Bloody fool.

Iain knew that she was up there. Cath would never sleep.

No dents but there were scratches on the wing and bonnet. The headlamp lens was broken though the bulb still burned.

Iain straightened, stepped around to kill the engine, dim the lights. The front door of the cottage firmly shut. The rain—straight, vertical—no wind. His key scrabbled in the lock. The smell of home. Darkness.

He hasn't been with *her*.

A doe leapt into a sudden white-light. Vivid. Bump. And a clatter. Her hooves on the bonnet. A hard, scrabbling surprise.

Iain stands, for a moment, in the high, quiet hallway. He does not switch on the light. He is wondering why he stopped back there. To check the wing, of course. Because that's what you do. You stop. Find out. This, after all, was different from those other, smaller, bangs—those nights he drove on through. This was big. Dark. B-road dark. Country dark. And it was raining.

Home sweet home.

He hasn't been with *her*.

He can't explain the lateness of the hour but Iain hasn't been with *her*.

Cath is not waiting at the stair-head, stern as Clytemnestra with her axe.

No dent. Some scratches. A roe deer. A doe.

She was already air-born, trying to break free of her predicament, the front of her lifted, her back-end springing up, the pale alarm of her haunches bobbing fear. Balletic, Iain always thinks; no other word. Only trained dancers achieve such weightlessness. So—being weightless—no dent, some scratches. But it brought him down to earth. The impact stalled him. He stopped to find out what happened—knowing full well.

But he hadn't been with *her*.

The doe was twenty yards back. He hadn't been going fast. The dark, the rain, the winding road—obviously. Hence, he supposed, the doe had *not* burst like an orange or twisted like a torn rag. Bright eyes in the flashing hazards. He heard her hooves on the tarmac. Not moving away. Scrabbling hard on hard—and Iain remembered one amazing morning, just past dawn. He was bivvied in the Spanish Pyrenees and watched a herd of Chamois scale what seemed to him a cliff, the click and clatter of hooves on bare rock, the silly giddy translation of the creatures, higher and higher up the face of improbability. Jacqueline was improbable.

But he'd been caught. Confessed. Cath had had her theories all along. The house creaked of its own accord. The dishwasher was sloshing.

Higher and higher those chamois climbed, pausing to look back at him, amazed that he should be there still, a bright blue tent in the perfect green of that meadow. Flag irises. Gentians.

Jacqueline had such wonderful breasts. In comparison.

Its back was broken. Only the front hooves scraped and slid on the road. The haunches slewed slack entangled. There was no blood that he could see. Everything was jaundiced and episodic in the flash-flash-flash of his hazard lights.

Inside the cottage, he closed the front door behind him, listening for Cath's footfalls on the bedroom floor above. He imagined her slipping back between the sheets, thighs pressed together tight to hold her knowing in. That bed had become her sovereign territory.

The doe was lying in the road. Not lying. Struggling to be up again, surprised how uncooperative she had become. She was three yards from the sheep fence and the thicket of gorse, flecked with yellow flowers, dense with spines, its branches wiry, fibrous, determined. She was a hazard lying there. Next car around the bend and crunch. Straight over her or swerve. He didn't want her burst like that or someone hurt because of him. He knelt beside her. Big raindrops. Cold. Her eyes dark deep. Breathing. No other sound. Nothing like moaning groaning whining screaming sobbing. Just breathing and the scrabbling of her two front hooves, confused. Such beautiful ears.

'Shhh.' That's what he said. 'Shhh.'

It does not take the hurt away. 'Shhh.'

'Don't sshhhhh me,' Cath had said. With Jacqueline he did not go back to look.

'Shhhh.' The doe was not comforted. It shuffled sideways, pushing carcass along tarmac towards bank. Iain reached out.

'Shhh.'

Her pelt was coarse. Hair not fur. Hard and functional. Like pubes. Beneath her ribs Iain felt her heart hammering. Hammering. No sound but he could feel her heart hammering for she knew he was a bad man and yet her only hope, her only solace.

The sky had been very blue that morning back in Spain. The tinge of dawn had faded but the sun was not yet up. The valley lay in grey-blue shadow. The chamois were climbing towards a blissful yellow light.

What do you do?

You take a firm hold of the head and wrench the neck broken. Best thing. One firm twist.

She wanted to live. This creature. Wanted to continue. Wanted to be away from this predicament. He recognised that. Wanted to be away from this predicament.

And who was he? Who was he to say? One firm twist.

There was strength in the creature's neck. Muscles knotted and twisted from strong shoulders to lean bone-sure head. Muscles which sprang. Muscles which now dragged her broken nether-parts towards the fence. He twisted and she twisted contrariwise, not ready, not cooperative. Live! Live! Live!

'Shhhhhhhhhhhhh.'

That twice and slamming Jackie hard against that wall and thrusting into her and feeling too her heart hammering.

'Shhhhhhhhhhh.'

He tried again but she resisted. She knew he was a bad man now and had become afraid of him. He had a penknife. A short, narrow blade. Blunt. No edge and hardly any point. He was soaked through now and trembling with chill. He opened out the blade. The neck, he supposed—with such a short blade. Find the vein and let her bleed out into stillness, quiet—no shame in that. He took her by the head again. Her frantic hooves stabbed sharp bruises into his thigh so he had to shield his crotch with upturned knee for fear of her, his palm set resolute against her cheek, the point pressed home into the coarse hair on her long neck. Iain thrust against the thick hide, hard muscle, terror. No blood spurted onto his fleece. She twisted away, the blade embedded in the muscle of her neck. He grabbed for it and she scrambled sideways, found some purchase only to fall again. He reached for the knife, pulled it free and stabbed. Nothing. And stabbed. Nothing. And stabbed. And stopped. Breath heaving. Heart hammering. Wanting to live. Hazards flashing. Scrabbling. The next car round the bend and who is he? What?

He took her by the waist, the forelegs live, the rear end a dead slump of ruined venison and bone and tendon. Her head twisted to look back at him as she rose in the air, rose effortlessly, lifting miraculous up and over the fence and crashing through the gorse. He heard her tumble down the bank into the field below, an eddy of limbs and confusions, pain, his penknife.

'Dear God, let it fall clear,' he thought, 'be lost in the long grass of the meadow among the cowslips and the thistles.'

He listened for a while.

Nothing.

He set his foot on the first tread of the stair.

8. THE WEDDING FAIR

by Sarah Hilary

Ella Derby's dad was in chocolate and her mum in shoes. That's how they met. Colin Derby was serving chocolate fondue in plastic cups with little pink umbrellas, and Laura Hart was arranging single shoes on velvet cushions. Harp music was playing. The hotel lounge smelled of lilies and coffee and Danish pastries. 'I really shouldn't,' said Laura.

There was a big arch of white balloons above her head. Her stand was next to Colin's and had a scarlet banner: Cinderella's Shoes.

'No pairs,' Colin said.

'Pardon?' Laura looked up, holding a satin mule by its dainty heel.

'Only single shoes,' Colin said. He adjusted the dial on the fondue machine. The chocolate made a sloppy sound as it was stirred by the plastic paddles. It was the latest thing back then, fondue. Colin was a pioneer.

'That's right,' Laura said, smiling. 'Just like Cinderella.'

'Beautiful shoes,' Colin said approvingly.

They were. White and ivory, satin and silk, with diamante buckles or grosgrain ribbons. All size five. Laura never showcased a larger fitting, although most of the styles went up to size eight. 'The chocolate smells nice,' she told Colin.

He filled a cup and arranged a pink umbrella with extravagant care. Then he placed the cup on a scrap of quilted paper and whisked it from his stand to hers, presenting it with a flourish: 'Compliments of Fondue Fountains.'

Laura laughed and took the drink, wetting the edge of the cup with her tongue to prevent lipstick stains before sipping at it delicately. 'Delicious! I'd let you try on a shoe but as you can see ...!' She gestured at the dainty footwear.

'Lovely cushions,' Colin said. 'Nice colour.'

'Claret. It sets off the ivory a treat.'

They both jumped when one of the balloons above their heads burst with a bang, leaving a gap in the white arch like the tooth missing from a grin.

'That's not supposed to happen,' they agreed, grimacing at one another.

Five months later, they were married. Laura wore the slippers with the diamante buckle and spiked heel. She was a size six. 'Nobody's perfect,' she sighed.

#

'Cindy, where's the sewing kit? This cushion's split a seam.'

Ella slipped down under the table, inside the folds of wine-coloured cloth that reached to the floor on all sides. Under the table was fusty, smelling of carpet and feet. The cloth was synthetic, alive with static like Frankenstein's monster. It clung to Ella, making the hairs on her head stand on end.

She rummaged around, searching through the boxes for the sewing kit. Most of the boxes held nothing but layers of tissue and the little padded toe pieces that helped the shoes keep their shape. Ella's mother always removed one shoe from each pair when they travelled to fairs like this one in Harrogate, leaving the spare shoes behind in the house in Ilkley, standing in a long row, toes to the front, on the floor in the guest bedroom.

'All that knocking about in boxes isn't good for them,' Laura said.

After being handled by prospective buyers, the single shoes would start to show signs of wear and tear. The satin would lose its sheen, the fabric begin to fray. Then it was the turn of the spare shoes to be liberated from the guest bedroom, and serve time on the stand.

Ella found the sewing-kit and set to work, mending the split seam with the tiny stitches taught to her by Laura for this purpose. When she was finished, she put the cushion back on the stand, underneath a brocade slipper.

A woman had wandered over from the Fondue Fountain stand with a little cup of chocolate. She put the cup down on the edge of the Cinderella's Shoes display and picked up the slipper in ivory brocade, holding it by a heel nearly as narrow as Ella's ring finger.

Laura smiled at her. 'Lovely, isn't it?'

'Gorgeous,' the woman agreed. She put the shoe down, took up the chocolate fondue and moved away, to the Vows and Wows stand where they were promoting venues for civil ceremonies. 'Who'd get married in a zoo?' Ella's mother always asked.

Laura Derby gasped and Ella looked up from the book she was reading.

Her mother was holding the brocade slipper by its pointed toe. 'Look at this!' She thrust the heel towards Ella.

Ella leaned and peered. There was a brown fingerprint on the heel. Chocolate-brown.

'I swear,' her mother said, 'some days I could swing for your father. Ruddy fondue.' She wagged the shoe at her daughter. 'Well don't just sit there, Cindy. Stain Devil—quick!'

Ella dived under the table, shoving the book out of sight into her pocket.

She was an expert in stain-removal. She knew exactly which Stain Devil to select from the box, a different one for each variety of atrocity, from blood to beer. It was astounding what got onto Cinderella's shoes during an average Wedding Fair. Ella crawled out from under the table and knelt on the floor with the spoilt slipper in one hand and the Stain Devil in the other. Dab, dab, dab. Never scrub. Her mum had taught her how to roll her wrist and the tips of her fingers: 'Coax the stain out; never attack it. If you attack, it'll dig in and stay put.'

Ella enticed the fondue from the heel with the lightest of touches, holding her breath until she started to see an improvement, and because lately the smell of the Devils made her queasy. The brown fingerprint lifted a shade at a time, from milked-coffee to pale hazel and then to a yellowy colour like proper vanilla ice cream. Luckily the shoe wasn't white. Ivory was much easier to restore, being a bit yellowy already.

She blew on the heel to help it dry, blotting it with a wisp of tissue, taking care not to let the tissue shred and leave fibres on the brocade. The slipper gave off the starchy smell of dye and glue. When she'd worked her magic, she held it up to her mother.

Laura squinted at the heel, turning it to the light in all directions. 'You're a star, Cindy-ella,' she said at last, placing the slipper back on its cushion and patting it into place, her fingers lingering over the pointed toe which looked from Ella's angle like the tip of a newly-sharpened pencil.

'Can I take my break now?'

Laura nodded. She was smiling in the direction of a shy-looking couple standing in the centre of the hotel lounge, gazing around them at the different stands. The girl was only a little older than Ella, holding her elbows in her hands, her arms tucked under her bust. The boy looked even younger.

Ella watched them for a while, even though she was wasting her break time. They weren't like the couples who usually came to these fairs, full of themselves, sneering at everything—until, that is, the girl would spot the tiaras and start squealing, or the boy would get talking to the Vows and Wows lot about ceremonies at Grand Prix racetracks: Getting hitched for a second time? Go around again at the Grand Prix!

Sometimes of course, the couples were excited—plain and simple. Excited by everything—the balloons, the music, even the vicar promoting church weddings in his parish. If the tiaras and tiered cakes didn't get them going, the wedding favours would—sugared almonds tied in stiff little bits of coloured net which spilled sequins and glitter when you opened them. Not even Ella could resist the favours.

Laura had caught the shy-looking couple in the beam of her smile and was reeling them in. Ella scooted for the revolving doors before her mother could change her mind. She was gasping for a cigarette.

At the front of the hotel, parked on the gravel drive, was a vintage car. Its driver was dressed in a steel-grey uniform and gloves, with a peaked cap on his head. He was smoking, strolling around the car with one hand in the pocket of his uniform. The gravel made a sharp sound under his shoes, which were polished like the peak of his cap.

'Could I borrow a cigarette?' Ella asked.

'As long as you give it back,' he said, a crooked smile creasing the skin around his eyes.

'Lovely car.'

'1929 Sunbeam convertible,' he nodded, adding, 'I put the top up because it looked like rain.'

The car was a brilliant peacock-blue, with the hard dazzle of enamel. Ella wanted to touch it, skate her fingers over the paintwork and feel them slide. She loved its severe lines and narrow nose, the round headlamps mounted on a metal brace like eyes on stalks. Peering inside, she saw the deep-buttoned pleats of its seats, the colour of clotted cream. The car smelt of wax and polish, a sweetly abrasive scent which Ella wanted to sniff and sniff until it filled her lungs. The car's top was soft and black, looking like leather or skin, faded in the places where it was stretched over a skeleton of struts.

'A beauty, isn't she?' the man said.

'Yes.... Thanks for the smoke.'

Ella made her way around to the side of the hotel. A fire escape led down from the top storey. She climbed its cast-iron steps to the fifth floor, where she sat, hiding her feet under her long skirt. She wriggled her fingers at the waist of the skirt, retrieving the strip of matches she'd lifted from the hotel bar. Scratching the match on the steps to light it, she held the cigarette between her teeth. There was an old burn on the inside of her left wrist—a smoker's scar—and she twitched at the sleeve of her blouse to expose it, shaking the filmy fabric back from the sharp bones in her hand. Her mother chose the clothes—floaty, romantic fabrics, using the soft folds to hide her daughter's awkward angles.

Ella leaned back, letting the cigarette hang off her lower lip, feeling the chill of the fire escape meet the cold of her bones. The cast-iron was hard, but she was harder. She shook out the match before it could burn her fingers. A breeze snatched the smoke away. Like the smell of the Stain Devils, the first drag made her queasy, but the second settled her stomach.

After a bit she sat up and started to finger the bones in her ankles. She wanted to kick the ballet pumps from her narrow feet and fling them over the fire escape. The pumps had rounded toes and had been silver but were scuffing to grey at the edges. 'Grey,' she recited. 'A colour for the mother-in-law. Provided it's dove, or ash. But lavender is better. Grey can be very draining.' She took the white stick from her lips and stretched out a long arm to tap ash from its end. 'Cinders.' She stuck the cigarette back into her mouth.

Under the filmy sleeve of the blouse, the old gold watch said her break time was up. The blouse was good for that—hiding scars and a man's wristwatch bought from a junk shop which would give Laura the shudders if she ever saw it, just like the boots Ella had wanted to buy with her share of the profit from the wedding fair in York. Brown boots with brass buckles up the calf and flat tyre-treaded soles. Great for keeping a faery-girl grounded; an angel earthed.

'You'll scare the customers,' Laura had said. 'People get nervous enough. Girls who've never worn a dress in their lives need to know they're not about to make a fool of themselves. Hardly anyone's in touch with her feminine side, these days. It's our job to reassure them that even the most tomboyish of girls can look dainty on her big day.'

So Ella's sharp bones were draped in gauzy cotton and linen, her long feet blunted by the round toes of ballet pumps. There wasn't much to be done about her hair, which was coarse and black and too often looked like a cloud. Laura despaired, she really did. Nothing would induce her daughter's wayward tresses into coils, or a sleek pleat. Ella was always pushing her fingers through her hair, making it worse.

'You'll have to wear a headdress,' Laura had decided when Ella was six. 'A chignon with seed pearls sewn through it—or silk flowers, if they're back in fashion by then.'

Laura had been planning Ella's wedding even before she was born. She was a peaches-and-cream girl herself but one look at her newborn daughter's sallow complexion and pinched features had settled it; this would be a winter wedding. Heavy damask velvet in a shade of dark red or plum, with ivy trailing from the bouquet. 'You'll look very striking,' she said to Ella. Striking was the word she used when 'beautiful' was out of the question.

In the lounge, the Wedding Fair was in full swing. The flower arrangements were shedding petals and rusty pollen onto the carpet and there were sticky pastry crumbs on the tables. Empty cups were everywhere, coffee and lipstick stains spoiling their white rims. The harp music could hardly be heard over the babble of voices.

At the Living Memories stand, Neil Riddle, the photographer, was chatting up a woman with nice legs. He was such a creep, always telling Ella to say cheese. 'The other kind of fondue!' he leered, fondling his camera, extending and retracting its lens.

Over at Cinderella's Shoes, the shy-looking girl had her left foot in Laura's lap, trying on a white satin mule. She was a size five; Ella could just tell.

At the Fondue Fountain, her father was serving a man who had a beer belly. Colin was pulling his sympathetic face and Ella knew he was saying the usual thing about 'bloody wives and daughters'—the preamble to convincing boyfriends and fathers that a wedding went off better if liquid chocolate was on offer. He meant it, too. Just like Laura and her shoes, Colin believed that chocolate fondue was a vital part of the recipe for romance; that a marriage which began with white balloons and real petal confetti would last for all eternity. And if it didn't, well, give it a second shot—try red balloons and rice.

'The bridesmaids and pageboys love it,' Colin Derby was telling the big-bellied man who looked as if he thought chocolate fondue was a waste of money.

Laura Derby's idea of a waste of money was a wedding on a beach in the Bahamas: 'Barefoot! And all that sand—can you imagine?'

Colin had imagined a punchbowl of white chocolate with kebabs of pineapple and mango. In this way, they took turns to be the silver lining and the cloud. 'It's called complementing each other,' said Laura.

Neil Riddle was showing the woman with the nice legs an album of his best work: glossy photos of happy couples, their relatives arranged about them in smiling semi-circles. Ella wondered what the woman would make of Neil's other albums, the ones he kept in his studio and only showed to special friends.

Ella had been in the studio. It smelled of chemicals, and he was always joking about the wedding photos which were strung on a line like little bits of washing. If the bride was older than the groom he'd say, 'Something old, something new, eh?' The other photos, the ones for his friends, were always, 'Something blue,' with a nudge in the ribs, 'Say cheese, skinny!'

At the Vows and Wows stand, they were playing a DVD of a couple skydiving on their big day, dressed in matching orange jumpsuits. The bride had a lace garter around her right thigh. The wind was making pumpkin grins of their smiles. Then the film changed to a couple underwater, wearing scuba masks and surrounded by shoals of coloured fish. They were sticking their thumbs up for the film crew.

Neil Riddle caught Ella's eye, and winked. The overhead spotlight was shining on his bald spot, making it sweat. Ella elbowed her way back to Cinderella's Shoes.

Laura was still cooing over the size five feet of the young girl whose boyfriend was looking aimless and embarrassed. Ella said, 'Have you tried the chocolate?'

He shook his head and she took his arm. 'Come along.'

When they both had a cup, Ella led the boy away from the worst of the crowd, towards the windows which looked out onto the peacock-blue car. 'So when's the big day?' she asked.

'Soon.' The boy gulped at the chocolate. 'We haven't set a date yet. But soon.' He shot a look at Ella. His upper lip was brown. 'We're having a baby.'

'Congratulations.' Ella tried to imagine the boy at the antenatal classes, holding the plastic doll out in front of him, looking scared.

To have and to hold. To have. And to hold. Is that what it boiled down to, always, in the end?

'Bev thinks it's a boy but I reckon it'll be a girl.'

Ella nodded, looking through the window at the dazzling paintwork of the old car. She'd only meant to rescue the boy from her mother's cooing; she didn't want to hear about him and Bev and their baby. She slid a glance back at the girl, trying to detect a bulge under the loose jumper she was wearing. How far gone was she? When did it start to show? Was she feeling queasy in the mornings, smoking to settle her stomach?

'We'll probably have a registry office job,' the boy was saying.

'Well, good luck.' Ella sketched a toast with the plastic cup of chocolate.

She needed another cigarette. Her father had smiled at her when she took the boy to the Fondue Fountain stand. If Laura asked where she'd got to, she could always say she'd been chatting to the groom-to-be about the catering arrangements for his wedding.

'Hey, Cindy-Sue.' Neil Riddle caught her wrist as she passed his stand. 'How's it going? Sold many shoes?'

'Get off me, you creep.'

His camera was slung about his neck on a stripy strap, red and green. He pointed the flash at her, its sunken bulbs shining like mirrors. 'Fancy a quick flash?'

His grip was grinding her wrist. It hurt. She jerked her hand and tipped the thick dregs of the chocolate cup onto the protruding lens of his camera. By the time he'd registered what she was doing, there was gloopy brown liquid all over his zoom. 'Silly bitch,' he snapped, thrusting her away and reaching for the Kleenex.

Ella ran for the stairs. She ran past the Fondue Fountain and the vicar in his dog collar, past the stand where they were selling silk flowers. The flat heels of her scuffed pumps thumped on the stairs. She followed the square spiral of the staircase up and up, right to the top of the hotel.

She looked down, seeing the carpet as a riot of giant roses under her feet, the flowers as big as millstones. It was always the same in these hotels—everything outsized, over-patterned, to accommodate the scale of the rooms and hide the dirt. She could see the hard spots on the pile where stray cigarette butts had burned holes, or guests had dropped gum and trodden it in. She held onto the broad wooden bar of the banister and leaned over until her hip bones hurt, seeing the Wedding Fair truncated to a rectangle of pink and white beneath her. When she straightened and looked up, she saw a stray balloon, buoyed by helium, trapped in the right angle of the high ceiling.

She turned to her right and faced the tall window which looked out over the town, past the gravel drive of the hotel and its ornamental gardens, over the red roofs of houses and the drab concrete tower-blocks that stuck up under the indifferent sky, to the humpbacked line of hills over the last of which lay Ilkley, and the house that, for as long as she could remember, had smelled of chocolate and shoes.

Ella stepped up to the window, close enough to spoil the glass with her breath. Directly below was the brilliant blue car, its soft top looking supple, corrugated like the cupped palm of a hand.

Her fingers found the latch on the window and tried to prise it open. It was locked fast.

She turned her back and thought how it would feel to throw herself, lightly like a bouquet, to have the wind take her, whisk her off her feet. To land in the deep-pleated seat of the car like a strawberry dropped in cream and be driven off, the longest way away, by the man in the peaked cap with the crooked smile.

From the hotel lounge, the sound of Laura's voice lifted: 'Cindy? Cindy!'

9. BIG SISTER

by Shola Olowu-Asante

Mama Kunle considered herself a connoisseur when it came to tea, spending more time than was necessary on elaborate arrangements: black and green teas in lace and muslin bags, white teas in lacquer boxes, herbal teas in hand-crafted wooden containers. When she gazed at her collection, which was significant thanks to her sons who indulged her passion by sending her regular consignments from their many trips abroad, it seemed that all was right with the world. Here was proof that she was indeed both elegant and civilised. At specific times in the day, she liked to sit back in a plush armchair, swirling the contents of the cup around, inhaling the strong, smoky aroma, and letting her thoughts roam. That day, as she looked ahead to the party, her imagination soared. She was sure that it would be the social event of the year. Soon though, she was wincing, as her reverie was broken by the familiar sound of a woman shrieking.

'Martins, you dey craze? Patience, move those chairs. Sunday, you are a lazy good for nothing! How many times do I have to tell you to clean this room properly?'

Mama Kunle did not need to put down her cup, walk out of her room and lean over the banister to see who it was but she did so anyway, deriving a perverse enjoyment from watching the erratic actions of its owner. In the hallway below, Kofo looked like a marionette with her flapping arms punctuating every word. She wore heavy make-up and a diaphanous negligee over pencil thin heels. Mama Kunle was used to seeing the younger woman parading around the house in her finest—silk and organza iro and buba, up and downs in guinea brocade, boubous made from the most expensive Woodin—outfits that were impractical for daily use. This wispy fabric though, that exposed so much more than it concealed—well she hadn't seen her like this since that very first day.

Mama Kunle had been walking down a lonely corridor in her too big mansion when a woman in a sheer nightgown skipped out of a room at the far end of the hall. The woman had a breathless laugh that made her think of the crystal bells that adorned her living room mantelpiece. She stood barefoot in front of a large window, her body, all contours and curves, visible beneath the gown. Squinting into the light, Mama Kunle thought the woman was an apparition, until she saw Baba's spindly legs and rotund belly behind her, his flaccid arms snaking their way across the woman's chest. Later, when he brought Kofo to her rooms for a formal introduction, the sound of their carefree laughter was still ringing in her ears.

'Bunmi, I have decided to officially invite Kofo into our home,' he said, in the manner of a hotel concierge. 'I am sure you will make her feel welcome.'

Turning to Kofo, his face worked hard to reflect the solemnity of the occasion.

'Kofo, Bunmi is my first wife. Show her the respect she is due and she will look after you, like a big sister.'

And then, meeting concluded, he trotted out of the room with the satisfied air of a man who had deflected a crisis. A seething Mama Kunle inspected the new Mrs. Bello through lidded eyes, conceding that Kofo was attractive. She had caramel coloured skin, huge almond shaped eyes, with long lashes that rested graceful as palm fronds on her cheeks. Only her mouth seemed out of place, an afterthought on an artist's canvas, a thin gash, puckered in a permanent pout that made her look like a surly schoolgirl. Mama Kunle treated her as such, her tone haughty and officious and while over the years their relationship mellowed somewhat, they became neither friends nor sisters. Each maintained a strained politeness, the only way they agreed, that two women sharing a house and a husband could co-exist.

Mama Kunle watched Kofo's demented pirouetting, as she chased and shouted at one servant after another. It dawned on her that Kofo had still not adjusted to the presence of Moji, the docile-looking third wife whose recent arrival coincided with Kofo's shrewish conduct and brazen displays of affection towards Baba. She had noticed Kofo hanging around his apartments with lingering looks and was thankful that she at least no longer hankered for those tedious night-time appointments, with the awkward grunting and groping in the dark. She liked to think that she handled herself with restraint at the top of their domestic hierarchy. Up till now she had observed Kofo's crazy behaviour with amused detachment but today was the day of Baba's seventieth birthday party and she felt it was time to intervene.

'Kofo, what is going on here? What are you shouting about?' she asked.

'Ekaaro Ma. These househelp are going to kill me one day. There is so much to do and guests will start arriving within a few hours.'

'Isn't that why we are paying the caterers and party planners?'

Kofo turned to face Mama Kunle, with both hands on her hips, a gesture that meant she would not shy away from a fight.

'Ejo Ma, please, Baba is my husband too and I want this party to be a success. I am just doing my duty.'

Mama Kunle would have arched a single eyebrow if she knew how, but made do with a slow pursing of her lips.

'Fine, do what you like. But keep the noise down. I don't need a headache today of all days.' Kofo was already gone, tottering on her heels, barking orders with a wild-eyed look on her face.

#

Back in her room, Mama Kunle's tea was cold, and try as she might, there was no getting away from the din downstairs. This will never do she clucked to herself. Over the past weeks, a beautiful image had crystallised in her mind. An air-conditioned canopy, perfumed with flowers would shield them all from the humidity and broiling sun: Baba's business acquaintances, the magistrates and politicians who enabled those connections to bear fruit, and the Obas, traditional rulers whose powers had long been reduced to a vague influence. Important family members were also there and she would sit next to Baba in the midst of all those elites, regal in her damask and blue aso-oke, with her sons fanning out behind. She could rely on Moji to be suitably demure in the background but who knew what kind of attention seeking stunt Kofo would pull.

She thought back to those early days of her marriage, that first unexpected opportunity to live in London with her husband, when most couples in their situation endured years of separation. She remembered the jobs as a cleaner, and later as a secretary, to pay for his tuition. Then there was the birth of her sons and the ensuing years in Lagos, watching Baba grow fat and flushed on oil and gas dollars while she felt herself diminish. Somehow she knew that it had all been leading up to this moment, when she would be restored in the eyes of the world to her rightful place and she was not about to let an hysterical harpy spoil her day.

So Mama Kunle was pleased when they all gathered in Baba's apartment— her three sons, Kofo with her sweet, dull-witted daughter Remi, who had never been able to endear herself to her father, and Moji, standing slightly apart, uncertain of where to place her allegiance. They all held hands and prayed for Baba's long life and good health, for the continued unity and prosperity of their immediate family. Spirits were high when she sidled up to Kofo and made her suggestion.

'Kofo, I was thinking that maybe we should change the seating arrangement.'

The younger woman furrowed her brow. 'Mama Kunle, ejo, everything is settled, let's not change anything at the last minute.'

'Kofo, calm down. Look there is no seniority amongst us and all those obas and politicians can be so dull. You are better in these situations, why don't you sit on the high table with Daddy.' She let her words sink in before adding, 'Of course if you don't want to ...' and then drifted away, leaving a confused-looking Kofo to chew on her words.

Later, over a steaming cup of chrysanthemum tea, Mama Kunle would tell herself that there had been no plan, that what followed was not her fault. For as they filed out of the room, making their way towards the party and their waiting guests, Baba's hand unconsciously skimmed Moji's derriere. Mama Kunle saw it as an act both innocent and tender, not meant for the eyes of another wife. Suddenly Kofo was storming forwards, her shrill voice halting everyone in their tracks.

'Stop. Stop. We have to get this right. We have to go in together.' She looked so eager and desperate. Her beautiful face was absurdly twisted and as she pushed past the boys and her daughter and reached Baba's side, she was panting. He turned to her, his eyes hard and contemptuous.

'Kofo, pull yourself together,' he said, while his fingers tapped away on his Blackberry.

'But Daddy,' she said, her voice rising, 'we have arranged it all between ourselves. I will sit with you at high table.'

'We are not changing anything.'

When she pulled at the sleeve of his agbada, Mama Kunle would tell herself that he was simply recoiling from her touch and did not mean for his palm to land so hard, so precisely on that smooth unblemished cheek and that the tremor she felt was from fear and not pleasure.

'Pull yourself together,' Baba repeated. 'We are not changing anything.'

And he marched away from the family's furtive glances, the accusing silence that hung in the room, marched ahead of all of them, through the sliding doors and out into the brilliant sunshine.

10. MISSY'S SUMMER

by Oonah Joslin

It was a scorcher of a summer the year Missy was born. Mammy had been running around like a headless chicken cleaning this and scrubbing that. She wasn't fit for the farm work so Liddy and I collected the banty[1] eggs. Daddy did the milking on top of the other work. We hardly saw him—just when he came in for his meals. Sometimes he took a piece[2] to the fields for lunch, and on market day, he went into the town and came back beery with a pocketful of sweets and some flowers. Mammy smiled and kissed him. It was only once a week he had a beer.

The day Missy was born, Liddy and I found Mammy hunched up over a chair with blood running down her legs. She told us to get Mrs. Black and we ran the lane like the bull was after us.

She was tiny. Millicent May, they called her. But I couldn't say Millicent, so she became Missy. I held her once, but she cried and frightened me so I gave her back double quick. Liddy was better at that sort of thing. Liddy helped change and bathe Missy and get her away to sleep—until Mammy was herself again.

Liddy and I were left to our own devices in those long, summer weeks. The cat preceded us into the shed, to get the indignant hens out, before we dared go in and collect their eggs. I'd clean the couple of dozen with a soft cloth and layer them up with newspaper in a basket. They were smooth, matt, and all different shades from cream to brown. I always picked out the one I was going to eat for my lunch, but Liddy thought that was childish so I stopped telling her which I'd chosen.

---

[1] eggs from a Bantam hen
[2] sandwich

Four years older than me, Liddy seemed to know what needed to be done and I followed her round as if she were a grown-up. We braved the sweltering mile walk to the post office every day to get the mail and odds and ends written on a note, and took eggs and milk for the woman there. Mammy seemed constantly busy with Missy and chores. I wanted to sit on her knee like before but she said I was a big girl now.

Thunder, according to Daddy, was the inevitable outcome of any prolonged spell of good weather. He'd welcome it, he said. The crops were in sore need of rain and the animals were all but cooking on the hoof. Mammy said she could feel something hanging in the air.

That day the cat was nowhere to be seen so we had to chase the hens out ourselves. They came straight at us, all claws and feathers flying. There were fewer than a dozen eggs.

'The thunder has stopped them laying,' explained Liddy.

When we got back to the house Mammy was clutching Missy, rocking and sobbing. Liddy went over to see.

'Get Mrs. Black!' she yelled.

I turned and ran. The rain fell in diamond-hard drops. In my plastic sandals and little cotton dress, I burst straight into Mrs. Black's kitchen without knocking and stood there panting and dripping onto the concrete floor.

'Good God, child!' said Mrs. Black, putting her coat on and throwing me a blanket from the couch.

Daddy never mentioned Missy after the funeral. Downpours continued into harvest time turning the fields to thick gunge and the peat bog was sodden, making a back-breaking job heartbreaking—if a heart could be more broken.

I started school. The teacher offered biscuits as prizes for good work. I'd run up the lane all excitement to tell Mammy, just as I'd seen Liddy do—for a hug. 'I got a biscuit today.'

'Did you? That's nice. Now away and wash your hands.'

She never looked up.

Daddy always had things to finish up in the shed. On Wednesdays he came home with sweets, flowers, and chocolates. Mammy accepted them without comment.

One frosty morning, I found the cat lying dead in the ditch with a litter of kittens. I picked them up one by one, and they each dangled limp in my hand. The last one moved and gave a weak miaow, so I brought it in by the fire.

'What's that you've got, girl?' asked Daddy.

'A kitten,' said I. 'The rest are dead, like Missy.'

Everything stopped. Mammy sat heavily on a kitchen chair with one hand across her mouth. Liddy scowled.

'Robert,' pleaded Mammy, 'Robert, get her out of here. Get them both out of here!'

Daddy took the kitten. 'Come on, girls.'

Daddy had always said death is part of life on a farm so we hadn't to get upset when cattle went to slaughter or a lamb died, or we'd be upset all the time. Mammy seemed upset all the time.

'Now, Lydia!' When Liddy heard her given name, she knew he meant it.

Things were never the same after Missy's summer. The hens kept laying, the work went on, but at lambing time Mammy went away. Every time she went away after that, it was for a bit longer. I wanted to ask where she went but Liddy shushed me. I knew if you upset people they go away, and I was too afraid to ask anyone if what happened to Mammy was all my fault.

When I held my daughter for the first time I thought of my mother, but the doctors said it would do more harm than good. The day that Missy died, a crack opened up in Mammy's heart leaving us all on the other side: a fissure that grew deeper and wider with time, a chasm that could never be spanned. It left each of us on the brink.

11. WHITE HORSES

by Stephen Tyson

When they were children, and played on Arncliffe beach, Corrine Gianni told Joel to lasso a white horse and one night he tried. But every time he threw the line out it came back empty. Years later, Joel would stare out to sea, watching the waves peaking like the curls on a baby's head. Sometimes he lost track of time, and that was when the sea would start to hurt his eyes.

On the narrow road next to the beach was the café that had once belonged to the Giannis. Marjorie Erin, the owner, bought fresh fish once a week during the season.

'There's five pound of plaice in that bag,' Joel said to the girl behind the counter. 'Put them in the back. I'll pick my money up tomorrow.'

Only Joel and Danny Reid still ran long-lines into the bay. Danny was nearly eighty, needed a stick to stay upright, and hardly stopped coughing when the weather turned cold. In the winter, when the catch was usually small, Joel would only take the fish off the lines every other day and leave a bucketful outside the Reids' cottage door in return for a few cans of beer.

Joel helped the older man towards a table by the café window and ordered two rounds of toast and a pot of coffee. Marjorie Erin said it was nice to see Danny up and about and handed Joel the money for the fish.

'Expect you'll get a good crop of Damsons this year,' she said, looking at Joel. 'There's plenty blossom about. Make sure you save some for me.'

\#

As the sea retreated, the two men began to paddle across the beach. When Corrine Gianni was sixteen, Joel had thrown her into the tide. She came out shivering and her hair looked like the slime that floated near the jetty. Danny had been the road sweeper then, and waited until Corrine ran back to the café before he shouted Joel's name.

Danny would start to rock on his stick just thinking about Corrine. If it was windy, you could hardly tell him apart from the sea, dressed in his green wellingtons and denim dungarees.

'Who do you think got her pregnant?'

Joel stopped. 'It wasn't me'

Every spring Danny asked the same question. Sometimes he would carry on asking for a few weeks. Joel was used to hedging around the subject and just carried on walking with the damp sand squelching under his boots.

'Thought you might know. My guess is that if it wasn't you it must have been Todd Hunter's lad ... saw her walking up towards the big farm once or twice early evening. Then again, could have been Reece Jones. He used to park his sports car outside the café and turn the music up until she came out.'

Joel bent down. 'Look like new casts. I'll come down later and dig some fresh bait.' He ground his foot down and the top half of a lugworm wriggled above the imprint of his boot.

'That's a fat bugger,' Danny said. 'We might pull in a few big ones if they're all like that.'

'I'll come down later.'

A line of flounders and plaice, the majority slightly curled as rigor mortis set in, lay hooked by pale, raw, bacon-coloured lips. Their flesh was speckled with spots and the two men nudged them with their feet.

'This one's diseased,' Joel said. 'But the rest are okay.'

'A bit small.'

'Big enough.'

'Hell of a chest that Corrine had.'

'Jesus.'

Danny started to laugh. Joel knelt and started to unhook the fish, hitting any that still flapped with a lump of blackthorn. After dropping the fish into the canvas bag and removing the tin of bait, the two men threaded fresh worms onto the hooks. Joel did thirty while Danny managed six.

'Expect we'll get rid of these at the hotel,' Joel said as he picked up the bag. 'You fancy a ride up?'

#

From the top of the rise, the line of the sea looked like ruffled silk. The engine whined as Joel ground the gears and Danny whistled. 'Bonny day,' he said. 'See for miles.'

'What's there to see?' Joel said as he pulled the van up in front of the hotel.

'Whatever you want. Helps if you keep cheerful like me. You should get yourself a woman.'

Joel shrugged and pocketed the key.

'Must be a few knocking about,' Danny said.

'In their forties?'

'Go into town.'

'I like it quiet.'

#

The chef poked at the white bellies of the fish, offered a price and waited while Joel and Danny exchanged glances. The older man raised his nose as he caught a whiff of cooking meat.

'Well?' the chef said.

'This time,' Joel said, 'but we'll want more in future.'

'You bring me big fish next time and I'll pay you more.'

'Bastard,' Joel muttered as he followed Danny towards the door.

'Till next time. You know I'm always fair.' The chef smiled as Danny turned and nodded goodbye.

'Fancy a pint?' Joel said. 'I'll park the van behind the café and pick it up in the morning.'

#

The vase on the windowsill was full of miniature daffodils with limp, fading petals. The water they stood in was pale green, ready to be changed. A few early tourists eyed the menu hung behind the bar.

'I hate that,' Joel said.

'What?'

'That Italian chef. Clever bastard.'

'He always pays up.'

'I suppose.'

'I never knew any other Italians apart from the Giannis.'

'What about during the war?'

'I was in Japan. You know that.'

'I forgot ...'

The jukebox came on and the two men gripped their glasses.

#

The sun was sinking when they staggered onto the street. Danny started to sing; something old, ripped, reassembled and resurrected by his gravelly voice. Joel knew better than to ask. Danny's melodies came with reams of history. Places, names, hurts. The two of them crossed the street and rested against the railing.

'Looks like someone's been building a sandcastle,' Danny said.

Joel looked down at the hump with the moat traced in the sand around it and then at Danny's lined face. The old man's cheeks jowled like a hound's. When Danny went, that would be it. He would know no one. 'It wasn't me that got Corrine pregnant,' he said.

The old man smiled and placed his hand on Joel's shoulder. 'What's it matter? I only say it to wind you up. You keep too much inside.'

'Might have been better if I had. That bastard Gianni said he'd buy me a net if I kept away from her.... You catch plenty big fish, even a mermaid....' Joel added, straining to mimic the foreign accent.

Danny shrugged. 'You're better off with a long-line round here.'

'I know that.'

'That sun's hurting my eyes,' Danny said, as he squinted at the sky.

Joel didn't answer—just stared out to sea, wrung out, his eyes smarting.

12. MANIC

by Juli Klass

The hallways are cool, painted that soothing pale green that always reminds me of hospitals. The floors are polished to a bright shine and I am conscious of my footfalls breaking the silence that aches over the place. I pass numbered doors left and right; my walk slows as I approach the reception to Unit 404.

I feel as though I have entered an aquarium, it is painted cerulean blue and baskets of trailing plants stretch tendrils to the floor. In the corner a large fish tank burbles and hums, its brightly coloured inhabitants go serenely about their business.

The nurse behind the counter looks up and smiles at me in a patronising way. She can't yet know whether I'm a visitor or an outpatient. I wonder whether she possesses some rare skill in divining my mental health from my physiognomy. Can she see some small, dark twist lurking in my future?

I try to look sane, composing my face into a mask, asking for Joseph, and explaining why I've come. In my informative teacher voice I tell her about the school, about how worried the children and teachers had been about him. I hold up the bright green handmade card, the garish 'WE MISS YOU' in black ink across the front. Glitter sticks to my hand and I suddenly feel silly, but I can't stop myself from wittering on about the gift.

She looks bored, waiting for me to finish prattling. Asks for my name and slides her finger down the page of a dog-eared book slowly searching for my clearance number. She can't find it and I point out that my surname is frequently misspelled with a C instead of a K. I feel embarrassed about this as though it's my fault. She starts again and finally hands me a grubby visitor's card and places a call to announce my arrival. I smile my thanks too brightly and realise that I'm nervous.

The woman who comes to me is statuesque and broad. A name badge is pinned to a great white expanse of bosom and says, 'Mrs. I.O. Potter'. I wonder what the I.O. stands for as I shake her hand and follow her to her office. I mentally list all the female names that I can think of that start with an 'I': Irma, Ira, Imogene, Iris? I am too timid to enquire but it annoys me that I don't know it, and I haven't even started on the 'O'.

I am invited to sit while she crosses the room to a battered metal filing cabinet. She flicks efficiently through the files and pulls out a pale yellow folio with 'JS Stander' printed boldly on the tab. Joseph's file.

I am told that today is a good day for him, the first in a while. She describes his condition as 'OCD' and I am finally prompted to ask a question. Obsessive Compulsive Disorder she tells me, I nod sagely. They changed his medication today, so they're hoping it will help him get back into the world and back to school. I smile now, wishing I looked more like a stereotypical teacher, bookish and sensible; I look down at my jeans and my glitter-coated hands. The interview is over and Mrs. Potter leads me to the visitors' area.

He looks so small and much younger than his fourteen years. He's got a pack of cards on the floor in front of him, he appears to be playing solitaire and then I notice that he's sorting them into groups. He's sitting on a fat book with 'Oxford English Dictionary' printed on the spine. Mrs. Potter announces my arrival and Joseph continues to sort the cards. I nod and smile at her reassuringly and crouch on the floor.

I greet him quietly. He finishes with the cards and looks at me, and smiles. I tell him how much we've all missed him and he laughs saying 'I'm crazy now, miss!' He's reassuringly normal. I hand him the card and as he opens it, glitter sticks to his fingers. I hold my breath, thinking it will bother him, waiting for him to freak out and pick all the glitter off his hands. But he doesn't, and I realise I haven't done my homework on this disorder. He reads the cheery messages with a faint smile and then carefully removes the wrapping paper from the gift.

He pulls the packaging off and flips open the matt silver console. It's the new Nintendo game and Joseph has briefly forgotten that I'm with him. As he fiddles with the keys, a tinny tune plays out while 'NINTENDO' flashes onto the screen.

He drops the game to the floor with a clatter and leaps to his feet as though shocked. He spins round, breathing hard and then picks up the dictionary and flicks through the pages, running his finger down the columns of words.

Joseph is muttering now, 'Nintendo! Nintendo! Won't get to heaven unless I know!' Louder now, and almost tearing at the dictionary before dropping it to the floor where it lands with a thud. He begins pacing and I run over to the duty nurse, feeling panicked by his behaviour.

She asks me what I said to him and I tell her about the gift. She looks at me uncomprehendingly, frowning and thin-lipped, annoyed that I have done something to upset this boy.

She marches over to Joseph and takes him by the shoulders. He's shouting now and crying 'Nintendo! Nintendo! Won't get to heaven unless I know!' She tries to calm him as he stamps again and again on the fallen game, breaking the screen while it beeps loudly. She turns to me saying, 'What have you done!' and I don't know. He yells out, his face turns red 'What does it mean? Won't get to heaven unless I know!'

Suddenly I understand. I grab the fallen dictionary and skim through for the word. I don't expect it to be there and it isn't. I root around in my handbag for my own pocket dictionary, frantically flipping the pages. Nothing. All the while he paces and screams, inflamed by his obsession. 'The word! The word!' he shouts. 'Won't get to heaven unless I know!'

I pull my mobile from my bag, my hands shaking, and dial my son. 'I'm fine love, can't really talk now, can you look something up on the internet for me? Quick as you can!' I can hear him typing and clicking on the other end of the phone, mumbling, 'Nintendo Nintendo, where are you?' and then, 'Um, Mum the company website doesn't say what the name means and I can't find anything immediately on Google. Let me keep looking and I'll phone you the minute I find out.'

I go back to the nurse and Joseph; he is calmer now that is he's stopped shouting. He's pacing and mumbling, back and forth, back and forth, catatonic. I feel like a criminal, feel like screaming myself. I ask the nurse where the bathroom is, she's been following my progress on the word search and is on my side now.

I walk into the ladies room and lean against the wall. Cold tiles are against my back and I close my eyes. I'm craving a cigarette but notice the smoke detector on the ceiling. I stand at the basin and run cold water over my wrists, damping my neck with my glitter hands. With a final look at the smoke detector, I head for the door to the garden. Outside there are chairs and umbrellas, stacks of magazines on wooden tables. I sit and light a cigarette, breathing deeply and willing my son to call.

I pick up a copy of The Economist dated 14 March 1992. Most of the pages have come out and the cover is faded, but I flick through it anyway, smoking and staring blankly at the marching lines of words. I turn the pages in a daze and when I reach the end of the tattered magazine, I put it back in the pile and pick up another one as I finish my cigarette.

Glitter glints and sparkles on my hand as I raise it to my mouth, I flick a small square of gold off my wrist. As I do, my cigarette ash falls onto the pages of the magazine. I swear and brush the ash away, sweating with distress. A headline catches my eye: Nintendo's Compact Console Will Turn The World Of Gaming On Its Head.

My mouth goes dry, the cigarette forgotten as I begin to scan the text. In the final paragraph, the article reads: 'Nintendo of Japan was founded in 1889 by Fusajiro Yamauchi. He was an artist and crafts worker. He started it as a playing card company. Nintendo means leave luck to heaven.'

I scramble out of the chair, shouting, 'Leave luck to heaven!' Dropping my handbag and clutching the article as though it will save the world, I run inside, laughing and chanting, 'Luck! Luck!' Nurses stare at me as I sprint down the corridor. I get lost; take a left, turn too early and back track to find my way. I enter the visitor's room shouting, 'I have it! I have the meaning!' The nurse is still with Joseph, they are both startled by my dramatic entry into the room.

I hand the article to Joseph, stabbing at the final paragraph, 'There there! Nintendo means 'leave luck to heaven'! He stops his pacing, sits down, and begins to read. Suddenly he freezes and looks up at me and says, 'Miss, what does Fusajiro Yamauchi mean?' My skin prickles and goes hot and cold. The nurse looks at me expectantly, worried. Joseph laughs and says, 'Just kidding, it's the guy's name, innit?'

Mrs. Potter sees me out, the I.O. of her name gritting against my consciousness. In the car on the way home I am agitated, chanting 'Isabella, Isis, Ivana, Octavia, Odette, Olivia' out loud as I drive. The moment I get home, I phone the hospital and speak carefully to the receptionist. 'I'd like to send a thank you note to Mrs. Potter, could you tell me her first name?'

The woman tells me it's Irene; I am annoyed that I hadn't guessed that one. I ask what the 'O' of her initial stands for and the receptionist laughs, 'All of the nurses ask Mrs. Potter, but she never tells.'

But I need to know the answer and the receptionist's laugh makes me want to break something.

13. PASSPORT

by Sarah Leipciger

My name is Heather-Leigh, but Tom calls me Heavenly. Everything's good except that Mom has a leaky heart and Kelsey's been away all summer. She came home last month with her new man who's got the same name as his grandfather, a famous Canadian poet. Meril Byrne. I've never read much poetry but I should have heard of him—he was an Okanagan boy.

Me and Tom were drunk on Buster wine when she came home. She came in through the front door and surprised us on the back porch; she must have crept through the house holding his hand, pulling him behind her a little (and he must have noticed the smell of our place in summer; a little sour, a little bit like sickness). She came out through the back door grinning at me with all her teeth, hoppin' up and down and presenting her man like a model on a game show would present a dishwasher. Her hair was too short. Her eyes were all puffed out because the black flies had got to her out in the bush there where she worked at a camp for people with problems in their head, and where she met Meril. He was a surprise, nothing like the bruisers she's brought home before. He was about an inch shorter than her, head shaved clean down to the skin and a thin beard pulled into a long braid that moved up and down when he spoke. He was skinny as hell, but then so is Kelsey, and had a long face, sunny eyes, long hands. His arm muscles were really defined, veiny forearms, hardly any hair. I felt like I was in the presence of a monk. 'It's a pleasure to meet you,' he said to me and Tom and sat down on the top step of the porch. He said *pleasure* like it really was a pleasure to meet us. Kelsey went back into the house to get him and herself glasses for the Buster wine, and this Meril just looked out over our river, his arms over his knees, his chin rested on his arms, and that braid of his blowing a little in the wind. After some time, with all of us being silent and Kelsey not back with the glasses yet, he said, 'do you ever swim in that water?'

'Only if you don't mind the weeds around your legs,' said Tom, comfortably, as if he'd known this Meril all along. But then again, that's Tom. It's never awkward with him. 'We got a paddle boat,' said Tom, 'if you ever want to go for a ride, it's just there, behind the shed there. Kelsey'll show you how to use it. You steer it with a little joystick.'

'I used one on the Seine.'

Kelsey came out then, with the glasses, and filled them from the plastic bottle we had sitting between us. 'This is Buster wine,' she said. 'Our neighbour makes it out of huckleberries.'

Meril smelled the wine like a connoisseur, sipped it, and smacked his lips.

'So what were you doing in Paris?' I asked him.

He looked like he had forgotten that he even mentioned it. Then he looked like he was surprised I knew the Seine was even in Paris. 'Oh, God,' he said. He pulled on his braid and smiled at his feet, which I noticed then, were bare. Me and Tom leaned back in our chairs, Kelsey gazed at him. 'I got mixed up with this woman who thought herself an artiste. We got into all kinds of things. We stayed in Rambuteau and became addicted to kosher falafels. I ended up busking on the Place de la Concorde as a golden Pharaoh, like a mummy. I wore an Egyptian mask, this thing with horrible blank eyes, and wrapped myself in this shiny gold stuff, this satiny material. I stood on a pedestal as still as I could, and bowed for people when they put money in a gold box next to me.'

'Why the hell do that?' asked Tom.

'It was easier than trying to play an instrument.'

Kelsey laughed hard then, slapped the porch and beamed at her man. She liked this one.

'So have you done a lot of travelling then,' said Tom.

'Tell them about New Zealand, Meril,' Kelsey said, and pushed his chest.

'What, all of it?'

'They don't mind.'

'You kids let me get you something to eat first,' I said. 'You must be starving. I'm starving.'

I realised just how gone I was when I tried to stand up, but then again isn't that always the way, drinking in the afternoon sun until it flies over your house and all that's left of it is its long legs stretching out on the yard to the river. Me and Tom, we'll do that sometimes, sit out on a Saturday and just drink. Buster wine or beer or rum n' cokes. We won't bother with food and we'll just smoke his roll-ups, and get slaughtered, and laugh and laugh until we cry. If I've got nothing else in this life, I'll always have these afternoons of recklessness with my husband, and the sound of our screeching, and that look he gets in his eyes when life is good.

I could hear Tom honking out there with those two as I leaned against the counter, eating pistachios out of a jar, looking in the fridge for something to feed them all. Mom called from St Mary's then, as furious as she was the day we moved her there, a few months prior. It was the hardest thing I've ever had to do, but with her heart, she needs 24-hour care and I was beat. She's only eighty-two. I was too drunk to talk to her.

'You left your bloody sweater here this morning.' Her voice was like acid.

'I knit that for *you*. You said you had a chill at night because they've been leaving the windows open in the common room so I knit that for you. 'Specially knit that.'

'I've got plenty of sweaters.'

'But this was special.'

'I don't want it. When you leave tomorrow you can take it with you.'

'Fine.'

She hung up. The phone rang again.

'You've always been an incredibly fast knitter,' she said, still accusing.

'So what?'

'How did you do this so quickly?'

'You said you had a chill. I wanted you to have my hugs, all the time.' I twisted the phone chord around my body.

'What are you talking about?'

'The sweater. It's a hug.'

'Well, thank you.'

'You're welcome.'

'Goodbye.'

'Bye.'

It really wasn't always like this. It was the thing with the home, now she's tried to escape, and we've had to call the police. There's all this water under the bridge now, and it's all full of turbulence.

I made ham and cheese sandwiches and found some crackers in the cupboard, a bag of oatmeal cookies, and washed a bowl of spectacular peaches. The three of them started right in on the food and I had to remind them we were waiting to hear about New Zealand, all of it. Meril took small sips of wine, like he only wet his lips with it, and Kelsey was doing the same. He rubbed his hands together and crossed his legs, and he grinned a few times so that beard of his wagged. Kelsey put her head in his lap and closed her eyes. The soles of her feet were black as the ace of spades. The sun was nearly down.

He traced those big veins of his on his forearms with these great boxy fingers as he began to speak. 'I was in New Zealand about six years ago. I was twenty-five. I slept in the back of a station wagon in a parking lot next to a marina up on the west coast of the North Island. I wanted to get a job on a fishing boat; I'd heard they were taking people on, like anyone, you needn't have fished before. You could go on as a cook, or just a hand to do the grunt work, or clean the fish maybe. I don't know. I never did get any work on any fishing boat. I had to leave because I'd found out that some beefcakes decided they didn't like me hanging around the marina. They figured I was plotting something, or maybe it was just weird for them to have some strange foreigner hanging around their town, eating in their greasy spoons. I don't know.'

'How'd you find out?' asked Tom, genuinely concerned. 'Who were these guys?'

'Oh, people would say things to me in passing, quietly. Then they'd act like they hadn't said anything at all. It took me a few weeks to realise this place was like the Twilight Zone. It wasn't a big deal. I took my station wagon down to Auckland, and it didn't take long to find some work there.'

Kelsey opened her eyes and grinned up at him, and tugged at his braid. She took off her glasses and laid them on her chest.

'Your poor eyes,' he said to her, and kissed her nose. 'They still look so sore.'

'So what job did you get?' I asked.

He looked at me and I could tell he was deciding whether or not he wanted to tell me. 'I'll tell you, but you can't make any judgements.'

I held my glass of Buster wine towards him, and he reciprocated with a clink of his glass, still barely touched.

'I stayed in one of those backpacker hostels. This one, people were staying there for months. They were mostly from England, some other Canadians, some Germans. Mostly English. And they were mad for drugs. They were working the shittiest jobs, like in butcher shops or pubs, or meat pie stands.

Really degrading stuff. Then they'd go and spend all their money on drugs, and complain that they had no money left over to travel with. I found myself in a pub with this English guy, from up north England, and he introduced me to this Kiwi called Max who he knew from his job on a building site. Me and this guy Max got to talking and by the end of the night I'd agreed to sell acid for him at the hostel—all the hostels.'

'LSD, Dad,' said Kelsey, and Tom nodded his thank you.

'Was the money good?' Tom asked, and that's how I knew he was really gone, because he wouldn't have been so bold to act that cool if he were sober.

Meril smiled at him, grinned at him, and nodded yes. 'It was great, until some guys ratted on me. I was arrested and spent nine months in the Auckland penitentiary.'

'No,' said Tom, aghast, and drained his glass. 'That must have been really something.'

'It was,' said Meril.

'What was that like?' I asked, and looked at Kelsey to make sure this was a suitable question.

'I met some really beautiful people. Some really sound guys. I spent a lot of my evenings singing with a group of Maori fellas—they call each other fella—and I studied Buddhism with a Japanese guy.'

'Meril is a Buddhist,' said Kelsey. 'He's teaching me all about it.'

Now here was something new altogether, yet I was still back at the Eiffel Tower or wherever it was, trying to picture him as a golden Pharaoh, bowing for coins.

#

Because of the heat, Kelsey and Meril decided to sleep in the sunroom at the back of the house. It was a little awkward there sometime around midnight when I woke up and heard them making love. I've never heard my daughter's fucking sounds before, why would I, I guess, and I have to say I was moved. She sounded like she was having a hell of a passion, and I could hear the way her voice excited him. I turned to Tom, to see if I could rouse him, play with him, but the Buster wine had him instead.

#

That Meril was already up before me, sitting at the edge of the river with his shirt off, trying to eat a crab apple. I came down and sat next to him, and laughed my ass off when I saw what he was trying to do.

'Tell me you know what a crab apple is,' I said, taking it from him, perhaps a little more violently than I needed to. 'You don't eat these, you nincompoop.'

'Nincompoop?' he said, and splashed me. 'Who uses the word nincompoop?'

'You sleep well?' I asked him, and my cheeks burned at the thought of it.

'It's like sleeping outside, that room.'

The sun was shining in our eyes and we had to squint. It bounced off the river in flints and reflected off our faces. This Meril had nice blue eyes, and he just kept smiling, and he was happy.

'So how'd you meet my daughter?'

'At the camp. We were in the same raft.'

'Like Tom Sawyer and Huckleberry Finn?'

He smiled, pondered the implication, and said no. 'Whitewater rafting. Down the Golden. She steered the boat. Grade three rapids too you know— no small chickens.'

'Where'd my daughter learn to drive a ship in the rapids?'

'They taught her, at the camp. They've really got it together at this place.'

'For people with problems in their head,' I said.

He spoke to the water. 'They encourage teamwork, initiative, trust. It's all about setting tasks and getting them done, and building confidence. Operating within a community where everyone is as crazy as everyone else. It's a trip man, I'm telling you.'

'So you like working there?'

He put his hand on his chest and feigned surprise, and laughed, and said, 'I'm one of the campers, dahling. I'm as crazy as snow in July!' He said July like Juw-lai, like he was from the Dukes of Hazards.

I looked at him sideways, and waited for the guffaw, or a slap on the back, or any indication that would tell me whether or not he was serious, but he was already pulling himself up, asking for something to eat.

#

A couple of days passed with me not knowing whether or not he was crazy; it was impossible to tell. I couldn't get Kelsey to leave his side without it being too obvious. And he was so full of these incredible stories. We'd all be sitting around on the porch with a couple of beers, or watching television and eating cinnamon toast, and he'd break in with some story about some country he visited. He once lived on an island in Honduras, Roatan, and he lived with this woman he'd met scuba diving. She was his instructor. She fell in love with him, he said, and asked him to stay at her house for a while. So he did. She was a marvel, he said. She was Spanish, and she could speak English, French, Yugoslavian, and a bit of Chinese. She played guitar in one of the drinking holes and where her voice didn't suffice, her humour kicked in. Well, he came home late one night, middle of the night, and walked into the bedroom, or maybe it was the kitchen, only to find her standing there, pointing a gun at his head. He said she was like driftwood. She'd left Spain so many years before, and she'd travelled so much, she'd lost her base. He found out that she'd been robbed at the house a few months earlier and they took everything. He said he couldn't really live with her after he found his nose up against the barrel of her gun, and it was sad, as he figured she had a lot of people moving in and out of her life. And she'd moved in and out of a lot of the lives of others.

Well I can't really fathom that—losing my base. These roots are deep. This was my mother's house. The furthest I've been is Toronto, and that was a five-hour flight from Vancouver so I'm thinking that's pretty far. And I've made plenty of trips down into Montana, through the canyons near Glacier National Park, to hang out at Red's cabin in Whitefish. Go skiing or swimming, depending on the time of year. But I've never been without family, whether it's Tom or Mom or one of my kids. Can't imagine that. That poor little Spanish girl, cooped up with all those languages and no one to speak them to.

#

I don't know what Meril said to Mom when Kelsey took him to visit her, but he sure stirred things up. This is the phone conversation I had with her a few hours after his visit:

'I'm going on a trip,' she said to me.

'Are you now, where are you going?'

'I've always, always wanted to see the Pyramids.'

'Well, everyone has always wanted to see the Pyramids.'

'What difference does that make? I want to go.'

'You need 24-hour care Mom. Who's going to take care of you? You can't go to the grocery store without your oxygen.'

'So it'll be the last thing I do.'

I put the phone to my boobs and took a deep breath, prayed to the ceiling fan, and continued. 'Now, did you want me to bring you anything tomorrow morning?'

'Do I have a valid passport? Can you look in my dresser, top drawer? I think it might have expired.'

'Mom, it expired sometime in the seventies.'

'That doesn't matter. I'm still a citizen. I can get a new one.'

'Mom, Meril told you some of his stories, didn't he? He's had quite the life, that Meril, hasn't he?'

'And he's got no regrets,' she said.

'Regrets? What regrets do you have?'

I heard her sniffling over the line. I knew her bottom lip was trembling, and her wrinkled hand, dappled with veins and blotched like water marks on the ceiling, was tight over the receiver. It was all muffles and sniffles for a good minute.

'I just want to see the Pyramids,' she said. 'I don't need to explain it to you.'

#

I watched that Meril at dinner. No way was he crazy. Me and Tom, we were taken with him, almost as much as Kelsey was.

'I spent a few months in Australia before I went to New Zealand, eh?' Meril started.

'You didn't hang out in the Sydney jail I hope,' said Tom.

'Tell us a nice story Meril,' I urged. 'Surely you've seen something beautiful? Have you ever seen the Pyramids?'

His eyes brightened and he put down his fork. 'Your mom was talking about that today!'

'I know she was. She thinks she's going to go see them now. You lit some fire under her ass.'

'I think we should help her,' said Kelsey. The puff was almost gone from her eyes now, but she looked tired.

'It would kill her,' I said, 'and don't bloody say so what. I know so what; she could live for a few more years.'

'We could take her,' Meril piped up.

Kelsey looked shocked; she put her hand over his hand. She smiled like she thought that was a bad idea. I didn't want to talk about it anyway, and I'd made this nice rhubarb crisp, and Tom had made ice cream, so we ate dessert. And I didn't sleep much in the night.

#

I was having a cold bath on the Saturday night. It was too hot to do anything else. Kelsey came in and sat on the toilet, started clipping her dirty toenails into the wastepaper basket. This was her way. She didn't say anything and waited for me to start talking.

'Why'd you cut your hair so short?' I began.

'Easier.'

'That camp is rough on you.'

She turned around and pulled the washcloth off the side of the tub, gestured for me to sit up so she could scrub my back. 'It's so good there Mom. People really—all people want to do is make others feel good about themselves. Meril, he's so amazing at getting people psyched up.'

'Like convincing Mom she should go to friggin' Egypt.'

'I would take her you know,' said Kelsey. 'But with both of them—I'd be the one on medication.'

I grabbed the side of the tub and looked up at her. 'So he really is a camper then eh?'

'He told me he told you, but I thought you would have cornered me about it days ago.'

'I'm not sure that it really bothers me.'

'I'm never sure what to believe.'

'What?'

'He likes to tell stories.'

'Well that's obvious.'

'No. I mean, all these places he's been to, I'm not sure it's anything more than bits and pieces he's picked up from other people.'

'He's a liar?'

Kelsey grinned then, and she had tears in her eyes. 'I'm not sure that it really bothers me!' She laughed again then, and pulled at the neck of her t-shirt and looked down at her boobs. 'Heavenly, tell me these tits aren't going to sag like yours.'

She wanted to divert me then, and I wanted to talk about it more. But she'd moved on. She's like her dad in that respect, so I left it, grabbed the pumice stone and went to work on my elbows and heels. That was the last we talked about it anyway because they left the next day. They confessed that they were only allowed a weekend away instead of a whole week, and there was going to be a bit of hell to pay when they got back. That Meril gave us a gift of crab-apple people, he'd done it well too. He scrounged bits and pieces from the kitchen—toothpicks, steel wool, cloves, a terrycloth, caraway and mustard seeds, a few broom hairs—and made a fat old couple with a jug of Buster wine between them. For the Buster wine, he used the cap from an Ajax bottle. He told me he'd learned how to make apple people from a guy who mended his shoes once in Mexico City. Great imagination that Meril, Mexico City or not.

As per usual, I felt like I was being ripped apart when Kelsey left. They wanted to hitch to the bus station, so we walked them up to Highway 6 and waited until they caught a lift. She hasn't lived at home since she was seventeen, well that's not true—she's come home for a few months here and there to help when Mom got really bad. But if you asked me how many addresses and jobs she's gone through in that time, I wouldn't be able to tell you. I would think it's somewhere in the twenties. Tom wouldn't even proffer a guess.

#

I think it was about a week after they left that St Mary's called me to say Mom had run away. We called the police right away and by chance, they found her at the bus station, half suffocated and delirious. So we didn't really sick the cops on her, as she now will have anyone who will listen, believe. An officer was at the bus station anyway and was alerted to her by the Quick Snack man who found her sweating and panting by the drinks fridge. When I got to the hospital she was hooked up to a couple of things, but she was bright as a Christmas tree, propped up and pissed off. Tom sat in a chair by the window while I fritted around her. There were other patients in the room, older and sicker, and the smell, one I always associate with the old and infirm, was like boiled chicken.

'Do you feel like telling me what happened Mom?' I asked.

'I was trying to get to Vancouver to renew my passport.'

'I told you, you couldn't go anywhere without your oxygen.'

'And I told you it'll be the last trip I do.'

That friggin' Meril, I thought. I considered telling her the truth about him, but it only would have been to hurt her. They brought Mom the prescribed soft lunch of rice pudding, over-boiled carrots, and pureed beef. She ignored it, which meant she was really and truly pissed off.

'I'm not a prisoner,' she said to me, and she looked at Tom. He nodded his agreement, but shrugged his shoulders too.

'Well, look how far you got Mom. How did you get to the bus station anyway?'

'Hitched.' She looked up, tried to cup her tears so they wouldn't fall. 'It's so boring getting old.'

14. THERE'S NOTHING I CAN DO

by Katie Mayes

I went to see Adam again today. My last visit before I have to go away. He was curled up, foetus-like on the sofa, arms crossed, wearing the same blue t-shirt and grey track-pants that he had on yesterday and, come to think of it, the day before. The Friday lunchtime news was on TV but he didn't seem to be watching it or even listening to it. He just lay there, silent, with a blank expression on his unshaven face.

I sat down in the armchair opposite him but he didn't pay any attention; he didn't look up or acknowledge I was there. I watched as his mother, Susan, came through from the kitchen and placed a fresh mug of tea on the coffee table, in the same place as the cold one she took away. Her hair looked lank and unwashed, she seemed tired and her hands shook as she carried the cold mug out to the kitchen. I followed her and watched as she bent double over the draining board, her face turned away from the lounge door, and I watched while she cried.

There's nothing I can do. I've tried to get them to listen to me, but it doesn't work. I've tried putting my arms around Susan but all she does is shudder and pull her cardigan tighter around her. I've sat next to Adam these past couple of days and tried many times to talk to him but he flicks at his ear with the back of his hand and draws his knees closer to his chest. I want to tell them that it's okay, but they won't hear me.

Susan hasn't stopped crying since Adam was brought home by the police on Monday. I don't think she cries for me, though; I think she cries for Adam. Of course, she doesn't even know me, not really, so she wouldn't cry for me would she? She did bring some flowers though, on Wednesday, beautiful, tiny, white daisies—my favourite. That was the day I first came to visit Adam so, I thought, if she can do that for me, the least I can do for her is to visit him.

I think she cries for Adam because he doesn't cry. He can't cry, he said, he can't because then he'd be crying in pity for himself. Which is true I suppose but then sometimes I wish he would cry, shout, scream, anything because maybe then he'd be able to get up off the sofa and stop thinking about it for a while. Maybe then, he'd allow his mother to hug him like she needs to.

I didn't stay long today, there didn't seem much point, he won't acknowledge me and there's nothing I can do anyway. I noticed his blue Marks and Spencer's suit hanging, clean and neatly pressed, in the hallway as I was leaving. I think that's the one he used to wear for work. Well, that's what he was wearing on Monday morning anyway. They wrote him a nice letter, the bank did. It came when I visited yesterday and his mother had to read it out to him as he showed little interest in it. Very sorry, they said, but in view of recent events we have no alternative but to let you go. Of course, they've paid him off and everything but even so, it's a bit unfair. What he did to me had no bearing on them whatsoever. But of course, depending on what happens in court on Monday, I'm not sure if he'd be able to go back to work there, or anywhere for that matter. He didn't react though, not a word, not a sigh, nothing—he just lay there, foetal, empty.

It's nearly time for me to go now though. It's funny but I don't feel much; I'm not sad about having to go, I'm not upset or in pain or anything like that. I've been to see my mum, she's inconsolable but, strangely enough, she did stop crying for a brief moment when I put my arms around her and whispered goodbye to her. I couldn't stay with her for too long, the dog kept whining and looking at me. Bless him. Poor little Scamps. Who's going to take him for his early morning walks now? Mum'll have to but I doubt she'll be able to get down there in her mobility-scooter. I can just imagine her wheel-spinning in the mud trying to get up and down those hills. Mind you, I don't think she's going to want to go down there much. The broken, splintered tree would be too much for her. Just knowing it's there as a permanent reminder, she'll probably find someplace else to take the dog.

So, this is it. The mists are rolling in now and look, over there, isn't that beautiful? If you stand there, on that bend, where Station Road meets The Causeway, the un-named road dips and curves off to the right, just stand there and look. Really look out over the landscape. The fields roll and rumble down towards the castle over there, isn't that beautiful?

That's where I used to walk the dog every morning before school.

That's the corner where I died, right there, can you see, can you see those beautiful white daisies laid beneath the splintered tree, there on that bend?

He was going too fast you see. He was late for work, got stressed out by all the rush-hour traffic, put his foot down, clipped the central reservation and spun out of control. I heard the wheels spinning and turned around just before he hit me. I will never forget the look of sheer terror in his eyes.

15. SHUTTERED LANDSCAPE

by Fehmida Zakeer

She pushed open the wooden latch and stepped into shadows bordering a pool woven of light and darkness. She carefully closed the door behind her, she did not think anyone would come to the tiny room where the steep staircase stood at the far end of the house at this time, but she wanted to make sure she wouldn't be disturbed at least for the next thirty minutes.

Razia dropped to her knees and crawled, unmindful of the fine dust blanketing the wooden boards. She hoped the planks would not creak and give away her presence to anyone sitting in the rooms below. The family had arrived from the city a month back to find their spacious ancestral home expanding in all directions. Now it was filled with relatives and friends waiting to celebrate the first wedding of the latest generation. Thankfully, no one had realised that the attic was clean enough to be a sanctuary from the bustle. She herself had found out only yesterday when she had come hunting for discarded cloth—the caterers, the maids, the cleaners—everyone needed rags and she was deputised to fetch them from the attic.

She made her way to the centre of the space where four triangular sloping roofs reached out and touched each other to form a hollow pyramid beneath, the roof was at its highest here, and she could safely stand up without the danger of bumping her head on the wooden rafters supporting the ridged, terracotta tiles. Skylights placed at regular intervals provided enough illumination to move around, though the dark corners were draped in shadows. She sat cross-legged on the orange and yellow cotton dhurrie she had spread out yesterday and closed her eyes. Even from here, she could hear sounds—the caterers getting ready, the lorry arriving with the chairs, the shouts of workers putting the finishing touches to the huge pandal[1] outside. She tried to block the noise out and looked around. Pale rays of light filtered in through the translucent panes bringing into focus the tumbling dance of the dust motes. She watched the particles whose flow trickled and tapered till they fell, their energies spent.

She noticed a familiar suitcase lying half-hidden in the shadows and opened it to find dozens of tight rolls of fabric—left over fragments diligently taken back from tailors after they had turned the material into outfits for herself and Reem.

How many times she had helped her mother choose bits from these for patchwork and quilting projects. She smiled, remembering the fun she and Reem used to have trying to guess the outfits the bits belonged to. Once they even got a piece of material that had come from a frock Reem had worn as a baby. She took some swatches from a few rolls and placed them on the mat.

The black and red kalamkari[2] fabric brought to mind a still summer afternoon in the year she turned nine. She had been standing on the ledge that ran along the outer periphery of the house her parents were building in the city. She was tugging a branch, testing its strength when suddenly her mother's voice travelled up to her, as tough as the branch in her hand. After finishing lunch, her mother usually took a nap, but not that day it seemed.

'Razia come down at once.'

Her heart had plunged to her stomach and the leafy bough leapt from her startled hands with a tittering sound. She groaned in horror as she looked at her partner in crime, Nitin, who seemed to have become a shade lighter. Razia followed him, trailing her hands on the as yet un-cemented terrace wall as they walked to the gaping window frame waiting to be secured with grills. They jumped inside and went down the stairs to receive the expected explosion of accusations and laments.

She grinned and wondered now what would have happened if her mother had not shown up. Would she have fallen as Nitin had insisted she would or would she have been able to climb down the tree as she had bravely maintained?

She picked up the blue and white seersucker on the mat and frowned as she tried to place it. Suddenly it slipped from her fingers and fluttered down to the

[1] marquee
[2] Patterns traditionally drawn on cotton using a reed stylus and vegetable dyes

muddy-white tassels of the dhurrie. Of course, the sleeveless shirt with the mandarin collar, again one of her favourites. One day she had inadvertently worn it to the religious education class and the teacher chided her saying that eleven-year-old girls should not wear such dresses. Her mother had been pleased when she decided not to wear it thereafter.

She shuddered as she picked the white hakoba[3] fabric. Her favourite wrap around skirt, ruined by a crimson blob that appeared on the back during a game of Kho Kho.[4]

'You are a big girl now,' her grandmother had said and grinned. From then on, whenever Nitin and Rajesh came to call her for their forays, her mother conjured up bizarre reasons to keep her at home—it was going to rain, tuition teacher had called and would come any moment, the sun would darken her milky white complexion ... soon her buddies lost interest and stopped coming.

She took the maroon fabric next and ran her fingers on the zardozi[5] filled petals of the flower encrusted with a tiny pearl at the centre. She stroked the pearl—suddenly it pulled loose from the material, unravelling along with the threads imprisoning the minute golden springs lending shape to the petals. She picked up a tiny piece and stretched it to make it a long string with unsightly undulations.

Tears welled up and threatened to fall from the cusp of her eye; she wished she could turn back time. If she had stayed at home in the city instead of coming here to her hometown to attend a far off relative's wedding six months back, those people would never have seen her, would have never sent word through a mutual friend that they thought she would be a perfect bride for their son in Riyadh. At this moment, she would have been exploring internship options with reputed psychologists.

At first she had not taken any notice, talk about her marriage was routine and she was used to it. She had known she was on extended parole even as she was doing her post-graduation. Inevitable though this was, she had hoped her luck would hold; that she could set up a practice. But this time phone calls went up and down and her father was hooked—a doctor, earning petro

---

[3] A cotton fabric with eyelet cutouts and patterned with machine embroidery
[4] A team game that involves taking an opponent across a dividing line
[5] A form of embroidery and embellishment that uses metal threads, gold and silver coils and other elements

dollars in Riyadh and also studying for his MRCP, an alliance fallen into their lap without any effort.

Her friends had come over dangling the tickets for the latest Aamir Khan movie in a bid to revive her spirits. Her aunt, who had moved in after her husband ran off, entered the room nonchalantly, 'Oh these are your friends ... hello ... Razia I hope you remember, we have to go to the tailor for the fitting today.'

Of course the fitting had been just an excuse, when she went complaining to her mother, her aunt piped in, 'Don't you know that well brought up girls don't go out after the wedding date has been fixed. Do you want to bring bad name to your parents?' Razia flounced off wondering whether her aunt had supersonic ears, teamed with her nosiness and flapping tongue it was no wonder her husband ran off to another woman, she'd thought viciously.

On the day of the fitting, her aunt handed over a slippery piece of chiffon edged with gold trimmings and said with pursed lips, 'Start wearing the hijab at least now.'

Suddenly a nasal voice pierced the stillness of the attic, her aunt again. She stiffened, sure that she would be discovered, but the wooden steps remained silent and the voice trailed away lamenting her whereabouts. Razia knew that she was expected to get dressed for the mehendi ceremony;[6] that people would start arriving in an hour's time and she could not remain hidden anymore.

She peered from the top. The ruckus from the other side of the house suggested that everyone was having tea and snacks. She walked to her bedroom silently, on her bed her pistachio green ghagra[7] with its profusion of creepers and stone studded flowers winked and glinted in merriment.

She gazed at it and was stuck suddenly by the tapering design of the embroidery on the skirt—an intertwined maze of silver threads, sequins and swarovksi crystals on the wide flare of the skirt rising up in sparse trails as it moved along the narrow cut of the fabric towards the waist—just like the spaces in her life.

---

[6] Event preceding a wedding when patterns of henna are ceremonially inscribed on the bride's and others' hands.

[7] An elaborately patterned floor-length skirt, tight at waist and hips and widely flared, generally worn on grand occasions.

16. SODA LAKES

by Liesl Jobson

Sunscreen, water bottle, towel, cap, socks. We set out the trestles, take our blades to the dock.

Soda lakes are mainly confined to subtropical latitudes in rain-shadow zones.

Sam's home club is on Strathclyde Loch, in Glasgow. 'A man-made lake,' she says, 'built on a demolished palace and an old mining village. The water is very shallow; we never get waves like you get out here.'

I can't imagine that. It sounds odd. And what's with no waves? Later I Google to check if she's telling a story. She's right on the construction details but I find nothing about there being no waves.

Often impermanent in nature, their terrestrial equivalents, soda deserts, represent their desiccated remains.

'Do you have to be licensed here?' asks Sam, who recently arrived in Cape Town. She's a microbiologist, a post-doc at the university for another year or two.

'Licensed?'

'In London,' she says, 'you have to have a license to row.'

'This is no London,' I say. 'You go. You row. You fall out. Nobody knows.' I don't want to scare her, don't tell her the horror stories.

'Which is our boat?' I point to the blue double. 'Wicked,' says Sam, 'she's brand new.'

'Ja, new enough.'

We slide Catalyst off the rack, roll her riggers, hoist her to shoulders. We settle her on the trestles, check the footplates, runners and seats. Then we carry her to the water, minding the molehills that can cause one to stumble. Sam says, 'If you win a race in London, you get points on your license.'

Owing to their hostile nature the soda lakes are often remote from the main centers of human activity and perhaps for this reason they have been little studied.

Sam drills me on the water: square blades, no arms, body swing and power strokes. 'Tap-down, slide. Drive and finish. Get out clean.' A pelican, more snowy than pink, swoops down and settles near the reeds. I catch my breath. I want to tell her about the intimacy I disturbed the other morning, but if I tell her about pelican sex she will think I'm weird.

The Great Rift Valley running through East Africa is an arid tropical zone where tectonic activity has created a series of shallow depressions.

'Did you hear about Andy Holmes?' she asks, but I'm a new sculler and don't know the big names of the sport.

'No,' I say, 'I only know Rika, the South African who went to Beijing.' God, what a goddess. I love Rika. I say, 'I used to go to her ergo classes. Brilliant. But they clash with my work hours now so I can't anymore. But, what's the deal with Andy Holmes?'

'He was an Olympic gold medallist. Paired with Steve Redgrave. Caught Weil's disease on the Thames.'

'Wheels disease?' I ask, wondering if the wheels beneath the seat loosen toxins on the aluminium slide. Maybe a spinal complication from the wheels' motion? But Sam doesn't hear because she's in the bow, and we're pitching into a head wind. The boat is moving and we're pulling together. Her voice behind me gives the instructions: 'Steady paddle at twenty. Prepare for pyramids.' I ready myself for the rate increase, slowing my mind, bracing my shoulders back and down. 'Next stroke, up two.' The first call unleashes a rush. We're at twenty-two strokes per minute. Concentrate; keep the balance. Quick hands. Don't rush the slide. 'Next stroke, up two.' Sam's fitter than me, and younger. At twenty-four strokes per minute I meet the pace, technique still clean. Shoulders over hips. Feet even. Strong thighs. 'Next stroke, up two.' Twenty-six. Not enough air. Boat wobbles. Breathe. Keep it neat. Never been pushed so hard. 'Next stroke, up two.' Twenty-eight. Brain-beat-heart-tight-burn-blind. Hit-hit-hitting. Hold. Focus. Panic. Coughing. God. Sam says, 'Down two ... down two ... down two ... to twenty, to eighteen.'

When we rest up at the Hart Memorial shed, it takes a while to catch my breath. My heart is a drum roll in my ears, slowing gradually to individual beats. How do you know if you're having a heart attack? What are the signs?

I wonder if Sam wants to hear about Keith Hart who had a coronary on the water. Probably not. When Keith collapsed, the boat tipped and his partner panicked. He couldn't keep him afloat and swam to shore to raise help. They searched until sunset but, mired in the deep mud, Keith was invisible. When the police divers found him at dawn the catfish hadn't considered his widow's finer feelings.

When I've emptied my water bottle, I ask Sam again about the disease that the British rower got. She tells me about the waterborne parasite that comes from the urine of rats. 'It's mostly tropical,' she says, 'but seasonal in the UK. Our coach in London really drilled us about keeping open wounds covered. Boat bite and blisters is how the parasites get in. Too sad it was.'

'Yeah?' I ask.

'Fatal it was.'

'Oh, fuck.'

'Andy Holmes was just fifty. He had a new baby. Just a month back. His fifth child.' Fuck, fuck, fuck.

'No parasites here,' I say, wanting to turn to sweeter matters, 'just jacanas and herons. Oh, and the hippo at Rondevlei.' But what do I know, really? There must be heaps of crap in this water, but I fell out of my boat about thirty times this year and never got sick. The hippo escapes when copper thieves cut the security fence to the sewage works. But they've tagged it now with a microchip for a quick retrieval. This, too, she probably doesn't need to know.

'This is supposed to be a *fresh* water lake. Ja right! The sewage treatment plant,' I say, pointing at the concrete tanks just visible over the ridge, 'washes out to sea, but when the north wind blows we say, wake up and smell the E. coli.'

These are often closed basins with no obvious outflow where ground water and seasonal streams flowing from the surrounding highlands collect to form semi-permanent standing bodies of water.

Sam works on my technique: feel the weight of the water on the blade at the catch; get a level draw through. Balance your body weight on the blade handle, like you're suspended in the air.

She emails later with the technical tips and balancing exercises. Her PS at the end reads, 'Don't try this alone.' I row alone. Well, almost alone. Last week while I rested after a sprint, my oars aligned on the feather, an otter on the bank caught my eye. The creature stopped, one paw poised in the air. Then it slipped below the surface without a splash.

Surface evaporation rates exceed the rate of inflow of water allowing the dissolved minerals to concentrate into a caustic alkaline brine.

Sam's professor said that one of the soda lakes in Kenya is home to a huge population of flamingos. Every two years or so, the toxicity gets too high and they die off in enormous numbers while the remaining birds settle at another lake. They suspect a nearby battery factory is dumping heavy metals into the water.

This year the flamingos came back to Zeekoevlei. They hadn't been around for six years, according to Old Guy, but the water was cleaner of late. That, he said, was why they were back. The queen of the club said he talked shit as they'd been there every winter, regardless, but Old Guy was a fair-weather rower. Was in the pub all winter, now wasn't he? Old Guy and the queen have a long-running spat. No point in asking questions. Unwise to take sides.

When I went out on the water again, the time after hearing about the flamingos' return, I set my mind to learning to row straight, and set my stern in line with the buoy. I held it there, inhaling down the slide, exhaling on the drive. With my left arm weaker than my right, my course was still a zigzag of drift and correct. Watching the buoy, I'd stopped minding my course. Didn't see the flamingos on a sand bank behind me until they were a vast pink flurry, neither cawing nor cackling, but a breathy beating of a hundred wings alighting and passing overhead. I wanted to weep at their beauty, afraid they'd leave again, never to return. But before my tears could form, the birds began their descent to the deserted beach in front of the old pump house.

'Too much politics in Kenya,' says Sam.

'Not just Kenya,' I say, thinking of the queen and Old Guy. The queen holds the club's purse strings. Old Guy coaches the disabled athletes in boats that are junk. There should be Lotto money for them, but it got lost on the way. Months ago, they were promised a new path to the dock to facilitate the wheelchairs and the blind guys getting down to the water, but the grass still grows in matted clumps through cracks in the old concrete. 'Promises and praise,' Old Guy said, 'are as cheap as Chappies. But it's all hot air and blow-offs that never deliver.'

'You can't get permits to take samples from the lake,' says Sam. 'Government wants it hushed up. The die-offs haven't been studied. Too damn sad.'

Seemingly hostile extreme pH environments are, in fact, curiously productive because of high ambient temperatures, high light intensities and unlimited supplies of carbon dioxide.

Last week, Sam met me early because I had to run a poetry workshop that started in town at 9 a.m. My catch was late; I rushed the slide. We pitched and jolted till she called, 'Easy up.' We drifted to a stop, panting and jangled. 'Where are you today?' she asked. ''Cause you're not in the boat.'

I said my mind was on the Rape Crisis workshop, which I wasn't ready for. How does one prepare for such a thing? She winced empathetically. We sat a while in silence.

'Well now,' she said, 'you'll need to return here before going there. Let's focus some, shall we?' I nodded. 'Even pressure on your feet and back straight. Engage your core.'

This remarkable photoautotrophic primary production stands at the top of the food chain and is presumably the driving force behind all biological processes in what is essentially a closed environment.

Today, again, the water is calm, our balance perfect. The riffle of bubbles bursting against the shell is a burbling whisper. As the bow breaks the surface tension, our blades pop in perfect rhythm. We head back from the weir and angle up to the dock in a smooth arc. Outside the boathouse, we wash off the boat. Sponge down the riggers, spray off the blades. I point out the waterline, a solid stripe from bow to stern.

'Wicked,' says Sam.

'Not too shabby, girls,' says Old Guy, 'but your body swing's still out of sync.'

'The easiest thing to spot out the boat,' mutters Sam under her breath, 'the hardest to fix inside it.'

When I rub the waterline, it changes from a solid paste into minute bright green specks on the sponge.

'This algae, Sam?' I ask

'Algae and nastiness,' she says.

'That nastiness,' says Old Guy, who has been bent over the adaptive boat, cursing all morning, 'is caused by high levels of phosphates in the water.' It's the third time he's had to repair the fitting for the amputees. 'Every idiot washing their car in the street on a Sunday morning, their detergent flows down the storm water drain and into the river. All the homeless washing their delicates in the river, their soap filters into the vlei.[1] And the oil and crud and laundry water from the informal settlements—ditto.'

Old Guy plucks at the pad of foam curling off the seat, where he glued it to prevent the paraplegics from getting pressure sores. 'The phosphates are what make the plants grow cyanobacteria—that's the photosynthetic microorganisms containing chlorophyll. You could say the bacterium and algae clump together in a symbiotic relationship.'

I figure Sam got her PhD on all this stuff. She could probably write the book, but she nods respectfully as she replaces her blades in the holding rack.

'Two or three years back those phosphates were coming from the sewage works, which was leaking into the vlei, but the council sorted that out,' he says, preparing to tell us the saga.

'Is that why the pelicans and flamingos have come back?' I ask, hoping to divert him.

'Yes,' he says. 'They thrive on the cyanobacteria.'

Our boat shed is a hundred yards from the water's edge. Could the dishwashing liquid we're using to clean the boats be seeping down through the Cape Flats sand and filtering back into the vlei as we speak? I wonder whether Old Guy has thought of this. Has Sam?

'And for the record,' says Old Guy, waving a spanner at us, 'those phosphates are highly corrosive. They'll chew up all the metal fittings if you don't wash that boat properly. So, girlies, make sure you do.'

'Yes, Sir,' I say. Sam rolls her eyes. I pull my cap down lower and stifle a giggle. If you don't concentrate while wiping the shell, you rip open your knuckles on the bolts.

Sam goes over my training program with me for the week ahead. I have to improve my cardiovascular fitness now. She throws her towel over a trestle and shows me how to replicate the technique in the boat on the ergo. 'For a sharp catch,' she says, 'engage your lats. Lift your sternum. Sit up straight.'

Tap-down, slide. Drive and finish. Get out clean.

Notes in italics taken from 'Microbial diversity and ecology of the Soda Lakes of East Africa', B.E. Jones & W.D. Grant, Proceedings of the 8th International Symposium on Microbial Ecology, Atlantic Canada Society for Microbial Ecology, Halifax, Canada, 2000.'

17. PLACES TO GO AND PEOPLE TO MEET

by Lisa Marie Trump

Cassidy was a rare thing, a Londoner with a Glaswegian accent. Life back at home had been hard and London had beckoned; after all, it was the city of opportunity. He now lived—if living is the right term, in a side road just off Oxford Street. It was a nice home, lots of gold ornament, colourful photographs, and sweeping marble stairs. He only had to vacate it between 7 p.m. and 11 p.m. Tuesday to Saturday. Old Bob didn't like it if he was around when there were visitors, 'Brings down the tone of the place,' he'd say. Cassidy didn't really mind because living on the steps of a London theatre you could expect little else, and anyway he had places to go and people to meet.

Leech was waiting in the rain at the corner of Tottenham Court Road, as always. Not much of a talker, he'd stand with his legs just far enough apart to make anyone else on his patch know that he, Leech, had the biggest tackle. He was leaning up against the glass of a television shop. Behind him, a giant matrix of TV screens all showed the same program. A wildlife documentary probably, thought Cassidy as he caught a glimpse of Leech's reflection in the rain-spattered glass. Nestling in the pixelated foliage of a Borneo rainforest, Leech looked like a rare gorilla, the alpha male about to scent his territory. It wasn't often that Cassidy noticed these things—colour and texture and form. Usually the dull throb of day would stab into his chest and press into his eyes. The nausea would rise and sour bile burn his throat. The ache in his right leg would explode, dripping the sticky canker of pain into his mind until there was nothing more of him left. Although the chill of the London rain trickled down the back of his neck making him long for Jade, his excitement eased his pain and he barely limped.

Leech carried a tatty khaki rucksack full of loose change, which hung, lumpy and jingling over his right shoulder. No words were exchanged—they never were. Like so many theatre-goers, night-clubbers and hen-party chicks, Cassidy passed Leech with little more than a glance. In the second of time that shoulder brushed shoulder, Leech spat out a small cellophane package and popped it into Cassidy's mouth, while he dropped change into Leech's open palm.

Transaction complete. Now Cassidy really had places to go.

#

Jade was having a party. Just a quiet affair, close family and friends, that kind of thing. Not far from the Waldorf, very nice. She'd thought about dressing up for the event: that shimmering silk strapless number in the window at Selfridges. Turquoise silk, sliding all over her like the cool rippling water of a Mediterranean beach. But the three coins in the torn pocket of her stained jeans wouldn't stretch to a Lacroix. A few drinkies, naturally, to get everyone in the mood. Start early, thought Jade, as she swigged the sour metallic beer from the can, there might not be enough to go round. 'Hop-along!' she shouted, as Cassidy limped into view. 'Join the party!'

'Is there room enough for me?' he joked, as he pushed through throngs of imaginary guests to reach Jade in the dark corner under the arches at Embankment.

'Always room for you,' she said, emerging from her blanket with her swollen belly peeking from beneath her jumper. She kissed him forcefully, the sour tang of beer wetting his lips and her warm round abdomen pressing against him. Her tousled hair fell forwards over her face and he gently pulled back to look at her. He'd never seen anyone as beautiful as Jade; her name matched her green eyes which sparkled through the grime of years on the London streets.

'What's this?' she asked, as if surprised, pulling out the cellophane package he'd passed to her mouth. 'I think this party just got better! I'll roll up.'

Cassidy sat down awkwardly and wiped the rain from his face. He felt his right leg pulsating just below the knee, a heavy, wet throb. But when he pulled up his blood and pus-stained jeans, the open, weeping sore looked just as it had the night before. He picked at it. It bled a little, crimson mixing into black.

'Perhaps you should get that seen to down at the hostel?' Jade said as she split the package and teased the sacred powder onto a cigarette paper lined with tobacco.

'Don't be silly,' Cassidy said, coughing through the black phlegm in his chest. 'This is my livelihood.' He took a long, slow drink from Jade's beer can. The sore gaped and oozed. He seemed satisfied with the result and displayed it proudly. 'This earned me a portion of chips, a coffee, and that little bundle, today. There was one chap, bus driver or something, judging by his uniform, nearly passed out when I showed it t' him. "Can ye lend me some change so I can get t' the hospital?" I said to him. He took one look at my leg and vomited all over his brogues. I walked him to the A and E and he slipped me a twenty for mah trouble.'

Foraging under a dirty grey blanket next to Jade, Cassidy pulled out a second beer can and drank from it greedily. 'Slow down!' Jade chided, passing the cigarette creation to Cassidy. 'I want some of it with this. Here, you light.'

A thin curlicue of smoke rose into the air and drew a hazy voile curtain across the cold wet night.

#

She smells musky and animal-like, Cassidy thought. I love you he whispered in his mind as the image of a lean white antelope nuzzling into him filled his senses. She wrapped her legs tighter round his waist in acknowledgement. How did she hear me? How did she get into my mind? 'I love you—your eyes, your mind, my child inside you,' he shouted.

Then vivid colours flashed across the underside of the archway the vibrant green of her eyes and the shimmering blue of her mind, then red came, the red of life. The colours lit their black little corner of London like an aurora. It made him long to see the sky. He placed his hand across her belly. He could feel the warm shape beneath that was growing and moving. A balmy rush of ecstasy swam through his body, starting in his chest and spiralling out towards his fingertips and the top of his head. It felt so good to be alive. 'Alive!' he shouted out, as if to check that the sensation was real.

Jade laughed, and she too shouted, 'Alive!'

Their echoing voices reverberated round the arches, like a choral praise to God in a baroque cathedral. 'Alive! Alive!'

Pure rapture coursed through Cassidy's veins; his blood tingled with the tang of it. He stood up, his arms above his head, the mother of his unborn child by his side. Every quick, shallow breath filled him with the sparkling fizz of what it means to be alive. I can do anything, he thought. Anything.

He took Jade by the wrist and pulled her out into the rain; it no longer felt cold, it was warm and running over their bodies like molten gold. He wanted to feel the canopy of the dense London sky over them, and they clambered up onto the bridge. They had freedom and power over everything other than that sky. The electric blue of the air sparkled all around them, cerise clouds exploding like fireworks overhead, streamers of orange and crimson flashing across the air and sending a rippling kaleidoscope into the river beneath their feet. Rosettes of pinks and yellows burst around their heads, and for a moment, Jade was surrounded with tropical flowers.

She stood beside him on the ornate bridge and the changing colours were reflected on her porcelain face. Like a pre-Raphaelite woman, Cassidy thought, and the only thing I ever got right.

'I can do anything!' he screamed, and Jade laughed a full, beautiful laugh that penetrated the deepest parts of his mind with the exquisite sounds of an orchestra. He stood on the ledge to be nearer the sky and made the surface of the mercurial river shoot lasers of blue, red, and yellow over the city. St. Paul's exploded in a shower of grey, silver, pewter, and gold—and spiky rubble rained down over London like confetti.

He turned his face to look at Jade and seeing the soft caressing spirals surrounding her, knew that she and the baby would be protected always. He breathed in the sky. The river water beckoned him and the tendrils of colour it sent towards him filled his lungs until he too was nothing but colour, light and sound. Elation filled his mind and he stepped off. The colours vanished.

But Jade could still see colour; repeated flashes of blue bouncing over the bridge and out across the black water. She could hear urgent voices and hissing radios. She moved to the dark corner under the bridge and pulled the grey blanket around her shoulders. She watched the swelling of the river, saw it lapping at the foot of the bridge, and she waited for Cassidy to appear once more, laughing and calling to her from the water.

18. RAPTOR

by Rebecca Lloyd

Robert had tried to get Violet interested in the owls *once*; he thought the two babies would delight her. 'Why are they so slow?' she'd asked.

'They're not slow, they're watchful; it's just in their nature.'

'They smell fusty.'

He'd laughed, and given her a gauntlet and persuaded her to take them onto her arm. 'I bet this one blinks first,' she said. 'Bet you a pound.'

'Would you like to work with them, Violet?'

She shook her head. 'There's too much waiting.'

'Would you like to work with the merlins, then?'

'I'm better at front of house, Robert. You know the others don't like me.'

She was right about that, his falconers were wary of her and although it annoyed him, he ignored it. They were secretive and careful and it would be in their natures to draw back from Violet's impulsiveness. He'd spoken about her only once, to Callum O'Connor. 'Complex woman,' he'd said.

'Fractured more like. Mass of contradictions if you don't mind me saying so, Robert.'

'I was hoping you and the others would give her a bit of support from time to time.'

Callum shrugged. 'I think she's got things pretty much worked out for herself round here.'

'I'll grant you she's a survivor.'

'Have you ever seen her in a temper?'

Robert had once or twice, and been shocked by it. He'd seen her kicking the barn wall and swearing in a way that made him shiver. He shrugged. 'It's nothing though, is it? It's just bluff—fake aggression.'

'What's the difference between fake aggression and real aggression, is there any?'

'I just meant she has other sides to her. She's vulnerable, you know, and she can be charming sometimes.'

'Yeah, I know about the charm. But if we behaved like she does, you'd sack us, wouldn't you?'

'I worry about her.'

'Don't we all?'

Robert felt himself redden. 'I think the business can afford to harbour one of life's little refugees, you know.'

'If that's what you think, you should increase her wages to stop her trying to get her claws on mine ... and Caroline's, and Jack's.'

#

Robert had been shaken by his conversation with Callum but he was sure Violet could be tamed if he was patient with her in the way he was with the more wayward raptors. He'd tried being hard, especially when she brought him gifts, but his desire to protect her was always there, a melancholic aching that sometimes turned to burning in him.

She once gave him an eggcup that looked like a sitting hen, and when he turned fifty-six, she gave him a bright blue tie with black swallows on it. He never wore the tie at work, but he put her bird of prey calendar on the wall behind his desk, and used the badly painted peregrine falcon paperweight she'd been so excited about.

When she came with a pack of playing cards, he'd had enough of it. 'I don't play cards, Violet.'

'Yes, but you might one day, you never know. Every man should have a pack of playing cards. These have got tropical birds on the back of them, look. I was sure you'd like them.'

'Please don't waste your money on me.'

'You always say that, but why shouldn't I?'

'Because you can't afford it; I hardly pay you anything.'

'Don't you like my presents, is that what you mean?' She raised her fingers and clutched them to her throat.

Robert turned the pack of cards over in his hands. 'Listen, Violet, I don't want gifts from you. I just want you to stick to our agreement and pay what you owe me on time.'

She laughed. 'That's the difference between you and me. I love it when people give me things. I mean, it's something for nothing, isn't it—everybody likes that, surely?'

'We're expecting a party from Manchester today. Shouldn't you be out at the main gates now?'

'I'm on my way, Robert. I really just came to tell you that Daddy sends his greetings. I was at the house last weekend. We had a big party in the ballroom, orchestra and everything, and the Italian Garden was full of pink lights. I danced all night,' she added quietly.

'Well, that's lovely, Violet.'

'And I was thinking of you.'

Robert laughed. 'I'm no good at dancing, so it's just as well I wasn't the one dancing with you.'

'Oh, I was dancing alone,' Violet said, 'I always do, you see.'

Robert tried to work again when she'd gone, but he had no heart for it. She made him restless. Her habit of jerking her head from left to right would've been exasperating in anyone else, yet it was fascinating when Violet did it; on her, it looked aristocratic. He waited for it, waited to see her curious round eyes blink or widen, waited to see the small quick movement of her hands as she touched her throat or her earlobe.

She'd been at Beechwood Falconry for seven years and over that time Robert had watched the streak of silver in her dark hair widen. She'd arrived in a man's coat one winter, asking for work, and he'd found her a series of simple tasks until he heard her talking about the eagles to a party of visitors at the gate, and knew she could do the job better than the other three. Her curious drifting life, about which he knew only fragments, began finally to make sense when she revealed the desolation of her childhood. 'And that's me as a little girl,' she said, turning the page of an old and brittle magazine.

Robert smiled. 'You haven't changed much.'

'Is that good or bad?'

'I mean I can see the likeness.'

'Yes, but is it good or bad, Robert?' She ran her finger across the tiny blurred figure of a child standing apart and to the left of the family group. One of the turrets of Maurice House rose behind her, colossal against the skyline. She told him how she'd wandered for hours through vast rooms with vaulted ceilings and between the marble statues in the Italian garden. 'There was one statue I used to talk to when I was miserable, and I swear he answered me sometimes. I suppose you think that's silly.'

Robert looked at her face. 'I think it's charming,' he whispered.

He'd never been to Maurice House himself, but the longer Lady Violet worked for him, the more inclined he was to join a group of tourists on a visit to the mansion, to get some sense of what life there must have been like for her.

When she came to him for money she was often in tears, and sometimes she trembled. She always began the conversation with the exact same phrase until it became a ritual between them. 'Oh, Robert,' she'd say, 'I'm in deep trouble and I don't know where to turn.' She'd pull up the neck of her sweater or t-shirt and try to hide her face in it.

'Dear girl, I'm sure it's nothing that can't be sorted out,' Robert replied each time. He knew that to stop her sobbing, he had to whisper, 'I can't talk to you if you're going to hide your face like that. Look at me.'

'But I feel so stupid and ashamed. I don't want you to see me.'

'What's happened, Violet?'

'I've lost some money again. I can't believe it, but I have, and I was being so careful.'

'How much this time?'

'A huge amount. I was trying to buy you something, and the next thing I knew all my money had gone.'

The change in her mood when he lent her money thrilled him. He hadn't properly understood her situation until she came to him in the barn once when he was with the kestrels. 'My real problem is Daddy. He won't let me get on and try to make my own money. Sometimes I think he'd bury me in money if he could.'

'Well, if you don't mind me saying so, Violet, you're lousy at handling it.'

'I'm useless at it because I've got so much coming to me, I suppose.'

'But do you really think it helps that I keep bailing you out?' He should've told her at that moment that there'd be no more loans; he'd increased his house mortgage to keep pace with her debt to him long ago, and now he was frightened for the business itself.

'If I can't make it alone in the outside world,' Violet explained, 'then Daddy would've won, wouldn't he? I couldn't bear that.' She began to weep.

'Look, I can let you have another five hundred, then that really has to be the end of it.

'You're the kindest man on earth, Robert Carstairs,' she said, 'You'll get every last penny I owe you, I promise.'

'It's none of my business, Violet, but when are you going to inherit? The loan worries me.'

He'd thought about selling up. He'd even practised writing a formal letter of dismissal to the staff, but when he read it out aloud to himself, it seemed so heartless that he knew if the business went under, he'd have to tell them straight to their faces. He could settle some money on them, but it wouldn't be much and he was ashamed of that. Over seven years he'd lent Lady Violet close to half a million pounds, and each time she'd returned some of it he'd been deeply grateful.

'I thought you were someone who didn't care about money. That's what you always say, anyway,' Violet said.

'I don't. Not for its own sake.'

'What's coming to me is far more than you could even imagine,' she told him gently. 'It's just a matter of waiting.'

Robert laughed. 'I thought you didn't like slow things. That's what you always say, anyway.'

'It won't be long. Daddy promised he'd settle some serious money on me next year.'

'I'd have thought a year is a bit slow for you,' Robert said. Her face fell. The light in the barn had softened her features, and the impulse to hold her came at him strongly, until he had to turn away. 'Please don't look at me like that, Violet. I'm only joking with you,' he whispered.

'Well as it happens, I have got a bit of money. If you come over to my flat this evening, I'll give it to you.'

#

It smelt sharp and stale in Violet's flat, and as Robert waited for her to move some clothes off a chair, he looked about quickly. Her half-closed curtains were too thin for the winter, and the ceiling wallpaper had peeled away in long drifts. Her table was strewn with piles of letters and old newspapers. 'They should be filed, or thrown away,' she said. 'They're mainly bills, though, so I can't. There you are, have a seat.'

Robert stared at her; she was innocent of the filth she lived in, eccentric like aristocrats were supposed to be, and the aching in him started again. Her fingers were at her throat, and her face was almost luminous in the shadows. 'It looks like this stuff goes back years,' he said. 'You could probably throw most of it away. I'll go through it with you, if you like.'

Violet laughed. 'I'll get round to it sometime.'

'No. I mean it. We could do it now.'

She turned away from him abruptly and looked through the curtains into the greyness beyond. For the last week, the sky had been heavy with water, but no rain had fallen. When she next spoke, it was so softly that he wasn't sure he'd understood her. 'I've never told this to a soul, Robert, but I have to keep things because I can't tell if they're important or not. They might be. You just can't tell.'

'But most of it looks like junk mail. That's not important to anybody except the bastards who send the stuff out.'

She turned back to face him, and Robert thought he could see tears in her eyes. 'I don't mean to be rude, Robert, but you're very simple-minded sometimes. You can't just go throwing things away willy-nilly, they might be lucky.'

'Lucky?'

'Everything in life is lucky or unlucky, even other people. Haven't you ever met someone who strikes you as so unlucky that if you don't move away from them fast, it'll rub off on you like a disease?'

Robert hesitated. 'I can't say I have.'

'And other people who feel so lucky that you want to be with them always?'

'It's never occurred to me to think like that. Is that how you live your life, Violet?'

'Maybe you don't need luck, but I do. You're lucky in my life Robert. That's why I've stayed at Beechwood for so long.'

'Other people would think you're the luckiest woman on earth being the only child of your father,' he said. 'But you can't live your life on the basis of what's lucky and what isn't.'

'Yes I can.' Violet pulled the curtains aside. 'I bet you ten quid it'll rain in the next hour,' she said. 'And if it does, then I'll be lucky tonight.'

'How can you know that?'

'Because I've just bet on it, and if I'm right, then I'm lucky and I can do anything.'

'Why do you have to be lucky tonight?'

'That's for me to know. Look, I can give you fifty pounds. Is that all right?'

'What're you going to do about the real money, Violet?'

'I told you, I wrote to Daddy. I said I wanted to buy a house. He's going to give me five hundred thousand soon; that's about the amount I owe you now, isn't it?'

Robert nodded and took the single crumbled note gratefully.

As he made his way back to the other side of town, he knew he shouldn't have gone to her flat—it had only deepened his pity for her. Just before he left, she'd darted forward and kissed him quickly on the cheek, and stepped away again, blinking. He could still feel the imprint of it as he reached home.

#

Everything Violet owned was lucky and certain things were particularly so because they'd been lent to her by people she hardly knew. She had towels, plates, saucepans, a good quality iron, and even a velvet jacket with embroidered pockets, all of which had become naturally hers through the passage of time.

She shouldn't have invited Robert to the flat; he'd gazed about in a way that'd made her feel uncomfortable, and she was a fool to have told him about the Luck. After he'd gone, she stood at the window watching the sky, it was as grey as pewter and still there was no rain. She'd given him a bit of money, yet he didn't smile at her as he turned to leave, and as she kissed him on the cheek he winced, and that wasn't usual in men she'd known before.

It came to her suddenly that she should leave Monmouth. Seven years was longer than she'd stayed anywhere—but she'd never come across anyone as kind as Robert before, and the thought of leaving him hurt her strangely. She'd come from a hard pinched place where men were frightening and the smell of rancid oil always hung in the air, but she'd had a good friend at the time who shared things with her, even her hairbrush. They'd come across an article about Maurice House in an old magazine they'd found in the women's hostel. 'Why is it that people like this have everything and we've got nothing?' she'd asked as they looked at the photographs.

'Because they're important people,' Petra told her, 'they're aristocrats and they're friends with the queen.'

'Monmouth,' Violet said. 'That's the place for me. That's where my luck will change.'

On the night before she'd walked into Beechwood Falconry for the first time, she'd slept in a barn with half a roof, and the old straw she'd scooped together as a bed had been foul with mould. Yet as she woke the next morning, she could feel her luck coming back to her, and it had made her bold and funny in her meeting with Robert. 'Anything,' she'd said, 'anything you've got. I can turn any trick.' She blushed.

'Well, we lost our cleaner a couple of weeks ago,' Robert told her, 'that's all I've got. Where are you from?'

'I don't think so much about where I'm from as where I'm to,' she said quickly, 'shouldn't we all do that?' and he hadn't insisted on knowing more.

If only it would rain, she could go to Fat Mack's in the blue sequined dress she'd bought in the second hand shop and win back everything she owed him, and that would put an end to her queer tender feelings and the curious idea she had that she'd wronged him. She still had the twenty-pound note that had fallen out of Callum O'Connor's pocket as she followed him to the display field that morning and it was enough to get into Mack's and buy a drink as well. She wouldn't even need to borrow from Ted Bullen, or do any other kind of thing with him.

She touched the windowpane with the tips of her fingers, and saw the first drops falling there like a miracle, softly at first, then hard and fast and running in jagged lines to the sill below. She caught her breath. Her luck was in then, and a person had to wait so long for luck to change sometimes. Only the most courageous and imaginative people could stand the wait, and she was one of them. She traced the path of a raindrop down the windowpane with the tip of her finger as the familiar trembling began deep in the core of her body and worked itself out in waves as if she was a still pool struck suddenly by a thrown stone. She knew she should eat something to calm herself down, but there was nothing in her flat worth eating.

She was tempted to open the bottle of brandy Ted Bullen had left with her, but he'd be displeased. He noticed small details. He wasn't one who came at a woman suddenly before she had time to even think. He was a cautious man who began the ritual with small circular movements of his fingers across a woman's thighs or at the base of her neck. It meant nothing to Violet, but she was happy to play the part of a woman mesmerised if he gave her money—and as long as she didn't catch sight of the place where his little finger should have been, she could almost persuade herself that he did arouse her. She turned quickly from the window and went to her wardrobe.

At Fat Mack's she went straight to the bar for a drink. Her face was burning, and her hands were freezing, but at least Ted wasn't around.

The bar tender shoved her drink towards her, spilling some and looking away quickly when she frowned at him. He was a grubby man, grubby like all the men in Fat Mack's, grubby like the walls, the maroon plastic seating, and the blue carpet covered with yellow slashes. Violet hated Fat Mack's Casino, but she always came back because as she'd walked through Monmouth after her interview with Robert, she'd discovered it. As she stopped in front of its metal doors, she'd spotted a bird of prey hovering in a patch of blue sky above, and she knew the place would be lucky for her eventually.

'Ted Bullen been in?' she asked the bar tender.

'He's out looking for some slut or other.'

She had no time to waste; he'd be back. She drank fast and walked over to the roulette table. Within the first hour, she'd won seven hundred and she was near crazy with joy. When she walked out into the rain that night, she still had four hundred left.

She'd be able to buy the brass eagle now. She wanted to see Robert's slow careful smile again and the special way he had of looking at her almost as if he was in a trance. She'd walk into his office the next day with the eagle and some of her winnings. She wouldn't fling the money in the air and let it settle round him like autumn leaves as if they were in a film; that would be childish. She'd hand it to him quietly, and then he'd know she had dignity.

#

Violet had always considered good and bad luck to be about as separate as any two human experiences could be. Yet as she left Beechwood Falconry with the police officers, it occurred to her for an instant that when good luck is in the ascendant, bad luck is in attendance as inevitably as night follows day, and you could never stop one from suddenly replacing the other. Yet months later, as she became used to the sound of the cell flaps closing in the evening she decided it must've been fear that made her imagine such a depressing thing.

Robert came to visit her every two weeks, and each time before he left, they touched fingers through the glass. He always began the conversation with the exact same phrase until it became a ritual between them. 'Violet, it wasn't me who called the police,' he'd say, 'you do believe that don't you?'

He'd bury his face in his hands so she'd have to tap on the glass to get him to look up. 'I can't talk to you if you're going to hide your face like that, Robert. Look at me.'

His business was gone, but that was no bad thing; the people he'd employed were suspicious and unfriendly, he was better off without them. In particular, Callum, with whom she'd had a brief and dirty meeting behind the barn shortly after she'd first arrived at Beechwood. She knew it was him who'd shopped her. But there were occasions when she was scared that Robert might not wait for her, and then she was obliged to show him with a small twist of her head that she did doubt him. She hadn't intended to manipulate him this way; it had started after he confronted her about her name. 'Of course Daddy would deny he knew me, what with me being in here,' she'd explained, but he'd cut her short.

'I know all there is to know about you now, Violet Wood,' he'd whispered, 'so you can drop the Maurice House rubbish. Violet Wood, tramp, gambler, and pathological liar.'

She'd wept noisily and their meeting had been broken up by the officer on duty. Yet, as she stared through her cell window that afternoon thinking about suicide, she saw a buzzard, or some kind of bird anyway, hovering high in the blue and knew he'd be back. And she was right; he came back, he forgave her, and he came back again and then again and a person couldn't ask for better luck than that.

19. MOTHER'S NOT HOME

by Jennifer Walmsley

Emrys sees faces in faded linoleum. Sneering faces like his Uncle Kendall's. He hears a voice calling out to him. He hears a fist banging on his back door. But he stays in his seat staring down at those faces, screwing his eyes almost closed to study the washed out pink and grey features swirling at his feet.

'I know you're there Emrys!' a crusty voice shouts. Silence. Then footsteps stamp back down the garden path to the lane.

Emrys shifts his ungainly body up from the chair and tiptoes over to the kitchen window. Outside, beyond grimy net and smeared glass, he sees his next-door neighbour bending over a stooped old woman who gazes up at his kitchen window as they talk.

Sighing, he flinches at the sound of the telephone ringing out in the hall. Leaving the window, sidestepping the cat he hates, he plods to the kitchen door, leans against the jamb waiting for the ringing to cease.

When it falls silent, the cat's body twines around his leg and taking the hint, Emrys returns to the kitchen to feed the beast.

After the cat finishes its meal and licks its dish clean, it stalks to the back door, tail raised up like a rod. Recognising the sign, Emrys lets it out and as he does so, that crusty voice calls out, 'How's your mother?'

Mrs. Jenkins is standing, he knows, on two concrete blocks. She peers myopically over the dividing wall covered in pigeon shit.

'Fine,' he mutters, about to shut the door, blocking her face out.

'I called round earlier.' Mrs. Jenkins is not ready to release him. 'Wanted to know if your mother needs anything from the Spar.'

'No, she doesn't.' He closes the door but remembering his manners, opens it up a crack, and adds, 'Thanks for asking,' and promptly shuts it again.

He goes to the window and sees his neighbour still standing on her dais. After a few minutes, she drops out of sight and he breathes in a wheezy sigh of relief.

Upstairs, his mother rests on the double bed she once shared with a father he never knew. Emrys looks up at the ceiling. A mental image of her huge frame rising and falling as she dozes makes him sigh again. He sniffs and thinks he can smell the baby powder he knows his mother likes after her shower.

Now he calls up, 'I'll bring your lunch up shortly, Mother!' but her reply, he thinks, is muffled by the constant sound of her radio.

Going into the larder, he pulls a face at how empty it is. A few tins, packets of biscuits laced in cobwebs sit on shelves that he knows need cleaning. He takes out a can of baked beans and soon they are bubbling on the gas stove. Spooning the beans out onto a plate, he places his mother's lunch on a tray and is about to take it upstairs, when he is interrupted by the sound of the front door bell. The tray in his large hands jerks as the bell chimes again. 'Damn!' Emrys cuts off the rest of the curse. Mother hates swearing. Putting the tray down on the floor, he creeps on slippered feet down the dim hall to the front door. From upstairs, the one o'clock news drifts down, declaring interest rates rising.

The letterbox flaps up. Two green eyes peer through the slit. 'Come on, Emrys,' Wendy, his mother's district nurse, cajoles. 'Open the door; it's bloody freezing out here.'

His cheeks grow hot and he is about to do as she asks, when he pauses. Mother dislikes being disturbed, especially at lunch times.

'Mother's not home!' His lie sounds weak.

'Of course she is,' comes the reply. 'Please love. It's cold and your Uncle Kendall's flu jab is due at one-thirty.'

'Go to him first then,' Emrys says, shivering at the thought of the man who's brought misery and confusion into his life. 'Don't tell your mother,' Uncle Kendall used to tell him when Emrys was a child, holding out a packet of fruit gums as an enticement.

Wendy, forcing lightness into her tone, a tone people often used when addressing him, says 'Please Emrys.'

Unable to resist her wheedling, he opens the door, saying, 'Mother will be angry with me.'

And Wendy steps inside and replies, 'I'll sort it out love. Don't you worry.'

Now she's running up the stairs, her black bag banging against a slender thigh and he hears her feet patter across the landing and his mother's door opening.

Slowly Emrys climbs the stairs and as he reaches the top, Wendy emerges from the bedroom, her face ashen. 'Go downstairs, Emrys,' she says. 'Put the kettle on.'

He starts to cry and takes a step towards Wendy. 'Mother said Uncle Kendall was coming to live with us.' And as his sobs turn into wails, the stench of death mingling with the sweet scent of baby powder wafts out of the darkened bedroom.

20. ADORATION

by Indira Chandrasekhar

I fell in love with her when I was nine. It was her skin, such a beautiful golden-cream colour, like condensed milk, but luminous. I felt that if I could lick it, secretly, without leaving a slimy trace of my saliva to sully its perfection, I would taste heaven. And I can't even describe the heights of heaven I reached a few years later when I imagined myself tasting other more secret surfaces.

All just foolishness—I will never get close enough to taste the great Devipriya, let alone smell her. I did see her once, at a function at the trade-fair grounds. The chain-link fences dripped with people and those who'd climbed the highest were triumphant. But all they could see, the saps, was the top of her head—her hair was orange-pink for the movie she was shooting then. I had arrived early, tied a scented kerchief around my nose, and clambered half-way up the fence to a spot directly over the canal that bordered the slum. It was the best spot. I caught sight of her face framed by the links and I thought I would die. But I willed my melting limbs to hang on because I didn't want the moment to end in the stinking canal.

The funny thing is, although seeing her like that was brilliant, I mean truly brilliant, it was also frustrating. She was gone in five minutes. I didn't have time to sink into the vision.

My neighbour has a DVD player. When he's away I climb in through his window. I can pause the disc when her smile is directed straight at me. They say that eyes define a person, windows to the soul and all. She has eyes to write poetry about. But it's her lips, that delicate bow dimpling into the soft roundness of her cheek; it's her lips that reveal her inner beauty. It's not only the shape, it's that fine ridge around them, luscious and pure. It opens up the contours just a little extra.

The film Basanti—Spring—is one of the few where it's not her face I want to dissolve into. When she lifts her arm to toss the colours of Holi[1] at the hero I see a slight crease in her golden skin where the material of her sleeve pulls at it. And if I manage to halt the film at the right frame, I can see a hint of the luscious weight that drags at her blouse.

Salim and I met as kids in the queue for tickets to Basanti. He lived in a joint family so no one noticed if he was not around. He'd sneak off to follow her wherever she appeared. In those days, you could get close when they were shooting on the streets. Not like now, where the outdoor scenes are shot in foreign countries, and the studios, where the indoor scenes take place, are impossible to get into. Except for Salim, who seems to have made it in.

I bumped into him at Orion Mall. She was expected at their first anniversary celebration. Salim was in the inner enclosure, part of her entourage, the slimy shit. I fought my way to the front and called out, 'Wow, Salim bastard? You look great. Muscles like the big stars, man.' His shoulders bulged under his tight t-shirt. Even his crotch seemed to have doubled in size, his thighs looking scrawny in comparison.

He laughed, let me past the security, slapped me on my back and said, 'Bastard! Mummy let you out today? Just teasing man, don't look so pissed. This bastard,' he said to the others, 'is a major fan. No movie he hasn't seen of our Devipriya-ji. His room ...,' I had made the mistake of taking him home once. My mother freaked at having a Muslim kid, practically from the slums, in our house. She counted her glass artefacts after he left. 'You've got to see his room man, papered with posters. Her breasts leaning over his bed ...' He shook his head meaningfully and added, 'Night-time ...'

The others laughed. I laughed too, feeling sick.

She didn't show up at the anniversary event. Held up at shooting they announced. Her troupe exchanged significant looks as they packed up.

'Shit, don't look so sad man, come with me. I'll take you to her.' I didn't believe Salim, but I went along.

The apartment building was on a corner of a quiet street, the entrance, narrow and grotty. I peered through the accordion grill doors as the lift rose past two empty floors. The light from the lift lit up rubble that crumbled off disintegrating walls. Water dripped somewhere and it smelled damp.

---

[1] During Holi, the festival of spring, people toss coloured powder at each other.

'Building used to belong to her mother, man, Supriya Devi. Remember her? She lived on these floors—abandoned since she died.'

Supriya Devi, she too had been a famous movie star. Stopped acting at the peak of her career. There was some scandal—the teenage daughter had an affair with the mother's lover, was that it? No it couldn't be, that was thirty years ago, my Devipriya was too pure, too young.

'Don't make a noise man, in case she's resting,' Salim whispered as we entered her apartment. It was practically dark but I could see marble gleaming and reflecting off opulent mirrors. We climbed a carpeted stairway.

'This is my room,' Salim said and turned on the light. It looked fancy but I didn't pay much attention for at that moment Salim reached into his trousers and groped, making little whimpering sounds. 'Wow, fuck man, it's so hot,' he said and yanked. As I backed quickly towards the door, something landed at my feet. It was a padded cup-shaped object, a sponge in a stocking, Barbie-doll-flesh coloured, pungent with sweat. Before I could exit, he removed his t-shirt. Underneath was another layer, skin-tight, that he stripped off. It flopped, grey-white beside him. Before me, sat the old, puny Salim.

He laughed at my look and said, 'No one but Hritik[2] has the real thing man. But those fucking ready-made padded suits are fucking expensive. My sister makes mine for me. Cool, no?' He held up his sweaty vest and palpated the sponge at the shoulder before tossing the vile thing on the back of a chair. 'Free, man, shit, I don't pay a paisa, they're her used cups.' He carved spheres in space in front of his chest. 'Poor thing, she has nothing man, almost flat, has to wear cups even in summer. Bad rashes.

'Come.' He led me out. 'You want to see her dressing room?' It was a long room finished in white veneer with ornate gold trim detaching in places. A cupboard door hung off its hinges. On a shelf against a mirrored wall were stands holding wigs, black, brown, orange-pink. 'Look, that's from the New York movie, you recognise?'

It wasn't her own hair. I thought I was going to vomit.

Then Salim began to finger her things with his unwashed hands. 'Careful man,' I said in a choked voice. He laughed and picked at a bead on one of her bodices. 'Take it easy, bastard. She won't be using it soon, too thin to fill her

---

[2] Hritik Roshan, a Bollywood movie star known for his physique

body-suits.' He pulled out a garment. It was body-shaped, a thick polymer material, golden-cream—a body stocking. I couldn't hide my horror.

'What? You didn't think her skin colour was real?' He cackled manically and led the way into the corridor. A large red-brown cockroach scuttled along the edge, keeping pace with us. Salim opened the door of a bedroom and the roach darted in, its antennae waving. A night light glowed on a bedside table on which dinner sat unfinished.

The room was chilled and stale smelling. A figure lay huddled under a quilt. Salim turned on a lamp with a dimmer switch. As the room brightened, I saw it was a woman with a ravaged, dark face. Her hair, sparse and wispy on the unwashed pillow was a coarse black but a band of greasy grey lined her face. An arm lay outstretched on the quilt, saggy skin an unhealthy brown.

The woman coughed and stirred. 'Salim? What took you so long? Have you got it?'

Salim stepped forward. 'Shhh,' he said. He picked up a hypodermic from a steel plate on the dresser and took out a glass vial from his pocket that he held up to the light. She grabbed his hand. 'Hurry Salim, hurry,' she quavered. 'You kept me waiting so long. Don't taunt me now.' He tapped the vial with a rusty blade. The cockroach, now sitting on the yellow dhal, raised its head and waggled its antennae inquiringly.

Revolted, I started to leave the room. Devipriya raised her head. She looked straight at me and smiled. The fine ridge around her lips picked up the light, opening up the contours that little extra and she seemed to glow, a luminous golden-cream. I smiled back, in heaven.

21. RABBIT CAKE

by Emmanuella Dekonor

I first learnt to make cake in Ghana, when I worked at Lawyer's house. Madam would call me from the servants' quarters, to stand barefoot and watch as she smeared imported butter all over a baking tin saying, 'Those other maids can't even pronounce the word "cake". Watch and learn. This will be good for you.'

Good for me? I was resentful. Why should I make my body stiff like a cement block to watch her make food that I would never eat? As if I didn't have anything better to do. And being around Madam too wasn't easy. One-two-one-two: *don't bite your nail* or *don't touch your face, hygienic this, tidiness that. Ah ah!* She was exhausting. The first time I stood in that kitchen, I eyed her proper. How dare she drag me from my room to watch her bake. Cake was for rich people. Who else would waste eggs like that? Mamie Bofroat's street doughnut was enough for me. What did I want with cake? Shia! But then one day, when the children were at school, Madam allowed me to lick the bowl. How it was sweet? I became determined to learn how to make a cake for myself. Madam said I was a good pupil and soon I took over all the baking in the house.

#

I made cake for Lulu after I arrived at her London door, in refuge from the chaos back home. I explained that it was a gift from me, to sweeten our bond. She laughed then made her face stiff, and at first I thought that maybe she had forgotten our language but then she raised her eyebrow and repeated the word bond as though it were a question. She narrowed her eyes at the cake then broke a tiny piece from the whole and continued picking at it until she finished the lot. Come and see how happy I was to see only crumbs remaining on the plate! For me it was a sign; soon she would regard me as someone special in her life. But now, eighteen months later, she hates my cake. 'So heavy, it feels like stones inside my stomach,' she says. It's true. My cake is stronger than Madam's. It has to be like that. So it can make any mouth sweet.

#

And on the day that I made the rabbit cake, my heart was filled with only sweetness. It was the last Thursday before Easter. I pressed my nose to the cold kitchen window to stare at a white-paper sky where grey buildings lined up like prison bars to surround our seventh floor flat. I shivered at the sound of the wind as it whistled past the window, forcing trees to bend and wave their naked branches at me. Lulu was wrong about The Cold. She said it would be gone in March but it was still here. I peered down from my high window to see English children running in the patchy grass. They reminded me of Easter time in Ghana when I would leave Madam's house at cockerel-crow to arrive at my village by noon, when the sun is sharp and my shadow cuts a long figure in the earth.

I closed my eyes and leant back against the kitchen counter to dream of village children running beside an old tro-tro[1] truck to escort their city relation back to the homestead. They are the only ones who will openly welcome me, shouting, 'Sister is back, O!' The other villagers ignore my arrival. Elders concentrate on their board games with deep frowns etched into their foreheads as they ponder their next deft move, cousins returning from market with baskets balanced on their heads cast their eyes over the length of my body, searching for signs of snobbery. And as for those mothers who take one look at me then begin to complain about city ways … hmm. I smile and agree with them that, yes, the city can change a person. But not me, O! Then I call one of the children to bring me water in a calabash—I refuse to drink from a cup—and my holiday begins. I rub my feet into the red dirt of the village and forget everything about everything: no English, no running water, I even forget about the flush toilet in Madam's house as I spread my legs to squat over the hole in the ground to relieve myself.

---

[1] A shared truck

When the evening comes and the moon is white like coconut inside, when the sound of a person clearing their throat signals the start of a story and people make a circle around that person ... eh heh! That's village life. One time, the women honoured me by asking for my opinion in the matter of a teenager who had become disrespectful. The next year they scolded me in front of that same teenager for losing too much weight. Village life!

On the day of the rabbit cake, I could think of nothing else. Deep inside of me the scent of firewood and goat soup teased and tore at me and I ached for my past. My ears filled with the rustle of palm fronds waving in the air as people dance on Easter Sunday for Christ who is risen! And then, I imagined Ma's voice on the day of my departure for England, her wrinkled fingers trailing my tears as she scolded, 'What kind of foolish girl will cry for going abroad?'

#

Lulu was losing patience with me. I could tell by the way her tongue clicked at everything I did, her eyes hardened at mine, and she now kissed her teeth whenever she approached the front door even though she was the one who suggested the bolts and locks so I would feel safe. The back-home food I often prepared for Chris, our white neighbour, now embarrassed her. But worst of all, her boyfriend did not return after he heard my nightmare screams. I tried to tell her that she deserves a man who will accept her relatives but she told me to mind my own business and, after all did I ever have a boyfriend? I felt like screaming, yes! And his name was Sandboy and oh, how he loved me. But I closed my mouth, resigned to her hostility. We were trapped between her filial duty and my hopelessness. It pained me that she no longer spoke to me. I resolved to make things better. My eyes searched the kitchen walls, the white units, the stove, the aluminium sink and finally the fridge pasted with Lulu's magnets of far away places. I pulled the fridge door open and saw that there were twelve eggs left and, like a blessing from God, the cake came to me.

#

I rushed around, excited by this new plan. We had all the ingredients. We always have more food than we need; it's Lulu's way of coping with this lonely London living. Oh, when you see her you will think she is a proper British, with correct accent and everything. Make-up here and there, always talking of old ageing, praying for a new man and weight loss. Yet every night, she forces big fufu[2] and palm soup into her mouth until she can eat no more. As if simple food can help her. But the craving that drives her to gorge herself, like her belly, only grows bigger.

The wooden spoon beat the ke ke ke sound of the atuman[3] drums as it folded the flour, eggs, and butter into the bowl. Ke ke ke. Lulu and I would become friends again: today, today, today. The words made a happy song. I was tempted to dance but I feared that my neighbours in the grey prison towers might see and judge me. I plunged my finger into the thick mixture and licked. Aha! This cake would sweeten any temperament. One taste and Lulu would speak to me again. Not that I minded her silence for I found my sweet Ma there. Every Saturday, when Lulu switched on the central heating, I would talk to Ma. I could hear her in the click of the radiator before the room became flooded with warmth. Then I would close my eyes and tell her about my fears and she would reassure me saying, all will be well. Sometimes we sang village songs together. Usually, when Lulu was out. I would berate her for hiding her sickness and ignore her until Sunday when she begged for my forgiveness.

The weekdays were cold without Ma. I would pull two, three of my sweaters over my head and run to stare out of the kitchen window, longing for blue Omo to paint a warm sky between those prison bars. I tried to imagine summer sunshine. But my body continued to shiver. Lulu had warned me not to go near the gas heater in her room but I was feeling bold on the day of the rabbit cake.

I filled as many baking tins as I could find with my cake mixture and turned the oven on. Then I went to the bedroom to pick up the box of matches hidden under my mattress. I marched into Lulu's room and tried once, twice, three times to light the heater. I turned the switch and placed the match to it but nothing happened. I was so cold I resolved that only a hot bath could warm me. I went to the bathroom, turned both taps on and ran back to the kitchen to check on my cake.

---

[2] Boiled cassava and plantain beaten together
[3] Atuman drums come in pairs, one female and the other male. They are made from antelope skin and used for a symbolic dance called the 'Adowa' dance that Akan people perform at ceremonies.

I swear, I didn't think of rabbit until I pulled out the baking tins. Then the picture formed in my head. I piled the cakes, one on top of the other and there it was. My eyes darted from the cake to the icing bowl and I knew what to do. I picked up the icing gun and set to work. I worked quickly and well. Then I stood back to admire my rabbit-shaped cake. Yes it was huge, but see how I had iced it with black and white oval shapes! If I twisted my head this way, the shapes looked like little eyes but if I turned the other way, they looked like bow ties. I twirled round the room and was about to continue with my little today-today song when I heard our neighbour, Chris, rattling his keys. Lulu would soon be home. I made space on the centre table and placed the big cake onto a tray there—no plate was big enough. Lulu would see the cake as soon as she walked in. I couldn't wait.

But first, my bath. I needed a warm body for our reconciliation. The bath water looked too calm for my excitement. I wanted it to bubble and spurt but it lay still and deep until I broke the surface with the tip of my finger. I stepped in and sensed my body begin to thaw. I closed my eyes and lay down so that only a small portion of my face was out of the water. From somewhere far away I heard Lulu's foot outside the door. Then she took her keys from her bag. Not long now, she would see the cake in a few minutes ... but oh, she has stopped to share a joke with Chris. I hear his laughter boom through our locked door. Lulu's giggle is a trickling girlish sound. I imagine her taking the cake to Chris. He will thank her and look into her eyes and she will realise that he is a special somebody for her. My cake will do that for her. Then they will include me in all their joking banter. I feel a drowsy smile stretch across my face as I imagine the days and weeks to come. Then my thoughts fly back to a memory of home and the scene beneath my lowered eyelids reveals a sunset sky stretching over my village.

22. HOLLOWS

by Stephen Tyson

During the summer holidays before I started secondary school, my father decided to dig a pond in the back garden. I think my mother must have encouraged him, because she loved animals and wild flowers. Large yellow and white dog daisies sprawled over the rim of the broad earthenware vase on the sill behind the sink, competing for space with the bamboo wind chimes that tinkled whenever the window was open. Even when my mother wasn't washing up, she'd rest her hands on the edge of the draining board and watch as a robin or some other feathered visitor plucked a nut from the wire cylinder that hung from the bird table.

As a reward for the hours I spent dislodging pieces of limestone from the ground with a small fork, my parents bought me a red Raleigh racing bike for my eleventh birthday. I hadn't objected to helping my father dig the pond, but hated getting soil stuck behind my fingernails and down the sides of my shoes. As soon as I'd finished in the garden, I'd scrub my hands until they were spotless, then change my socks and put on my black pumps.

My friend Billy didn't have a bike, but used his older brother's. In early August, we spent nearly every afternoon cycling around the back roads and lanes of Greyseaton. One afternoon, as we tore along a strip of tarmac behind a new housing estate, less than a hundred yards from my parents' bungalow, Billy's front wheel snagged in a rut and he landed on the road.

When he picked himself up, a stream of blood was running from the gash above his right eye. I looked down and saw the shape of half his body—a long uneven shallow cast. He scraped away the granules of sticky tarmac from his arm, then pulled out his handkerchief and pressed it against his forehead. Nearly five minutes went by before he stemmed the flow of blood, and we both realised the tarmac hadn't hardened off properly. If there'd been a sign to warn us the surface was still pliable as clay, we hadn't noticed it. We left our heel marks all over the road.

Billy didn't look too bad when we parted, as he was still holding the handkerchief against his head. But as soon as he arrived home, and removed the temporary bandage, the bleeding started again. So his mother took him to see the doctor.

'I've had three stitches,' he said, when he rang me that night. And my brother's taken the bike off me. The front wheel's buckled.'

'We could go looking for newts instead. You said you'd show me where they were.'

'I'm not allowed out, not for a while.'

'Your mother can't keep you in all through the holidays.'

'I suppose not ...'

She didn't. Two weeks later, I followed Billy back over the tarmac, which was hard by then, and had lost some of its rubbery shine, and turned onto a narrow path that led into a wood. Eventually, we passed under a low canopy of leaves, scrambled up a mossy bank and came to a wall. We rested there for a second, as an unseen bird cawed from the treetops.

Billy found a footing in the wall and started to climb. When he'd clambered over the top layer of stone, I followed him into the field. A dozen or so black and white cows were lying in the furthest corner, legs hidden, twitching whenever a fly buzzed around their eyes. It was a hot day, grass seeds and pollen rising in the breeze, a dusty looking haze over the horizon. Billy had started sneezing when we'd left the main road, but it hadn't lasted. I was glad; I didn't want to go back because he'd suddenly developed hay fever.

We ducked under a barbed wire fence at the edge of the field and headed towards a patch of chest-high bracken. Billy knew where the newt pond was, but I knew more about newts than he did. I knew they liked basking under rocks during the day, deep in the silt, out of view, and that they made a popping noise when they came to the surface at night. My mother had bought a book on amphibians, and I'd read a few pages.

The pond was behind the bracken, and looked slimy and dark. I thought I might get a rash or start to itch if I even touched the surface. Strands of sticky weed covered the water, as though a giant green dog had stood astride it and moulted. I knelt down by a rotten tree branch, and passed a jam jar to Billy.

His wavy fringe dropped over his right eyebrow as he squinted at the sun. When he pushed it back, I could see the scar where he'd cut his head. The worm of puckered skin was pink and wrinkled.

He took off his yellow t-shirt and spread it over the trailing vetch and clover. The water must have been warm, because the air above smelt of molasses and mouldy bread. The odour was so strong you felt as though you'd only have to slap your hands together to send a stream of tar back into the pond.

'How many do you want?' Billy said.

'As many as you can catch. My father was going to fill our pond with fish, but my mother said they'll eat all the wildlife. They keep arguing about it.'

Billy was lying on his stomach. He must have been holding his breath, because his rib cage never moved. And he remained still when a tiny insect, hardly bigger than a flake of black pepper, landed on the smattering of freckles that ran over the curve of his neck. Then suddenly, like a falling guillotine, he let his hand break the surface of the water. The jar made a glugging sound, a spray of droplets arced then plopped back down, and series of ripples ran towards the reeds across the pond. I tried to visualise the path of Billy's hand, but even his shoulder was submerged.

The girl must have crept up on us. I never heard her moving through the bracken until she coughed. When she stopped, a metre or so away, her shadow moved over the edge of the water. She was wearing a pleated red skirt and a khaki halter-top that stopped above her thrusting belly button. She stood with her back to the sun, glaring in my direction.

'I'll tell on you,' she said. 'I'll tell the farmer.'

I scowled back at her. 'Tell him what?'

'That you're stealing.'

'We're only catching newts.'

'I know what you're doing. It's cruel.'

She shut up but didn't move away, and continued to stare. I don't think she'd washed her hair for a week. I'd never seen such lank hair. Billy withdrew his arm from the pond.

'Who is she?' he whispered, and put the jar down.

I flicked a ball of clover with my middle finger. 'Just some stupid girl.'

'I haven't caught any.'

The jar was empty. I took hold of the wet rim and placed the makeshift trap by my side. Then I wiped my fingers on my shorts.

'Where do you live?' Billy said to the girl.

'On the new estate.'

'Did you walk through the woods?'

'It's hardly far.'

Billy looked impressed, so I mimicked the girl. 'It's hardly far.'

'I bet you wouldn't have come on your own,' Billy said, and rolled over onto his back.

The girl strode toward us, skirting the spongy grass where the water had overflowed. 'You're wasting your time, anyway. All the newts are at the back of the pond.'

Billy looked disinterested. He'd closed his eyes. I felt like shaking him. But I was certain he'd try again.

He didn't, though. He started whistling, a shrill rendition of the Hokey Cokey, which made the girl giggle. The two of them were starting to get on my wick.

'If you know so much,' I said to her, 'let's see you catch a newt.'

'I could, easily,' she said. 'But I'd put it back.'

'Go on then.'

She smirked, flaring her nostrils, then jabbed her small pink hand towards me. Her fingers tapered, spear-like. Everything about her was jutting and bony, even her knees came to points. And she smelt of washing powder, the blue grainy sort my mother packed into the retractable drawer before the cylinder started to spin.

When she'd taken the jar from me, she sidled around the edge of the pond. Billy sat up, and pulled his t-shirt back over his head. The air was cooling a little as the haze was spreading inwards from the horizon. The sun looked like a smear of butter.

The girl stopped next to the narrow dyke that ran along the edge of the grass bank behind the pond, then stepped onto a stone a metre out from the edge of the water. Her legs looked shaky at first, but she quickly squatted. She'd have to get lower, I thought. And as though she'd read my mind, she edged her feet slowly back, until she was kneeling.

She lowered her arm slowly, taking her head down with the motion. When she was nearly curled into a ball, she touched the surface with the bottom of the jar, but gently, without a splash.

'I bet she'll catch one,' Billy said. 'I can just tell.'

'She seems to think she will.'

I wasn't going to admit her stealth impressed me. But she worked silently, gradually trawling her arm from side to side. Her gaze was intent, probing. I got the impression she could see right to the bottom of the pond, beyond the weed, right into the silt. When she eventually lifted the jar back into the light, she got to her feet without saying anything. She was smirking, triumphant.

She retraced her steps, cupping the jar at waist height.

Billy got up as I buttoned the top two buttons of my shirt. I took my time. I tugged on my laces until they wouldn't go any tighter and knotted them. And as my belt felt slack, I unfastened it and stretched the soft leather until the metal spoke nudged into the last hole. Then, when I was ready, I sprang to my feet.

I stood next to Billy, and at the very moment the girl held the jar up, I grabbed it. The newt's spotted belly touched the glass—then all I could see was murky water.

'That's not right!' Billy yelled, as I dashed into the bracken.

I was never a good runner, but I didn't think they'd chase me. The tougher bracken stems scraped against my shins as I ignored the foot-worn path and headed in what I thought was the quickest way back to the wood. I wanted to stop, to cup my palm over the jar, but I sensed I was being followed.

They might have caught up with me if the girl hadn't fallen. The only time I dared to glance back, Billy was trying to untangle her halter-top from the barbed wire fence.

#

The newt died. My father continued to state his preference for kio and water lilies and my mother stuck up for tadpoles and dragonflies. The ceremony I'd imagined, where the three of us stood in the back garden and watched the newt slide from the jar into the clear water above the butyl liner, never happened. They never even knew the newt was in my bedroom, behind the blue cotton curtain, waiting for their stalemate to end. One morning, before I'd even brushed my teeth, I pulled back the curtains to find a stiff green corpse, like a shrunken dinosaur, floating on the surface of the stinky goo in the jam jar.

Billy hadn't called round for me. But I saw him, a few days before I was due to start secondary school, horsing about with the girl. She had a Chopper bike, an orange one with cow-horn handlebars. He was pedalling, and she was sitting on the seat behind him, holding his waist. They were cycling on the tarmac, round and round, in a figure of eight.

23. FALLOUT

by Trilby Kent

Twenty-four biscuits steam like cow pats on the cookie sheet. When they are cool, Delphine will top each one with a generous splodge of marshmallow Fluff and squash them into sandwiches. Twelve in all: enough for ten children, one for Hank when he gets home from work, and an extra one for Lou tonight. Whoopie cakes are his favourite treat, and you only turn six once.

She can hear Lou rattling about upstairs, restless for his guests to arrive. They'll come bearing Slinkys and pogo sticks, roller skates and Frisbees and Mr. Potato Head, perhaps a Davy Crocket hat or a cap gun like the one advertised on *The Roy Rogers Show*. This is what she has told him. For the first time in his life, the boy will have a proper birthday.

You only have to look at the effect of two institutions and three foster homes on his sister to see how lucky Lou has been: he's young enough to still have a shot at a normal childhood. At sixteen, Iris is already a lost cause. They'd fought again this morning, when Hank had told the girl that they were expecting her to help with the party.

'I'm not wasting my Saturday wiping snotty noses,' was the reply.

'Now listen here, you got home three hours past your curfew last night, young lady. That may have cut it in Newark, but not in my house.'

'So?'

'So, consider this your due.' Hank pressed his beefy pink palms together, fixed her with a stern look. It is easy for him to be the disciplinarian. He works six days a week at the plant, leaving Delphine to deal with the fallout at home.

At times like this, she is glad that Lou is hers—and that his sister isn't. Iris's adoption papers have yet to come through, and Delphine sometimes hopes that they might never arrive. That morning, the girl's plump lips had twisted into a sneer as she planted both hands on her cinched waist. The little hussy was leaning into them, pressing for a fight, and Delphine noted her plunging neckline, that molasses-smooth cleavage, with rising disgust.

'He's your kid now. He's your problem.' *Slam.* The fly screen clattered against the closed door, exposed latch scraping a groove into the fresh paint.

Delphine straightens the gingham cloth that covers a foldout table sighing under the weight of Ritz crackers and stuffed eggs, trembling Jell-O moulds, hot dogs with Cheez Whiz. Casting a hawk's eye over the gleaming linoleum tiles, she spots a burst of flour exploding like a powdery firecracker beneath the counter, and she reaches for the broom.

As she passes by the window, Delphine allows her gaze to wander outside. She might suggest that the mothers sit outside this afternoon. The yard is as tidy as her home: Hank's lawn neatly mown, pebble path wending towards the gazebo, flowers blossoming to a strict colour scheme. Her husband once observed that her eyes are the exact colour of the ceanothus, and Delphine considers how she might drop this into conversation without sounding vain. Although the air is beginning to sweeten with the smell of summer fading to a close, it is still warm enough not to need a jacket.

If her garden is anything to go by, all should be well with the world.

#

Iris presses one foot against a concrete bumper and leans against a shaded patch of wall. The parking lot is empty but for two cars, and she wonders who else would come in to school on the weekend. Teachers, probably—and kids getting dropped off for detention.

A cigarette dangles between her fingers, tipping sprays of ash. She wears jeans cropped short and cut tight because she loathes skirts. She stopped wearing bobby socks when she was ten. Suburbia does not suit Iris. Perhaps it's because she is too old for hopscotch and bicycles, tree houses and Scouts; things that still make Lou's world go round. The other girls in her year at Bayonne High hang out at the soda bar a fifteen-minute walk down the main drag that connects the school to a strip-mall and, beyond that, a gas station. Clutching books to their pointy chests, ponytails swishing to and fro, they exchange gossip and plan parties which will be supervised by their parents in sprawling homes. Lawn, pool, games room. Dad by the barbeque, tongs at the ready, Mom preparing a tray of cookies and Tang and giggling along with them as they discuss their crushes on cute football players.

Delphine would love it if Iris brought home some of those girls. 'A civilising influence', she'd call them. They might teach Iris to avoid red nail polish, or to grow out her kinky black hair from a fuzzball to something that the boys will like. More time with the girls might also mean less time with young men (the only remedy for a girl with her reputation is marriage, and Iris has no plans for domestic bliss just yet). Delphine would have them all sit together in the garden, surrounded by the ridiculous figurines that her neighbours give as Christmas presents every year. Iris finds herself making a mental catalogue of the saccharine child figures, the smirking terracotta frogs, the bloated putti astride dolphins, the novelty toadstools, myriad gnomes. For Delphine's birthday this year, their neighbours had presented her with a painted Negro jockey—'I could just see him perching on the stone wall by your hyacinths!' Mrs. Lambswith had gushed. It's the kind of present that white people give each other all the time, judging by the other gardens in their neighbourhood. The dwarf has an idiot's grin and cartoonish features that look as if they have been smeared with chocolate sauce.

Iris hates the jockey; hates it even more because she knows that Delphine doesn't like it, either. Something about him makes her feel guilty; perhaps it's because he's black, and you can't treat Negroes like entertainment any more. Then again, Delphine doesn't like most of the garden trinkets that Mrs. Lambswith keeps buying her; they're tacky, middle class. But what can you do? The Lambswiths are good neighbours, so the figurines stay—tastefully, discreetly, peeking out beneath the hydrangeas and swaying spires of foxgloves, the toads lurking in the shade, the Greek statues by Hank's workshop.

That was her only remaining cigarette, and it's too soon for Iris to return to the corner store where she lifted the last pack. Sighing, she drops the butt and lazily grinds it into the ground with her heel.

#

Moments after little Steve Kennedy knocked a bowl of tomato ketchup onto the patio, smearing the flagstones with indecent scarlet sludge, one of the Simmonds twins managed to knock Jimmy Wagner in the eye with a T-ball post. Over the boy's howling, Delphine is struggling to measure out equitable slices of birthday cake while the other children clamour for corner sections with extra icing. At the centre of the horde, Lou's face is like a shining coffee bean, broad with delirious satisfaction.

He doesn't appear to have noticed that only four of the invited ten children have turned up for his party. Marcia Simmonds was one of Delphine's oldest friends—they had tried out for the Bayonne cheerleading squad together three years running—but she does not know Mrs. Kennedy or Mrs. Wagner very well.

'Can you believe it—even Ike got involved,' Mrs. Kennedy is saying. 'Sending troops to escort the students and all. The pictures on TV made it look like a war zone, not a school.'

'I wouldn't want my kids there, that's for sure,' nods Mrs. Wagner. 'What with all the media attention, and the threats—and I'm not just talking about white folk, you know.'

'Course not!'

Marcia glances at Delphine, who has paused over the slices of cake. 'Well I think it's a mark of progress,' she declares, slightly too loudly. The other mothers purse their lips. 'This desegregation thing, I mean. Just look at Hank and Delphine, and the good they're doing here.'

Delphine feels the heat rise to her skin, forces herself to smile modestly at Mrs. Wagner. Forget the fact that she and Hank never managed to have their own children; that beggars can't be choosers. Steve's mother has platinum blonde hair that has been teased into a bouffant, and Delphine's auburn curls feel lank and untamed; she wishes that she had made time for a poodle cut. All that time spent on careful preparation, and now her garden is beginning to resemble Hill Eerie.

'You're absolutely right, Marcia.' Mrs. Kennedy carefully returns her cup to the table, brows furrowed. 'But Hank and Delphine are getting on with it quietly, aren't they? Not raising a hullabaloo like those people down in Little Rock. Best that these things are done quietly, I say. No need for all that negative attention....'

When she hears Iris entering through the front door, Delphine tells herself that things cannot get any worse. Minutes later, there is an almighty smash. The mothers turn around just in time to see florid shards of plaster scatter across the lawn, flitting through the flowerbeds like fairy tumblers, spinning and toppling and skidding in all directions.

'What on earth was that?'

'Stevie, now look what you've done!'

The cap gun's first casualty: all that remains of the painted jockey are the jodhpured legs, daintily crossed at the knee.

'It was Rob's fault, Mom. He pushed me—I wasn't aiming at it, honest ...'

'She's right. The boy wasn't aiming at it at all. Strange ...' Delphine rummages on hands and knees beneath the camellias, feeling for the statue's head. 'If I didn't know any better, I'd say something else hit it from above.'

'What? Dropped by a bird or something, you mean?'

Delphine peers up at the window above the kitchen. Iris leaves it open even now that the evenings are cool; perhaps she has devised a way to clamber down the back of the house to steal off to the drive-in on Saturday nights. The jockey usually perches directly beneath that window. Delphine scans the patio ground, but the tiny intaglio crystal paperweight has shattered into a fine powder, perfectly camouflaged amid the plaster debris. She does not have time to consider the items lined up on the windowsill of the upstairs bathroom; and by the time Iris makes her appearance, she no longer cares.

'How's it going, gang?' The girl has changed into an emerald swing skirt, and her Peter Pan blouse is buttoned up to the neck. She deftly opens a bottle of cola and play punches her brother. 'Looks like your bash is cookin', bro.'

When the dusky air begins to shimmer upon the hosta, the guests say their thank-yous. Once they have left, the first thing Delphine does is flap open a garbage bag and plunge the party debris inside with a weary sigh. Iris perches on the back step with Lou, watching Delphine gather up the larger bits of the painted jockey and toss them into the bag.

'Shame about your figurine,' she says.

Delphine glances up sharply, straightens. 'Next time, just aim for the pissing cherub, okay? Come on, Lou.'

She retreats indoors with the boy, leaving Iris alone to clear the table. The evening air carries the scent of white primrose, and the girl smiles.

24. THE UNDERCURRENT

by Clayton Lister

Mina watched the car enter the reservoir car park from a long way away—or as if she only now were waking from a deep sleep—with little comprehension and still less interest. It was the old man scrabbling out of the car that drew her in.

On foot, and with some urgency, he set off along the path that ran between a high hawthorn hedge and the stream bordering the Water Treatment Works. Blackberries were mixed in with the haws, and another black fruit: *Buckthorn berries!* It delighted Mina to identify the tallest reeds in the stream, not bulrush, as often mistaken for, but *Reedmace!* She wanted to share, or boast, her knowledge.

But the old man had moved on, off that shady footpath to the broad verge where the long grass bowed and tangled, rainbow-sparkling wet. Mina would have loved to stop and play. The spiky heads on those big ugly plants—what were they now?—were ripe for picking. They would have stuck to the old bloke's cardi, maybe his bum, and later he would have sat on them. *Yow!* But he was having none of it. 'Great burdock!' Mina exclaimed, and off he sped.

That was how the game started, as a celebration. That she could name the plants was marvellous to her. 'Bees in the bindweed! Snuffle-snuffle, oink, oink ... hogweed!' Chasing after the old bloke, the louder she exclaimed, the faster he ran. So that by the time the footpath had taken them behind the village, she could barely keep pace for laughing. '*Moo* parsley!'

Only toward the end of that creepy, long tunnel of coppiced willow did Mina begin to suspect that it was not a game to him. Here, for lack of light, the lower branches were spindly and leafless. Noticing a single straggly shoot of bittersweet nightshade twining through the canopy, she cackled witchily. The old boy spun fearfully on his heels, toppling and nearly falling.

Mina resolved then to keep quiet. She wasn't a wicked girl. He slowed his pace; the old boy clearly was not enjoying this walk of his. When they turned into the field of tall grass all gone to seed, she feared he might not make it back to the car park. He'd clearly forgotten about the hill. But at the top, he stopped and shook his fist. 'Bloody vultures, I ent dead yet!' he said.

Mina forgot herself and corrected him. 'They're not vultures. They're rooks!' she laughed.

He hurtled down the other side. If he lost his footing now, he'd fall into the river. He ignored the greeting a jolly-looking fat man gave him from the cratch of his moored narrow boat, and he ignored his barking dog.

Onward he raced without so much as a glance at the Pinkhill hide, over the bridge at the inlet works, past the reed lagoon, all the way to Shrike Meadow. Only then did he allow his old bones a rest. At the meadow's edge where it fell into the river, he picked his spot. There he dropped, deadweight, swung his legs over and dangled his feet in the water. Mina giggled. He all but fell in.

'You're funny,' Mina told him. By stepping out from behind the hawthorn tree where she was hiding, she meant to put him at ease. But while he'd certainly been aware of her before now, he hadn't actually seen her. He gasped, and buried his face in his hands. Mina was sorry to make such an impression on him. 'You've still got your slippers on,' she said, but could not understand his muffled reply. 'What was that?'

I said, 'I ent here for your amusement!'

Mina felt terrible, but it also dawned on her, studying the old man's weathered features, that she hadn't been so far off the mark thinking he might enjoy her little game. 'It was you what learned me all them things!' she said, recalling it only now. She knew by the guilty glance he cast her that she was right about that, and, "He's a mine of useless information," she quoted from someone. Mina herself didn't know who until the old boy made the enquiry with a raised eyebrow. 'It's what Mum used to say,' she said out aloud, only now remembering.

'That so? What else did she say?'

Mina thought hard. "Never there when you want him—which is never. Always when you don't, which is ... always."

Mina knew now that the feller was her granddad. He snorted. But if he *was* her granddad, how come he'd been scared? 'You,' she guessed, 'didn't come here to see me.'

It was a little hurtful that he hadn't. His response, though, was to laugh grimly, and that hurt outright—as did what he said: 'Your mother must be right. I am losing my marbles.' In fairness, sensing her umbrage he tried to make it better. 'If I ever had any. Always was a distraction, you.'

Mina swallowed hard. 'Ent distracting you now, am I?'

He only laughed again. 'I'm still here, ent I? Ten years after. Who'd have thought?'

Mina was nonplussed. 'Ten years? After what? That can't be. I *ent* ten yet. I ent even nine years old.'

'Oh,' he said, regretfully, 'Oh. Well, spose I might be wrong.'

But he wasn't. He knew it. She knew it.

'Blow me down,' Mina said. 'I'm dead, ent I?'

#

Yes. He was sorry, but there was no denying it. The last time he'd seen her she was quite dead. He himself had identified the body once they'd fished it out. 'Hadn't even cleaned it up for me,' he said. 'All bloated and blue, you was. Dirty. Didn't looked like you at all.'

Mina sat down heavily on the sward's edge next to Pops, her own feet not quite reaching the water. He clearly needed it, but she daren't hug the old boy. The dead cannot touch the living. Everybody knew that.

It'd been a day just like today. Or a day like this was set to be. 'Blistering.' That whole summer had been, unlike this one. 'Miserable. Bloody miserable.' First time he'd been back since what happened. But no, he had not been expecting to meet her here.

Mina listened, sympathetic but dazed.

He'd done what he could, of course—in the first place had not wanted her even to paddle; had warned her not to venture any further from the bank. But she was stubborn-headed. Not unlike her mother in that respect, who in all these years had not let him forget it was his fault. Since Mina was here now, he hoped she appreciated the heartache and bad feeling she had caused. But he must have recognised the extent of her dejection; he didn't push the point, only muttered, 'They said some awful things.'

What they, or anyone said wasn't of much interest to Mina. But she ought to respond in some way, she thought. 'Blaming you?'

'Because you didn't have no clothes on! I told you keep 'em on.'

Funny how the memories returned to Mina only when she reached for them. 'I had my knickers on,' she said.

Pops only snorted, as much to say, 'All the difference that made!'

But she'd been swimming. Why would she have swum dressed? That really would've been silly. She was dressed now. Barefoot but dressed. It felt good to flex her calves and ankles, dabble her toes in the water. The flesh on Pops' legs between his trouser hems and socks was pasty, bluish even. Much more like a dead person's than hers was. As if oblivious, or, as if they belonged to someone else, Pops let his feet dangle half in the water. He still had his slippers on.

'So you,' she said, 'came here today ... what for?' At the back of her mind she could feel something surer than mere suspicion forming. He'd not sat down to cool his feet any more than he'd come to visit her. He was here to do himself in! But how could she ask her own granddad about something like that? He'd been in such a state even when he'd arrived. 'You didn't shut the car door,' she told him.

Pops seemed genuinely surprised to learn that—surprised then brightly amused. 'Well, that'll serve her right, 'n'all!' he said, and with all his might he hurled the car keys into the river. He was old, though, stiff-limbed and clumsy. They plopped a short distance away from his knees, and Pops followed.

Again, Mina felt the need to say something. But she thought it'd best not be about his mishap. Seated waist-deep in water, he made no effort to climb out. So, at length, she asked, 'How is mum?'

'*Hah*!' Pops slapped the water. What did he care? He slid a little deeper. 'She's got a new man.'

Curious. It was so curious that Mina doubled forward the better to read Pops' expression. 'Who was her *old* man?' It seemed a reasonable enough question. But Pops glanced at her sharply.

'I don't *know*,' she said. 'Tell me.'

Pops winced, shifting uneasily as if, after all, he had damaged something slipping down the bank. His tailbone maybe? But Mina knew he hadn't. 'We've had this conversation before, haven't we?' We have. I *never* knew who Mum's man was. Granddad, you've got to tell me who my dad was.'

'Ask your mother!' Pops snapped. 'She's the one got bloody pregnant, bloody stupid.'

'I did ask,' Mina told him, 'lots.' Even as she spoke it was coming back to her. 'But Mum said to stop asking because the time would come when I'd realise who it was.' Pops didn't have an opinion on that. None that he wanted to share, anyway. 'So tell me,' she said, 'about this new man.'

The old man huffed. 'She wouldn't be talking of buggering off if it weren't for him, I'll tell you that much! Bloody old folks' home! They've no right!'

Mina didn't care anything about old people's homes. But this conversation about her dad, that was interesting. The very last time she was here, that's when they'd had this conversation. Unwilling to drag up the details of the actual drowning, Mina had imagined she'd entered the river in high spirits stubbornly resisting his pleas to her to come out—hadn't Pops hinted as much himself?

She remembered that she'd been furious. Backing in deeper, she'd believed she was safe.

The river was running a lot more slowly on that day than this. She'd been so angry, though, would it have made any difference if she had realised the danger? *Why* would he not tell her?

Then another memory surfaced. She knew well enough how babies were made—didn't like it; but those kids down the road from where she, Mum and Pops had all lived together, weren't lying about it. She'd asked Mum. Who, though—who with Mummy—had made Mina? They had lied about that, those kids. Surely. Hadn't they? It couldn't have been ...

'*Granddad!*' Mina shrieked so loudly and shrilly that Pops flinched. In flinching, he slid a little deeper into the water. He had to scrabble to regain the seat he'd found. Mina fought an urge to strike him, kick him back down. She must *not* touch the living.

He was muttering. What was he muttering? 'You raise a child ... I taught you everything you know!'

'My *daddy's name!*' But he only shrank from her, deeper again into the water but not intentionally. Not by choice. 'So, *do* it,' she said. 'What's stopping you?' The old man shook his head. 'What you came to do, *do it*.'

He seemed all at once to have become more conscious of his vulnerability. Pops scrabbled onto his knees and now facing Mina, begged permission to climb out. Mina stood up. That he could look so pathetic repulsed her. The muddied water lapped at his chest and throat. His mouth worked, but wordlessly. Mina pointed. Best not fight it and prolong the agony; what was he waiting for?

Now he found his voice. 'But,' he said, 'I love you ...'

It was Mina's turn to smile grimly. What, that smile said, in the same way you loved Mum? It was a very effective way of driving someone backward into deeper water; dead or not, it was much more satisfying than physically forcing a person ever could be, Mina was sure.

There he slipped, so easily away. It was child's play. Mina was so intent on his silent passage from the bank that until now she hadn't registered the jolly-looking fat man they'd passed earlier. Neither had she noticed his dog although the mangy old thing had bounded ahead of its master to bark furiously at her. The man watched Pops' body, rolling, submerging, re-emerging as it passed. He looked for a moment as if he might plunge into the river to intercept it, but saw sense.

Would this mutt never stop its yapping? '*Boo!*' Mina said, alarming it into a spin.

Then it did lose interest—as, so Mina realised, she herself began to withdraw not just from the dog, but the entire scene. She saw it as if from an increasing distance. Pops' body slipped under one last time. Just how far would it carry she wondered. All the way to Pinkhill Lock? How far had she been carried? That was a memory beyond her compass. Had she gone too far driving him all the way to his death?

Not that guilt or remorse afflicted her particularly. But then the thought struck: where would that part of Pops go that wasn't his body? Would he simply fall asleep, as she felt she'd been asleep these past ten years? True, she had returned—woken—when the opportunity to avenge herself arose. She did recognise now that she hadn't come here today to play with Pops at all. But what if, just as they'd needed to be in the same place for Mina to wreak her revenge, they needed to be in the same place for him to wreak his? There in sleep, their eternal death-sleep, together they would be.

Mina was going under even now. She could feel it—feared it, as when alive she'd feared sleep for the nightmares that she could not always wake herself from. Now, as then, more than anyone, more than she'd ever wanted a dad, Mina just wanted her mum.

25. LOVEFM

by Sarah Hilary

Johnny should have told her—would have told her—that Elvis was his first love. But the time was never right.

That song had been playing all summer as they lay on the beach, love's jetsam, her long hair roped with sand, his skin grainy with goose-bumps: 'Love me tender, love me long, take me to your heart ...' and then that last line about dreams coming true, sung so beautifully Johnny felt his heart break each time he heard it. She got sick of it in the end. 'Dumb song,' she said, and reached a sandy hand to switch the radio off. It was a vintage Roberts radio, contemporary to the King, finished in Ferrari yellow leather. Johnny had told her he didn't want it touched.

#

The trailer park was the lousiest, most godforsaken spot Johnny'd ever seen. It might've been a shanty-town but for the gaudy ghetto touches: neon signage on the biggest of the trailers, gold paint peeling from the window-frames, stars and stripes slung in fraying swags everywhere. Mired ankle-deep in garbage, the place stank of petrol, cooking fat and waste. The trailers were packed cheek by jowl, hundreds of them, set up from the dust on cracked concrete stilts or sinking into pits of mud and worse.

The ranks of dirty-white boxes gave the place a mausoleum air. Strung between two posts, a banner was sagging in the wind, bearing the name of the park, 'Graceland 2', above a scabby daub of Elvis with a half-eaten hamburger in his fists. Propped against one post were the remains of a wooden Indian, stolen from outside a tobacco store some place, his face and torso peppered with buck-shot. Bullets had removed his nose and broadened his mouth from ear to ear, leaving shards of wood hanging like loose teeth.

Johnny shivered despite the damp heat curdling the air around him. He had the feeling he was inside a dream, but one so real he'd wake with the taste of petrol in his mouth and the stain of neon on his skin. He wasn't sure how he'd got here. The last thing he recalled with clarity was driving his beat-up Buick away from the beach, away from her.

There'd been days of driving, tires choked with desert, windows caking up so bad he'd had to stop and clean them every few hours. He remembered the heat and the car radio—*You've lost that lovin' feelin'*—the road ahead bubbling like a swamp. Then the trailer park had shimmered into view, dazzling him.

He'd stopped the car and walked, stumbling in the potholes, his legs stiff from sitting so long behind the wheel, a bottle of Coca-Cola hanging from the numb fingers of one hand. The park was deserted, the only sound the snagging of the wind shifting the flags and the faded image of Elvis. The sun made a blaze of the trailers, crazing every ugly angle, lifting a smog of fumes that turned the air to treacle.

Johnny took a slug of cola, grimacing as the metallic-sugar taste found his tonsils. What was that slogan? *Life tastes good*. Life.

He scrubbed the back of a hand across his eyes, tired beyond belief. The stars and stripes billowed and boomed about him, their red white and blue exaggerated to crimson, silver and sapphire. Like her eyes.

Passing the remains of the Indian chief, he entered the trailer park. He expected a dog to run up barking, or a kid. His boots were muffled by the thick dust, making him another non-sound in the place, an extra layer of emptiness. He approached the nearest trailer and peered through the grimy window at an unmade bed, film posters on the wall—*Full Metal Jacket, Jaws*—empty beer bottles spilling like bowling pins in all directions. The next trailer was the same, and the next. No people, but plenty of signs of recent life: plates of food left out on tables attracting flies. In one trailer, a TV was tuned to the shopping channel, its volume turned down low.

After passing a dozen trailers, he reached the largest, a palace by comparison, with a plastic awning set around its roof like the icing crust on a wedding cake. One side was defaced by a sprawling picture of Disneyland, all sickly-pink turrets and phony sunshine. It was the same box as the others, just larger and gaudier, with beaded curtains at the windows and a scarlet neon sign in the form of a Smith and Wesson. It winked at him and from the muzzle, the word 'Bang!' flashed on and off, on and off. The place had the sweet meat smell of barbecued ribs.

Feeling nauseous, he leaned against the side of the trailer, remembering the way her fringe curled on her forehead, cradling it like a hand. He felt his gorge rise and thought he might puke, but the feeling passed. 'The things we do for love,' he muttered when he got his breath back.

The dry beat of the sun on his head urged him to get inside. It had beaten like that on the beach, drumming down on his body and hers. He swung up the short flight of stairs to the front door of the trailer.

It was unlocked, opening onto a dim space striped with colour by the bead curtain, stretching back into a darkened right-angle where he could just see a couch. He blinked, waiting for his eyes to adjust to the change in light, and heard music. The tinny sound of loud speakers was stripping the sentiment from the song, 'Love Me Tender,' reducing it to a ringtone, raucous with feedback: 'When at last my dreams come true, darling, this I know, happiness will follow you, everywhere you go.'

The tune looped back on itself, starting over: 'Love me tender . . .'

Sitting on the couch, propped by plush cushions in every shade of pink, was the King. He wore a white jumpsuit, its belt and a bib a riot of rhinestones. His face was half-hidden by mirror-framed glasses and his hair was coiffed and brilliantined. Who else could it be but Elvis?'

The song rumbled on and the King joined in, a live performance from beyond the grave: 'Love me tender, love me sweet, never let me go . . .'

That's when Johnny saw her. Dancing. A slow, hip-slinking dance, her skin stained strawberry by the lighting. Her face was turned towards the couch, her back to him. She looked drunk; the slutty moves only needed a pole. It didn't seem decent, dancing like that in front of the King.

'You have made my life complete, and I love you so.' A hand, flashy with rings, waved in his direction.

The King. It really was. Which could only mean ...

Elvis raised a hand and plucked the glasses from his skull, the dying ember of his eyes glinting across the trashy expanse of trailer. He dropped his gaze to the girl. 'Shake those tail feathers, baby.'

The music squawked on and the girl kept dancing, her limbs sinuous, sinful. The red tip of Elvis' tongue tapped his upper lip, keeping time.

'What—what's she doing here?' Johnny managed to ask at last.

Elvis put a finger up, hushing him.

The girl danced her way back, away from the King and towards Johnny, turning at the last minute and draping her chin over his right shoulder, chest to chest with him, her face hidden in his shoulder.

Johnny could smell her hair, the salt that still clung to it and another scent, rusty, russet, beneath. His skin itched all over with the memory of what he'd done.

He stared across the lurid space of the trailer at Elvis. 'Am I dreaming?'

'You want me to pinch you?'

'Oh,' Johnny said. 'Oh, no. This can't be right. You're Elvis. You should be in heaven.'

'We reap what we sow.' The King looked at him, rhinestones winking. 'Where should you be, sonny?'

The girl lifted her head, the long hair parting like a curtain on her face. Johnny could see the imprint of the radio dials across her forehead, a rank of bruised and bloody indents. From one crimson socket, the ruins of a sapphire eye, silvered by the antennae of the Roberts radio, gazed on him with unquiet reproach.

'Welcome to hell,' drawled Elvis.

Hell. It was almost worth it, to be sitting in the same room with the King.

26. BREAKDOWN

by Vanessa Gebbie

Tom's hurting. He writes to try to stop the hurt but doesn't want to think about wives, daughters, sons, love, or mental illnesses, so he keeps a list of other things. Always has a list; today it's 'elephant' 'New York' 'leather' 'the fall of stone' 'pink'. And photos. He has photos in books, in magazines, and his own stuck in albums. They're on the floor in the front room, by the sofa. Today he's going to pick a photo at random, flick through a book—eyes closed—and stab with his finger, stop the pages, write about that one, use his list.

The photo is of a car crash. What was a pale blue car, concertinaed between a lorry on the left and a wall on the right. It's dark, raining. The tarmac glows. There's a single streetlamp, orange light fizzing in a puddle, like a kid's spilt drink. Tom would usually note that down, but this time, he doesn't. Not that his kids are of an age to spill orange fizzy drinks, but the mix of kids' drinks and the broken body of the car might say something. The door of the driver's cab is hanging open. The letters N and Y are just visible in yellow on dark green on the door, and there's a sheaf of papers on the floor. Hanging from the rear view mirror is something on a chain. Tom pushes his glasses back up his nose, peers at the photo. It's a crucifix. A rosary. It's almost moving, swinging.

Tom can smell incense, feel starched cotton over bare knees, smell mothballs. The hairs on the back of his neck are prickling. Has he remembered to polish his shoes? Will his father see dirty shoes beneath the robes, get the stick out? Will his mother pull his father by the sleeve, try to stroke the leather patch, will his father push her away, tell her to get the food on the table only this lad'll have to eat his standing up?

In the photo, the wall is cream-painted brick. Some has been bounced off by the impact. Tom can see flakes of cream paint on the wet tarmac, and a few on the bonnet of the car, although that might just be where the metal is folded and the vehicle paint layers are cracked and standing proud.

Tom's hands are cracked. The skin down the sides of his nails is cracked and sore, like a miner's. On the mantelpiece in his front room is a miner's lamp. It's dented, like the car bonnet, and then the room is filled with dark dust, he can't breathe, he hears horses whinnying, the screech of metal-rimmed wheels careening off metal rails, and a tumbling of rocks into water, and the creak of timber, the fall of stone. Tom looks at the yellow N and Y and sees a man standing at a door holding a hat, and he's blocking the sun, handing Tom's father, who is young and will never be happy again, his own father's lamp, and he's saying something, keeping his eyes lowered.

On the tarmac, too, in the flakes of paint, and the orange fizz, is glass. Glass that has burst out of its frame like a live thing, and heaped itself all about in fairy cubes. He thinks, stupidly, of confetti, and cries. He makes a note about multicoloured confetti and blood, and thinks of saving up for a trip to a place in London with the wife and kids to see sculptures made from cars. And an elephant's head made from ribbons of steel from a car door, the frame lying there like a skeleton, the elephant looming up and out, ears flapping and the distant sound of trumpeting from a loudspeaker while people pushed and touched and the sign said 'Please don't touch.'

The car door here, this car door, is buckled but still latched. The window has burst, the door is almost folded in two, but it is still latched. 'Always lock the car when you're driving at night, love.' And Tom doesn't want to see into the car. Behind it, in the background, is a breakdown truck. Its door is open, there is a bloke in a uniform sitting on the tarmac in the glass and the damp, leaning against the broken car, one arm over his eyes. He's resting his head on his knee, and Tom can see his hair is thinning. That pulls. He maybe tried to do something. Maybe he got a callout, 'There's a car broken down, Victoria Street, near the old cinema.'

Maybe he got the message it's a girl driving, a dark-haired girl with shoulder-length hair and earrings in the shape of sailing ships. On her own, a bit scared because it's dark. And someone said, someone at the office who took her message from the mobile, 'No problem darling, stay in the car. That's the best. The van's on its way.' And Tom wonders if she put the radio on, or whether she got out her handbag and did something with lip gloss, or whether she called home. He doesn't think so. But resting on the wheel—he can see it now, he can look—there's a hand holding a mobile. A white mobile with a pink ribbon for a strap.

Tom remembers a pink ribbon on a nurse. Pinned to her top, and he got confused, said it was in the wrong place, went to get it back because it belonged on a mobile, not twisted into a loop on a nurse, and they pulled his hand away. Then someone was shouting. It sounded a bit like his father and Tom flinched, waited for the stick, then slid down the wall and put his forehead on his knees because suddenly, his head was so so heavy.

Tom puts down his pen and looks at the photo, the press gets everywhere, he thinks, and the bloke with his head on his arm didn't see the flash. He looks at the dark head resting gently on the wheel like she's asleep, he can see an earring in the shape of a sailing ship and he's at a twenty-first, and his daughter is saying, 'Oh Dad, you shouldn't have,' he's kissing her and saying, 'I know ... I'll take them back ...' pulling the little box away and she's laughing and hugging and her hair is dark over his face.

He hurts. He can't write about love, or mental illnesses, or wives who have left, or sons who moved away, or Tom, him, himself, the breakdown man, being too slow to stop a lorry skidding down Victoria Road and into the wall of the old cinema, or a lorry driver who probably never noticed the little blue car stopped, or a dark haired girl on a mobile phone who once saw an elephant's head made out of a car door and laughed.

27. SOME GAME

by Sarah Leipciger

The reason I was even out that night was because my friend Stephanie talked me into going to a party at her cousin's house. I was still pretty vexed over some madness that happened with this guy I linked, Rommell, and I was planning on staying in for the rest of my life. But Stephanie wouldn't allow it. Her cousin's ends were in a different area than ours, but we didn't have to worry about that postcode rubbish like boys did, like if you were in an area that wasn't your own you might get shanked or shot. We were neutral. And also, I liked the idea of going to a party where I didn't know no one.

The thing with Rommell was ugly, still. I really fell for him, which I knew was a dumb thing to let happen. But when you're in it, sometimes you can't stop yourself. And guys like that are brilliant at making you feel like they really like you. He would come over to mine on a Saturday morning when Mums was at work and we'd fuck in my room. If he didn't have football, he'd stay for a while and we'd be naked in my bed, smoking draw and watching cartoons on Sky, which Mums put in my room because I cut a deal with her that I'd do my GCSEs. (She didn't need to know that I would of done them anyway). About a month after we started seeing each other, we were at mine watching Spongebob Square Pants and Rommell reached over the side of the bed to where his trousers were on the floor, and came back up with this little, black velvet sack in his hand. He tossed it onto my tummy. I loosened the little string tie and held it upside down over the palm of my hand, and a thin silver chain and heart locket slid out. It landed softly in my palm, like a tickle. I asked him to put it on me, and he did, and when he did the clasp, he kissed my neck in tiny kisses all the way up to my ear, and around to my lips. Goosebumps came up all over me like some big wave. You couldn't blame me for thinking this made me his wifey. So I wore the necklace to school on Monday. In the lunchroom this grimy girl Sharon from Rommell's year came up to me and grabbed the necklace off me and threw it at my chest. It slipped down into my bra like something wet. Everyone was laughing and calling for a fight, but I was too shocked. And I wasn't much for fights. If Stephanie had of been with me it would of gone that way, but I was alone. I looked around me and saw Rommell standing there up against the wall with his bredrin. They were laughing like they had their mouths full of cake, like it was so funny they were trying not to choke. Someone in the crowd called me grimy. Some other prick called me a slag. Rommell just shook his head at me and walked away. I found out from one of his boys that Sharon was his wifey and when Rommell found out she cheated on him, he stole her necklace from her bedroom and gave it to me.

I'd never been so humiliated before, never been so hurt.

So I was glad to go to this party where I wouldn't see any of the dickheads from my school. I could be anonymous.

We could hear the beats from halfway down the street before we got to the house where the party was at. Some boys who stood out the front looked us up and down when we walked up the steps, and nodded to show us their appreciation. Inside the house, it was dark and body hot, and the music was so loud it made me feel like I was trapped in some kind of bubble. Me and this other girl Kara followed Stephanie from room to room looking for her cousin, squeezing around hard elbows and shoulders. I guess trying to find some place to kick off from. Her cousin, Jeremy, was in the kitchen and he was already so high, he couldn't converse with her. They did this mad thing where they kept asking each other questions that made no sense to either of them. Finally he told her to go away, that she was fucking him up, so we went back into the sitting room and found an empty bit of floor in the corner, and sat down to finish the ciders we were drinking on the bus. Then Kara pulled out a litre bottle of vodka and we started to pass that round, trying to get pissed so we could have some fun. It wasn't long before we started chattin' to some people, mad drunk conversations that didn't mean nothing, and this boy came and sat next to me on the floor, and was all 'Wha' g'wan?' He told me his name was Theo and all I could think of was how I wasn't going to let no boy charm me tonight. He was a couple years older than me though and pretty buff, so I sort of turned my body towards him and answered whatever dumb questions he was chattin'. Asked him some questions too. He seemed safe though, so when he asked me if I wanted to go out to the garden to smoke a spliff, I took his hand and let him pull me up off the floor.

The garden was just as packed as the rest of the house but at least you could breathe. We stood against the wall and I looked up at the grey-black sky while he dug in his coat pocket for his zoot. He told me he wrote lyrics, but every second boy in my school wrote lyrics, so I asked him to spit some to see if he was for real. So he stood back a little and started to bounce his shoulders, and pulled his cap down on his forehead. I rolled my eyes, waiting for the same old gangsta bullshit, but then he moved his body right next to mine and his lips were in my ear, his hot breath in my ear, and he was chattin' about London, about how he was nothin' but a brand name in London, about how the city stuck to him like summer smog. I started to move with him. His lips kept tickling my ear, like he was breathing his lyrics right into me. When he was done, he stood back and asked me what I thought. I gave him this big flirty smile and said, 'Standard.' He grinned and asked me if I wanted to go to a club. For some mad reason I said yes (like wasn't the thing with Rommell enough shit for one year?). I told him I had to go and tell my girls first before I jammed. Kara was on the couch with her hands up some man's shirt and Stephanie was in the kitchen doing C with her cousin, so I didn't think they'd care too much if I left.

I took a black cab with Theo and two of his bredrin, Binz and Jason, to Brixton, to this small club I'd never heard of before called Green. In the cab they were chattin' about some beef they had with some boys from Hackney but it was the same rubbish I'd heard a million times before from boys in my area, all like, *some mandem come into our yard chattin' shit blood, swear down, wan' get on my ting, shanked my cousin, bangedmywifey, robbed mybredrin, still blood, they was all batty boys got no respect, blood bring it on next time they show their batty boy faces they get tin shankedinnit*, like a broken fuckin' record, as my Mums would of said. Most of the time, boys in different areas didn't even know what madness it was they hated each other for; they just hated. I didn't really listen to what they were saying, because Theo was getting more buff by the second, softly playing with my hand and rolling his eyes and whispering, 'Oh my days,' like he was above all that beef.

There was a long queue outside the club but Theo knew the bouncer so we went right in. He knew the coat-check girl too, kissed her on both cheeks as he handed her our coats. She put her eyes all over me like she thought I was grimy. Green was a sweet club, just one room underground with a bar at the side and a stage at the back. No fancy decorations, just good beats and some lights and a dance floor. The people there were older and way slicker than the people I was used to seeing in clubs. They looked rich. Smart. Theo bought me a vodka and orange and got himself a Hennesee and we went and stood by the wall. His bredrin went straight to the dance floor and disappeared in all the other bodies. The beats were too loud for us to talk, so I just drank my vodka and orange. When Theo saw my empty glass, he took it from my hand and went back to the bar. I watched him, wondering what I was doing there and wishing that I didn't come, because I knew that after all this, these drinks, he'd expect me to fuck him. Or at least go down on him. He was hot, but after all that business with Rommell, I wasn't really feeling sex with someone I just met. When he came back with the drinks, I thought I should just tell him what was on my mind so I told him I wasn't going to shag him. He told me he didn't think I was grimy like that anyway. That might of been the truth, or it might of been what he thought I wanted to hear, but it didn't matter because I felt a lot better after that. We had a few more drinks and then I wanted to dance. He didn't want to, said he preferred to keep his back against the wall, so I went onto the dance floor by myself. I was just getting into it when he came and told me we were leaving. Jason and Binz were hungry. That pissed me off a bit because there we were in bloody Brixton, at this fly club, and now we were leaving. I felt like I didn't have any choice, because the tubes weren't running anymore and I didn't have enough cash to get a taxi home. I had to go where they wanted.

We walked a few blocks from the club towards Brixton Academy, a place I did know because I'd been to a few gigs there. It was after two in the morning but there were loads of people about, and bear dealers hissing at you from dark doorways. '*You want hasheeeessshhh, I got craaaaackkk, I got browwwwnnn...*' We found a kebab shop with a queue out the front door, but it was the only place open where we could get eats. We queued up and after a few minutes of standing still I realised I really needed to pee. I pushed through the queue into the kebab shop, all full of loud people, and asked the guy behind the counter if he had a toilet. He ignored me the first few times I asked but when I got his attention he just nodded no, all vexed, without even looking at me. If I was like Stephanie, I would of given him some serious shit for that, but I only ever got pissed off on the inside. I walked back out and told Theo I really needed to find somewhere to pee. He said there was an alley that we'd passed one block back. I asked him if he'd come with me and stand guard, but he just laughed. He said, 'if I have to watch you piss, I might not like you anymore.' His mate Binz looked at me all funny and said he'd come, but I said no thanks.

I was just doing up my jeans again and about to leave the alley when Binz showed up. 'I had to piss too,' he said, undoing his trousers. 'Will you stand guard for me?' I told him, 'I don't think so, bruv.' I had to get pretty close to get by him and back onto the street, and he grabbed me by both arms. His trousers were undone, and I could see the top of his stripy boxers. 'Why don't you at least suck my dick?' he said, 'since you told Theo you wouldn't fuck him.' He kept hold of both my arms and pushed me against the wall. He didn't look very strong, wasn't much taller than me, so I was surprised how tightly he had me. I wondered what he would do to me if I rammed my knee into his balls. I started shivering so hard that my shoulders kept jerking up and down. A girl and guy walked past. The girl looked at me, but then looked away fast. Binz put his knee between my legs and pushed up against me, like pressed his whole body against mine, and held my arms tighter. His face was right next to mine now and I could see his jaw muscles going, like he was trying to decide what to do. I could feel his heart beating against me and I worried if he could feel mine too. I didn't want him to know how scared shitless I was, because it was hard to believe this was for real, still. Part of me thought this was some mad test to see if I was safe, like, if I screamed he would laugh at me. Another couple of people walked past and this time some guy in a blue coat stopped and asked me if I was okay. Binz let go of me and started to laugh. He held his hands up sort of like he was surrendering and said, 'safe' to the guy, and backed away from me. The guy ignored Binz but kept looking at me, waiting for me to say something. I smiled at him and told him I was fine. He nodded and walked away, looked back once or twice.

I couldn't move for a minute, like I could feel Binz's hands on my arms even though they weren't. But then I sort of peeled myself off the wall and started to walk back to the kebab shop. He skipped along like a little kid next to me and said, 'Safe, innit?' And I was just like, 'Ya, whatever.' I wasn't going to say nothing to Theo—I didn't think he would care if his friend tried to link me.

When we got back, Theo and his other mate Jason were inside the kebab shop. I was cold and still shivering. All I wanted to do was go home and be alone in my bed with the covers pulled up over my head. I decided to just get a taxi, and wake my Mums up when I got home so she could pay for it. I would bell her on the way. She'd be pissed at me for waking her up and begging money off her, but she was always saying I should bell her if I got stuck. Binz went into the kebab shop without saying nothing to me, and I started to look up and down the street for a taxi. A few black cabs with their lights on drove right past me like I was invisible. One pulled up a ways down the road, but someone else got in. I was getting vexed.

And then I heard shouting. The shouting was like, so serious, and sudden, out of the blue—it made me jump. And someone was screaming, like really scared. It could of been a boy or a girl. All sorts of people came out of the kebab shop and walked away down the street really fast, looking back at the shop like it was going to blow up or something. A guy came stumbling out. Theo and Binz and Jason came out right behind him and circled him. He was crouched over, holding his stomach with one arm and covering his head with his other hand. He kept saying, 'I didn't mean anything by it, I didn't mean anything by it.' I saw he was wearing a blue coat and that's how I knew it was the guy who stopped before to see if I was okay. His mates were standing on the pavement behind him, yelling at Theo and them to leave him alone, but I could tell they were too scared to actually do anything. Binz had a knife. It was some expensive-looking one. Big ass shiny blade with a fancy shape, like a leaf. Binz waved his knife at the boy, told him he should learn to mind his own fucking business.

I was shaking all jerky up-and-down again. I didn't want anybody to know I was with them lot, but I felt like it was my fault this was happening. I yelled at Theo, tried to make my voice hard, but it came out sort of all wet. I just stood by and watched after that. Theo wouldn't of heard me anyway. He and Binz and Jason were smiling at each other, like everything was a game they were really good at and they didn't give a shit about nothing. It made sense. Nobody seemed to give a toss about nobody else.

Binz kicked the boy in the back, his lower back, and he fell onto the pavement, on his side, curled up like a baby. After Binz kicked him, he backed away and Theo stepped in and stomped on the boy's ankle. Then he stepped away and Jason went in for another kick to the lower back. The man from the kebab shop opened his door and waved his phone around over his head, said the police were on their way. I thought he was going to help the boy, but he just closed his door and locked it. Some boys in a car slowed down right in front of where we all were and honked their horn the way people do when their football team wins. They were laughing and brap-brapping out the car window. After a minute or two, the boy in the blue coat stopped moving. You could see his shoulders shaking a bit, like he was cold. One of his mates finally got in front of him. He held his arms up and was just like, 'Stop! Stop! Leave him the fuck alone!' Binz walked right up to the boy's mate and slashed his knife down the side of his face like it was nothing, like he was cutting nothing. The guy who he shanked, he just looked surprised more than anything. At first there was a white line down his face where the knife cut, then bright red blood started to seep out. The blood started to trickle down his face, and drip off his chin to his jumper. Some blood dripped onto the pavement and for some mad reason that made my throat go tight and my mouth fill with spit. I had to turn around and gob on the road and try not to throw up. I could hear laughing. Theo and his bredrin were just walking away, patting each other on their backs and laughing like they were the rulers of the world or something. I didn't know if he knew I was still there or not, but Theo didn't look back.

The guy in the blue coat, and his mate, they were sat on the pavement and their other mates were around them. Other people stood by looking all shocked. I saw a taxi with its light on and practically jumped in front of it to get it to stop. Driving away, I felt like I'd knocked over something delicate and rare, and instead of cleaning up the mess, I just stepped over the broken pieces.

28. THE WORLD'S END

by Andy Charman

Dorset, Late Summer, 1846

The mid-morning sun has beaten the world into hiding; the fields stand motionless in the ripening heat and only the crickets raise a sound, filling the air with their cree-crick-cree-crick, making it seem all the hotter.

Bill and the chestnut mare are in the shade of the stable. He has a hand palm-flat on her shoulder as he brushes her quarters with a reassuring rhythm, the hiss of the brush marking long, drawn-out beats. Drops of sweat fall from his brow, splashing darker colours onto the cobbles, and when he draws breath, the scents of horse and straw sting his nostrils.

The mare flicks her tail in agitation. He keeps to his rhythm. Then her near hind-leg comes up and smacks the cobblestones. He hardly blinks.

'Yeah, a'right. I know.'

She's having none of it. She stamps a second time. The clatter echoes sharply from the farmyard walls. It seems to cast her anger like a shadow on the hot stillness around them.

He stands back and straightens, and looks her in the eye. 'C'mon Penny. It's naught. Ee'll be gone tomorrow.' He moves closer to her and strokes her neck. She nods a little. 'S'alright,' he tells her. 'S'alright, now.' Soon she is calmed, while the crickets still call.

He runs a hand over her muzzle, picks up the leather harness that needs mending and ambles to the stable door. His eyes are way off on the horizon as he mumbles his agreement with the mare. 'You're right, though. Should'n be a-feared to see us own brother.'

He reaches over the door for the bolt, slaps it open and steps out into the sun. And there he stops. There is a figure at the far end of the track, just coming through the gate.

He shades his eyes and watches the man striding towards him.

"Ere 'e is then.'

As his brother approaches, Bill has time to appreciate the changes that time has made. It is a surprise to see such an old man. Cornelius' face is tired and lined and his eyes are squinting and small. He has nothing of Bill's weight or strength—his arms are thin and wiry. Bill remembered him bigger. Without removing his hat, he nods slightly. 'Corny.'

His brother stops and grins at the reception, shaking his head but not commenting directly. 'You knew I was coming then.'

Bill nods. 'I hears you're out by Stur.'

'Rooms at the World's End Inn.'

'Oh aye? They's having a good old get-together is they?'

The smile fades from Cornelius' face. 'They've not seen each other for a long time. They're brothers, Bill.'

But Bill hardens his jaw. He stares at Cornelius. 'Dare say,' he concedes.

A bead of sweat forms on Cornelius' brow, breaks from the pore and slides down his cheek. His tongue laps it from the corner of his mouth. His eyes tighten. 'I was asked to bring word that your master, Squire Guthrie, requires his horse and trap.'

Bill nods again, managing to show his disapproval with just the weight in his eyelids. 'Say which? Bay? Chest'nt?'

'Black stallion.'

Bill snorts at this. 'What's that then? Women out there?'

'My master was entertaining Miss Emily Bankes, who has lately been joined by her sister.'

"Lately bin joined?' Sort o' talk's that?'

Cornelius doesn't answer, sticking instead to the stiff formality of his task.

Resigned, Bill shakes his head and turns towards the carriage house. 'Ha. 'Lately bin joined!' Come on. The' can help me hook 'em up.'

Cornelius follows him and is directed by his grunts and nodding commands. They put a saddle in the trap for Bill's return, harness the chestnut mare to take the trap out to the inn and tie the stallion behind.

All the while they work at it, Bill watches his brother with sizing eyes, noticing the scar on his neck and the forefinger missing from his right hand. He can't deny his brother's efforts but when he has to lift the canvas cover back on its shelf, Cornelius hasn't the strength and Bill all but takes it from his hands. He looks as if that alone proves many, many points. Cornelius won't meet his gaze.

With everything ready, they climb aboard the trap.

'Walk on then, Penny,' Bill directs and the chestnut mare tugs them forwards, before settling into an easy amble. It is hot. The horses must be spared for their masters and delivered untaxed.

Cornelius is watching the chestnut mare, and peering out from under his hat as if he has nothing to answer. Bill can think of plenty of accusations and he glances sideways at his passenger as each new one occurs to him. They reach Julian's Bridge and are crossing the river before either speaks.

At the top of the arch they meet an old man with a handcart and two dogs by his side. Bill draws Penny to a halt. 'Art.'

'Bill.'

'How's she doin?'

'Ar, she's a tough ol' bird, Bill, she's a-coming right.'

Bill nods with satisfaction and the old man whistles his dogs away from the horse.

'Much on?' Bill asks.

Art dips his head back the way he came. 'Drayton's 'erd. Cassn't find else. Gertie'll harvest soon mind, so he'll see us through.'

'Well, you send word if there's ought the' needs, now.'

'That's right kind of you Bill. God keep 'ee.'

Bill clicks his tongue to get Penny moving again and they resume their steady rhythm.

'Who was ill? His daughter?' Cornelius asks.

But Bill won't answer. His sideways glance is full of contempt. 'Much as thee'd care,' he mutters.

Cornelius chews his lip for a little distance, sweating, as they both are. Then Bill starts shaking his head. 'Your ma ... cried for a week she did. Then another week when she hears you've taken to soldiering.' Cornelius keeps his gaze contritely focused on his boots. 'You could ha' just told her. You could ha' just a-said goodbye.' Bill stares at his unanswering sibling. 'Could'n you?' he demands.

Cornelius looks up. 'William, we had no time. Major Guthrie was told he could join the army and leave for India or stay and hang for murder. We left that night. I had no choice.'

'So that's the first week. And the next fifteen years when you sent no word, nor wrote nor nothing? You should ha' seen your ma, Corny. You broke her heart, you. You, her favourite. Went to her grave weepin' over you.' Cornelius sits quietly penitent as the road-side daisies drift by. 'Didn' hear nothing 'til old Healey come home one leg short of a wicket. Poor soul. An' that were five year. You could ha' sent word, but no. An' I'll tell you the wherefore. You've a cow's heart, that's the wherefore.'

'I had no choice.'

'Cow-heart.'

'If they'd have known where I was they'd have followed. Guthrie and I swore secrecy when he asked if I'd go with him. I swore, Bill. How could I have broken my word?'

'Broke your mother's heart instead.'

'I'd no choice.'

Bill has no answer for this. Instead, he broods over the reins and watches the road. They ride out past the water meadows by Cowgrove and onto the Mill Lane. They nod at the few other people they pass, but the silence between them seems to grow. Eventually Bill is chewing his lips, regretting his outburst, uncertain how to retract his angry words. 'India was it then?' he grumbles. Cornelius nods. 'What's that like then?'

Cornelius smiles as he glances up the road to review their pace. 'You've not been outside Wimborne, have you Bill? Not past the World's End, I shouldn't think.'

'Nope. No reason to.'

Cornelius cannot suppress his grin. 'If I told you what India was like, you wouldn't believe me.' Bill has no answer to this. Cornelius chuckles. 'Ain't you ever wanted to, Bill? You've never even seen the sea.'

Bill shrugs, head sideways, like a tortoise wriggling to return to its shell. 'No reason to,' he repeats.

'But wouldn't you like to? Just to see a little more of the world beyond the Stour?'

'Why?'

'Why to see things ... to grow ... for betterment, for self-improvement!'

At this, Bill raises his eyebrows. 'Oh ar? Improvement is it?'

'Yes,' Cornelius insists, 'improvement.'

'That an improvement?' he checks, nodding towards Cornelius' missing finger, 'or that?' he asks, looking at the scar on his neck.

'No...' Cornelius concedes.

'Good. There's no need to lose parts, then, to improve the' self?'

'Lor' me Bill. That was just the army. No, I'm talking about progress. D'you understand? Like the railways. Tell me you've at least seen the railway?'

'Railway? Progress?' Bill shakes his head. 'Look, see that field there? Week or so, it'll be harvest. Then'll plough him an' lay seed. Then'll grow again an' ripen an' harvest again. It don't need no progress.'

Cornelius is grinning and trying to interrupt, but Bill will have none of it. 'I seen your progress. Art Hanham an' all his gang spent two summers in no work for them steam thrashers. They's no food an Barkham's paying less for his harvest, but can't sell grain for tuppence and who the blue-blazes do you think's improved by all tha'?'

Cornelius's mouth hangs open as he looks around the landscape for his argument.

'That's politics, not progress.'

Bill grunts, and for the time being that is the end of it. They sit, rumbling down the road without a word, before Cornelius picks up the point. 'That was him we saw earlier was it? Art? Are they all working now?'

'Some on 'em. There's them as burnt the threshing machines, they's in Australie. There's Ted Crick and Jerry wassisname—Thatcher—they's both hanged. Chapman's Common got took over by the Vicar French an' his board. But ar, they's working now. Banke's banned them machines. That's the wherefore. God knows there's enough others that isn't.'

'Jerry Thatcher, hanged?'

'Ar. Bloody fool.'

'You don't think they should have burned the machines?'

'Don't think they should a' been a-caught. Machines? I dunno; don't make sense to me ...'

At which point they suddenly lurch forwards because Penny has stopped still in the road. Bill fumbles, rushing to regain his seat, coughing self-consciously, as though he was embarrassed by the antics of the horse. He clears his throat before clicking his tongue, 'Get on now, Penny.'

The horse moves on, but Bill is still rolling his shoulders to re-position his shirt. Cornelius smiles as he looks from horse to driver. He watches them for some time, travelling in slow, steady silence. Bill unwraps some buttered bread and two apples and they eat as they drive.

Eventually Cornelius gestures at the chestnut mare with his half-eaten apple. 'How does she know where we're going, then?' he enquires.

'What? Penny? Does as I tells her.'

'But you've not so much as twitched those reins since we left the stables.'

Bill shrugs, unable to answer.

'She know your thoughts?'

Bill stares at his brother, squinting for the sun, but scowling too. 'See, you make that sound like a wrong-un. That's what you do. Sommit I's never so much as thought on and you make it out as it's wrong. Sure enough, Penny understands me, much as an old mare might, which is better'n some folks, but it's just as it is. That's all. Just as it is. There's no need f' you to come an start a-making it right or wrong, no need at all.'

'I haven't said a thing about it!'

'No, but there's plenty as said as needs no words. That's the truth.'

The two men stare at each other. Bill's gaze jumps from his brother's face to his tunic and back again.

Cornelius' look of wounded innocence melts into concern. 'Bill, I'm sorry. I meant nothing by it, really I didn't. You and I, we just live different lives now, that's all.' He licks his lips and searches the floor for something more to say. 'I've seen things, see. I've seen a lot of the world. It's exciting, Bill! That's the thing. I've always been excited by it. And you would be too, if you'd seen what I have.'

'You reckon?'

'Of course! Look, I'll tell you what. What if we go up to the railway tunnel once we're done with the horses?'

Bill shifts on his seat and rolls his shoulders. 'Can't think as I needs to visit no railway.'

'No, Bill. No need. But it's a thing to see, truly.'

Bill looks up to see the broad thatch of the World's End Inn curling into view. He shrugs and starts wrapping up the remains of their meal. 'If you like.'

#

They prepare the horse and carriages for their two masters and Bill is surprised how familiar the major is with Cornelius. Compared to the squire, Bill's own master, the major is almost friendly. Once the courtyard has stopped echoing with the clatter of hooves, Bill remarks on it. 'Part of the family then, eh?'

'He treats me very well,' Cornelius agrees.

They both know the same cannot be said of the squire, so his change of subject is welcome. 'Come on. I'll get a flask of cider from the landlord. We'll go and see the train pass by.'

And so they do. Cornelius carries the stone flask and they walk until they reach the embankment where they sit to watch the tunnel mouth for the train.

'So what happened with Chapman's Common then?' Cornelius asks.

Bill smacks his lips savouring the cider. 'That's all beyond me,' he mutters, 'they fixed up some Board, the Vicar and that. But first, no one's allowed no trapping or shooting, and then no pasturing. Can't say as I understands it. Not common land no more like tha'.'

'And the threshing machines?'

'Ar, well, that's all about the same time. Sprung up like daisies they did. Suddenly there's a whole crop of men, Crick, Thatcher, Johnson, they've no work in the harvest an' French has taken over the common so they can't even put a cow out to pasture, much less shoot a rabbit for the pot. No surprise they took to burning the things.'

'And what happened?'

'Word comes out of Lacey. Old man Bankes just bans the lot of them. No machines on his land. Course there's plenty of others that uses them, but there's not many cares to cross him. Hard times, though. Hard times.' He takes another bolt of cider and hands the bottle to his brother. 'What you do for Guthrie then? Tickled his teats wi' summat?'

Cornelius peers over the cider bottle and into the past. 'He was set upon in the streets of Calcutta. I grabbed the cutlass that was swung at his neck. He kept his head, I lost my finger.'

Bill nods, trying to imagine. 'That India, was it?'

Cornelius cannot help but grin. 'Yes, that was in India.' He looks up towards the tunnel as the shrill whistle of a train breaks in on their conversation.

Bill finds himself tensing. It is a ghostly sound to his ears—screaming and unearthly.

'Here it comes,' Cornelius mutters, but nothing could have prepared Bill for what comes next. The thing that roars out of the tunnel explodes into the space before them. There is first a puff of smoke and then, like a terror-stricken horse bolting from its gate, a huge black cylinder screams into the cutting, blowing out immense breaths of smoke, one on top of the other, roaring, thundering and burning at once.

Bill jumps two feet back up the slope in the instant it appears, scrabbling for grip. 'Oh The devil!' he cries. 'The devil!'

The train's whistle blows again and Cornelius turns to see his brother's fear. For an instant, he is amazed but then he bursts out with laughter.

Bill won't let go of the grass, as though his grip on the ground might save him. 'What?' he demands, eyes still wide, 'what's so funny?'

He is glancing anxiously after the train and its carriages as they curl beyond a growth of young beech trees.

Cornelius has tears of laughter glinting on his cheeks. 'I've a cow's heart!' he calls, 'just look at you!'

#

It takes a while for Bill to see the funny side. He defends himself at first, saying it just shocked him, that was all, then explaining that it came at such a pace as he had never seen, until he can finally laugh at his own surprise. As they walk back to the inn, they are chuckling together.

But the sun sinks low and the shadows stretch too long.

'If I'm lucky, Bill, I'll have some time tomorrow. I'll call in and see you if I can. I should like to see where Ma and Pa are resting.'

Bill nods, keeping his eyes on his brother's golden-lit face. He tells him of the churchyard and the flower-covered corner. They shake hands before they part.

By nightfall, Bill and the chestnut mare are back in the cool of the stables. There's barely enough light in there to pick out the walls, but he knows the place for everything and has time enough to feel his way. The horse is steaming, for the night's air has turned cool, and the vapour catches what little light the moon yields. Penny raises her near-hind leg and stamps on the floor.

'S'alright, now,' Bill mutters, 's'alright.'

And when everything is hung in its place, he shuffles to the stable door. His hand reaches for the bolt; he slaps it open and steps out into the night. His eyes do not focus on the stars as he mumbles his agreement with the mare. 'You're right, though. Progress. I hope they knows what they's doin.'

29. MATILDA AND THE MISSING

by Caroline Robinson

Isaac could find things, anything that was lost he could quickly locate. When he was tiny, barely able to toddle, his mother would fret after some missing article: favourite brooch or the green-handled scissors. She'd slam about in the bedroom muttering, opening drawers and rummaging the contents into tangles. Doors ajar, dresses slumped over the bedstead, jewellery box contents tipped amidst the melee of dishevelled sheets, and Isaac would shuffle on his bottom across the pink Axminster, point a chubby finger and make a soft-sounding oink. It wasn't a grunt as such, just a nasal whisper—if you like. At first his mother didn't notice this ability, took it as coincidence that her son pointed at that which had eluded her. Then she understood and attempted to exploit his agility for finding things.

At his parent's dinner parties, items were hidden for Isaac to find. Minnie would carry him in and he'd be sleepy and slightly grizzly in smart, starchy pyjamas. The first few times he performed, he came up with the goods, went directly to the cushion, or ornament or whatever concealed the quarry. The guests 'oh-ed' and 'ah-ed', the women made a fuss of him and the men folk ruffled his hair and patted his father on the back. Then they'd be back to their gathered groups and their glasses, and their eye-flirting and sneaky glances. Isaac saw all this over Minnie's shoulder as she carried him out, he heard the babble of chatter and the chink of empty bottles carried away by waiters.

He stopped performing when he was about four. Minnie would bring his supper up to the nursery and she'd sit with her plate of cold cuts and pickle balanced on ample knees watching him eat his meal at the little table in the window recess. Then he'd be bathed and she'd tuck him tight into linen sheets that felt like ice. She'd heat a tiny pan of milk on the gas ring and pour it into his china beaker, the one with the circus scene. Minnie would retrieve a nutmeg from her pinafore pocket and grate a shake of it over the hot milk. Isaac would sip as Minnie read. Warm milk, nutmeg and the odd waft of coal smoke mingled with the scent of lavender that seemed to cling to the air at the top of the house. He didn't go down to the dining room again until way past puberty and then only the few, odd times when there were agendas that he couldn't quite fathom or his mother was drunk and needed an ally.

He never felt like an ally; never felt he knew his mother enough to be considered a protector or guardian—possibly a witness, a chaperone if you will.

She seemed to shrink. Each time he came back on leave she appeared less, seemed to get nearer the carpet each visit.

Once he had found the dining room to be a jungle of wooden legs: the chairs, the fat table. And all the flesh legs—the silk stockings and the black dinner-suited legs with shiny patent leather shoes—were like undergrowth that he crawled through on his mission to find that which had been hidden such as a cigarette holder, an ivory brisé[1] fan, or a tiger's tooth that had been capped with gold. When he had grown, he'd seen the surfaces, the sun-bleached tops of Victoriana, and the scratches. He could see the cigarette burns on the edge of the bureau; he could remember his father balancing his Capstan Full-Strength there as he held Minnie—quickly, as Isaac crawled around the undergrowth looking for things his mother had lost.

Now he looks for bodies, children that have been misplaced, husbands that have gone awry, or Aunts that have wandered astray. He sits with a map, a glass of port and what he calls a witness, a clip of hair—even a few strands plucked from a hairbrush, a comb or a piece of clothing that belonged to the person who is sought, is missing. On his desk, in a silver Art Nouveau frame is a sepia tint of his mother, Matilda. She stands resplendent in a fox fur, cloche hat with a sprig of cherries and she wears a brooch fashioned as a spider. Isaac found it many times: down the backs of chaise longues, once in the orangery and often in the potting shed.

Isaac has his own office: a spartan Formica affair. He's handed a file: photographs, biography, last sightings etc. He'll fan them out, all the papers, on his desk. He'll shuffle them, light a cigarette, go across to the window, slide a chubby finger along the Venetian blind, lift a slat and stare down into a back street where his mother was found. He still writes to Minnie, keeps in touch, sends her money each month by direct debit.

---

[1] Consisting of pierced sticks of ivory, horn or tortoiseshell

30. STEALING THEIR CHURCHES BEHIND THEM

by Trilby Kent

The Stolen Church—what remained of it—rested between converging slopes high on the Little Karoo. Wildflowers and weeds sprouted brazenly about its whitewashed walls, bending in the same dry wind that whisked sprays of sand against the bolted door.

Cupping his fingers around his eyes, Wilf Beatty pressed his nose to the only window that had not been boarded over. He counted fourteen pews and six plaster columns—the pale green paint long since reduced to defeated shreds—but no organ, no altar, no pulpit. A bit of a washout, really. With a sigh, he gingerly edged himself from the crumbling stoep—there was no railing, and his balance, like his eyesight, was not what it used to be—and paused to consider the building.

The name used by locals was actually something of a misnomer: the church had been relocated, not stolen, shortly before the outbreak of the first Anglo-Boer War. Dutch faithful had dug it up by the foundations, lifted the clapboard frame onto sturdy runners, and hauled the whole thing twelve miles north to build a new Jerusalem further inland.

Out here, the land smelled of men. The earth was so hot, so dry, that raindrops would sizzle as they struck the ground. Taking his thermos from the car, Wilf indulged in a long sip of tepid water, trying to ignore the tiny particles of sand that slid meanly down his throat as he thought, this is it: Africa. An electric sky gilded the distant fields, shimmering layers of wheat rushing from the creeping dustbowl. The sublime evening light suggested it was time to head home. Throwing one final glance at the church—the culminating stop on a three-day pilgrimage—he hauled himself into the bakkie[1] and began to consider his route back to Cape Town.

His friends would be waiting for him there. They had come down from London together two weeks ago: Stephen and Marie the wine enthusiasts, Mike and Gretchen the game spotters, he the lone war hack. It was his first visit to the country of his birth in thirty years, and their impending departure made him acutely aware that it could be his last.

Navigating the rocky descent to the main road, Wilf began to fumble with the radio controls. Rock 'n roll, kwaito, a call-in programme, a prayer show. A smile brightened his creased features as he recalled the story of a devout Afrikaner who listened to one such radio show on his daily commute. So devout, that when the presenter called the faithful to clasp their hands and close their eyes in prayer, the farmer did just as he was told—and drove straight into another vehicle.

It was easy to laugh: coming from an English family, it had always been easy. His father had been a lawyer, while his mother had grown lavender and ran a small business selling ostrich feathers to local ladies. Every evening, she poured her husband a brandy sundowner as he tuned into the BBC and flipped open the Times crossword. Their cook, smelling sweetly of sweat and molasses, would prepare dinner and bellow with the might of a rhino on heat if Absalom helped himself to one of the peas she had shelled for the baas[2] and his family. Absalom, with a face like a peach stone, who was paid in dop[3] by the next farm down and who frequently staggered into the garden stone drunk in the middle of the night. They were all gone now: by the time Wilf made the decision to emigrate in '75, there had been little to leave behind besides his practice and a few casual acquaintances.

He had reached the outskirts of a small town where a cattle auction was drawing to a close. Stern-faced farmers whose khaki shorts contained bulging bellies hunkered around the enclosures in thick knee socks and baseball caps with two burly Staffordshires trailing the group on short, sturdy legs. Passing them, Wilf drew up to an intersection where the traffic lights were broken and a uniformed warden had stepped in to maintain control. He was a young

---

[1] A pickup truck

[2] Boss meaning a supervisor or employer, especially a white man in charge of coloured or black people.

[3] Informal term for a drink, especially of brandy or other spirits.

man, probably Zulu, and his crisp white gloves were sizes too large for his hands. But what was most extraordinary was his technique: rather more like conducting an orchestra than directing traffic, as he waved both arms simultaneously, as if inviting all the vehicles to move in at once.

And then Wilf recalled something that Stephen had mentioned the other night over dinner. They had been discussing race, as people invariably did here. Stephen, who was something of a Wagner aficionado, said that the composer had always worn gloves to conduct Mendelssohn's music. And they had debated whether or not this had been as a show of disdain for the Jew, or, alternately, as an expression of respect for his music. Try as he might, Wilf could not remember what, if anything, they had concluded.

#

The first time it happened, Verity thought nothing of it. The instructor was demonstrating an eyebrow wax on one of the other students, a girl from the township bordering Verity's own. It seemed only sensible that she should stretch the latex gloves on over her porcelain fingers before beginning the procedure; it set a good example to those students who came from towns where hygiene remained open to loose interpretation.

And yet Miss de Proux forgot to don the gloves the following afternoon, when she had shown her students an alternative to hot wax. Samantha Fraser had volunteered herself for the threading demonstration—she was one of three white girls in the class—and Miss de Proux blithely started to wind, twist and jerk the thread, follicle by follicle, without so much as running her hands under a tap. Verity did not feel that it was her place to question the oversight.

But today it had been her turn to volunteer. Before tying Verity's oiled kinks beneath a crisp white headband, Miss de Proux took a moment to put on her gloves. And in that instant, Verity realised that there had been no oversight. Miss de Proux did not like touching black students.

Home was a two hour walk through Cape Town's less salubrious neighbourhoods; she did not like wasting money on the bus fare, and a young woman was just as safe on the streets as in an overcrowded people-carrier. Strong, brisk strides helped to temper her racing thoughts, as she breathed the cool air swept in by the mists over Table Mountain.

If she could just stick it out, tolerate the indignity of it, she could leave the Technikon at the end of this term. She'd be a qualified beautician then:

manis, pedis, facials, waxing … soon she could be earning 2,500 Rand a month. Not that Verity planned to stay here: it was a job on a cruise liner that she was after. Sailing around Europe and the Middle East, perhaps even the Caribbean—anywhere but Africa. A decade after apartheid ended, and what did girls like her have to show for it? Equality is not the same thing as respect her mother had said all those years ago as they watched televised coverage of Mandela emerging from prison to cheering crowds. Now Verity knew how true this was. A person can respect something and fear it at the same time. Fear breeds hate, her mother had said. They hate us because they're afraid of us. But what did Miss de Proux have to fear?

These were the thoughts that distracted her attention from the road ahead, from the screaming traffic, from the blind corner concealed by jacaranda trees. As the bakkie rumbled across her path, she only had time to register mud-splattered chrome and two white hands on the steering wheel. The vehicle bounced as it shaved the pavement, swerving out of her way a second too late.

The girl fell with a gasp, seeing her bag tossed into the air in the same instant that he did, hitting the ground as he had hoped she wouldn't. For that instant, they were one audience sharing in the same horrific performance.

Then, as she propped herself onto her elbows and peered up at the vehicle in confusion and awe, he decided to retreat. She was not hurt. It might be a stunt: carjackers could be lurking in a side-street, waiting for him to take pity on her and venture out. With a wave of one hand—a half salute—and an apologetic bob of his head, Wilf reversed his vehicle and turned back down the drive, toward the city.

# #

The lonely clatter of Karoo windmills had long since faded. As he commandeered the bakkie through Cape Town's urban sprawl, Wilf tried to shake the memory of his encounter with the girl—he was already thinking of it as an encounter, not an accident—but found his thoughts returning to the Stolen Church.

We have a nasty habit of running away, he thought. It all started with the voortrekkers retreating inland from the British, dragging their church with them. Then the English themselves, turning a blind eye to the injustices of apartheid. Next, the young exiles—he had been one of them—who had fled at the height of the violence, fearing an oppressive government but hoping to bring about change from across the seas. Now, it was the white professionals fleeing to Australia, Canada, and England in their droves.

Even those who couldn't leave were finding other ways to retreat. Homeowners built higher walls around their houses and invested in expensive security systems. Politicians obfuscated questions about soaring crime and the AIDS crisis. The desperate escaped into drugs, a kind of assisted denial, while the stout hopefuls—the precious few that remained—retreated behind veils of blind optimism.

All running away, stealing their churches behind them.

His friends would be waiting at the hotel, pouring him a gin and tonic while they reminisced about their day at the wine estate. Stephen would be recounting a bit of local lore he had picked up—perhaps this time, the story about the little girl who asked her mother for a saucer of milk to put outside each morning, until one day the woman was shocked to discover that her child had been feeding a black mamba. That's not the sort of creature you tackle without a good pair of gloves, Stephen would laugh. And the others would nod knowingly and wonder aloud whether the tale could possibly be true.

31. HUNTER'S QUARRY

by Dee Weaver

There's a dead hedgehog by my left hand. It's lying in a pool of blood. My blood. I cut my wrist. It was an accident but, God, wouldn't that make Hunter laugh if he understood irony? He thinks I'm such a loser, but I never feel more like staying alive than when he's on my trail. Trouble is, I'll bleed to death if I don't do something about it. But I daren't move. If I move, I'll be seen. If they see me ... well I may as well be dead. They'll take me back, and I can't face that. So I lie here and bleed.

Nearly got caught this morning. Damn foxes kept me awake half the night so I ended up sleeping long after the sun came up. Had to run like hell, through the grand ballroom and along the full length of the portrait gallery. Normally one or two guys turn up, I can stay ahead of them, moving from room to room. This lot, though. All over the place. Every way I turned I could hear their heavy boots clomping the floors.

I doubled back through the dining room and climbed out through the door at the far end of the conservatory. That's when I cut my arm on the broken glass and it's bleeding like hell now. I need something to stop it, but I've got to stay hidden in these rhododendrons until Hunter's men go. Shit! One of them's seen the blood on the path. He's calling the others. They're getting close.

I make a run for it, crouching low, crashing through the bushes in the hope they'll think I'm a fox. I'm in luck. A pheasant clatters up ahead of me and takes off. I drop to the ground beside the kitchen garden wall and lie still, praying it's enough of a distraction, and that I'm hidden from view. I'm shaking now. This is worse than the last time when they came in the night with thermal imaging cameras.

I hear them laughing. They sound embarrassed. They talk, goading each other. 'A fucking pheasant. Wish I had a twelve-bore. Be good in a pie, that.'

'God's sake don't tell Hunter. He'll have us walled up.'

'So where's the kid? He must be here somewhere.'

'Don't fucking know. Don't fucking care. We tried. Let's ring Hunter, tell him the place is empty, and split. I'm ready for an early pint.'

Their voices and footsteps fade into the distance. I give them two more minutes and then raise my head. I'm facing an old peach espalier, still pinned to the high brick wall although it died years ago. Hunter's leaning against it, his shoulders jumping as he laughs at me. Bastard's fooled me for once.

'Come on, son.' He puts on that false-sincere voice I hate. 'You can't run for ever. Give up quietly and it'll be easier for you.'

I stand up. Slowly. Gripping my wrist to slow the bleeding. 'Okay,' I say. 'But I need to get this fixed first.' I haven't been this close to him for years and I don't like it one bit.

He nods. 'Fair enough.'

#

We're in the hospital emergency department and he wants to handcuff me to the bed. They won't let him. One arm is injured and they need the other for a drip. That pisses him off no end but he can't argue with them. They make him wait outside and I take my chance. As soon as they've fixed my arm, I say I need to go to the loo, and make a run for it.

He doesn't chase me this time. He knows I'll go back to the Hall in the end. He knows I can't stay away. It's my home. My inheritance. He'll leave me alone for a few weeks and then, when he thinks I've dropped my guard, he'll come for me again.

I get a bus back to the village and pick up some fish and chips from the shop on the square. They're cold by the time I've walked back to the Hall so I re-heat them in the Aga. My legs are trembling, loss of blood I expect, so I sit at the long pine table in the kitchen while I wait. I'm dizzy and thirsty. I go down to the cellars and dip the well. It's the best water in the country, this. Cold enough to clench your guts, and so clear it's invisible. And it's my secret. Hunter had the water supply turned off to try and flush me out. He doesn't know about the well ... flush me out? Ha! That's some joke, especially as he also doesn't know that the water pipes collapsed years ago. God, I need to sleep.

#

The principal bedroom has huge mullioned windows that look out over the parkland towards the trout lake. Trouble is, it doesn't have a floor so I can't use it. My bed is an old mattress and a sleeping bag in one of the smaller rooms in the North wing. It's the only part of the house with a roof that doesn't leak. To be honest, it's the only part with a roof of any description. The whole place is collapsing. If I stay here, one of these days it'll bury me.

That'd be cool if I could be sure Hunter would leave me here. But I know he wouldn't. High-ranking conscientious policemen can't knowingly leave dead bodies under piles of rubble, even if they wanted to. And he wouldn't want to. He'd ... I don't know what he'd do, but he wouldn't let me lie here in peace, where I belong.

#

I'm standing on the terrace. For the first time this year the breeze is mild against my face. There's a mass of tiny wild daffodils skirting the edge of the wood, and the hawthorns are misted with new green. Trout are rising in the lake. It's clogged with weeds and the boathouse has collapsed. I could do it up if I had the money. Like the Hall, it's criminal to let it rot this way.

Hunter's back. Alone this time. He gave me a couple of weeks for my arm to heal. He has that kind of honour. He likes the chase to be evenly matched. He's standing at the other side of the terrace, watching me. I spread my arms, as if I could embrace it all. The Hall, the gardens, the lake. Everything.

'Look at it!' I shout. 'My family created this!'

'Bollocks!' Hunter yells at me. 'Get real, lad! They were servants. Cooks, cleaners, gardeners. You don't know shit about them, or the people who paid them a pittance and treated them worse than dogs, who put them out of their homes when they decided to abandon this place.'

I clench my fists. Glower at him. I want—I so want—to hit him. He always makes me feel like a mulish kid. I hate him. He keeps asking why I live like this. He should know. He does know. Because I love this place. And he'll never understand that this is where my roots are. I hate him so much. He knows that too but I never miss an opportunity to tell him.

I scream at him. '*I HATE YOU!* Don't ever forget that. I hate you.'

'I know, son,' he says, suddenly quiet. 'I know. But I love you. And so does your Mum. Don't ever forget that.'

32. CITY PEOPLE

by Shola Olowu-Asante

A cockroach graveyard—that's what I stumble into when I enter my kitchen. A crunch underfoot and I scream, first from shock, then at the sight of a dark mangled body, oozing its thick, purulent liquid onto the sole of my sandals. There are a dozen or so more strewn across the tiled floor, upside down fossils, fixed in that final gasp for life. I shudder with relief that this last batch of poison has worked, although I remember reading somewhere that the species has been around for 350 million years. So not only am I the interloper in this house but as it's always thirty degrees and humid in Lagos, I'm probably fighting a losing battle.

Leaning down, I slip the sandal off my foot and tiptoe out of the room, as if in fear of waking the dead, returning a few minutes later, with a fresh pair of sandals and a dustpan and broom, poised to sweep the corpses into the afterlife.

'Where the hell is Francis?' I hurl the question into the empty room. Francis is our steward. Leke and I decided against live-in help after our last housegirl, Charity, turned our home into a bordello, 'entertaining' the local mechanics and gatemen whenever we were out. Still, with a husband perennially chasing contracts in Abuja and a litany of domestic woes—if it isn't roaches then it's rats, leaky faucets or blocked drains—I've been wondering whether we made the right decision. He's supposed to start at 7:30. It's already 8:00.

I gather the carcasses into a pile in a corner of the room, holding the broom far away from my body as if playing a game of hockey. Just then, my mobile phone rings. I read the marine blue screen—it's my mother.

'Mummy, can I call you back?' I'm not in the mood for her histrionics.

'No, you can't. We need to talk, Lola.'

'Alright then. What's the matter?'

'Nothing's wrong. Do I need to make an appointment to speak to my daughter?'

'No,' I say, trying to sound patient. 'It's just that I'm busy at the moment.'

'Doing what?'

'Cleaning the kitchen. I told you we had a problem with cockroaches.'

'Where is that man, Francis? Why are you doing manual labour in your condition?'

'Mummy I'm pregnant not an invalid.'

'Well then if this one dies too, don't say I didn't warn you.'

I count slowly to ten in my head. It's been a long time since her words have had the power to hurt me. Even so, I place a protective hand over the swollen bulge that is now my belly.

'Thanks. I'll remember you told me so when it happens.'

Silence. I think perhaps I have shamed her a little. I should have known better. 'I need some money.'

I sigh. 'How much?'

'A hundred thousand—just to tide me over. Mr. Afolabi is taking me to London tomorrow so I'll pay you back by the end of the week.'

This is a story I've heard more times than I care to remember. Portly Mr. Afolabi (who already has two wives and an unfortunate lisp) is the closest she's come to a stable relationship but there's been no noticeable improvement in her finances for the five years they've been together.

'Fine, I'll call the bank and do the transfer today. Anything else?'

'What do you think we should get for Papa's birthday?'

'I don't know what *I'm* getting but maybe *you* can pick something up for him in London.'

When she hangs up, I feel drained. My mother is an emotional succubus and our conversations usually end up the same way, either with a plea for money or an invitation to join a hare-brained scheme. I close my eyes and place my cheek against the wall. It feels smooth and cool against my clammy skin. Even though I would never give her the satisfaction of agreeing, I know she's right. This is my fourth pregnancy, a blood clotting disorder having miscarried the three before, so I need to take it easy. I let the broom slide onto the floor, hitching up the elastic waist of my maternity trousers. Looking around the kitchen and through the open doorway to the living room, I notice the dust that has settled across the furniture and terrazzo flooring.

I make a mental note of things for Francis to do. There is the daily mopping and dusting. We need eggs, milk and fresh vegetables that he'll have to buy from the local market and not the air-conditioned mall with its shiny, uniform produce because 'import taxes' will inflate even the basics fivefold. The freezer is on its last legs and needs a new stabiliser, thanks to NEPA, the electricity provider that's cut our power supply every day for the past fortnight. We probably need to buy diesel, seeing as we use the generator every night and now that I am expanding into my pregnancy, in the daytime too.

I grimace as I remember my soiled slipper and pick it up by the tips of my fingers. I can't decide whether to leave it for Francis to fix or clean it myself. I step outside into the garden—a concrete expanse with a smattering of shrubs and potted plants lined against the wall—swaying uneasily as I experience the full assault of the sun. I close my eyes and white spots blaze like comets across my eyelids. For a second I almost succumb to a feeling of weightlessness until firm hands grip my shoulders.

'Madam, Madam,' Francis says, his voice full of anxiety. 'Madam, Are you alright?'

I shake my head and step back inside the house.

'Madam, sorry I'm late. The go-slow today was too much.'

I glance at his pinched face, his concern is palpable, although by now I'm sure it's no longer for me but for his job.

'Francis, how many times must I tell you it's not go-slow, it's traffic.'

'Yes Madam, tr-a-ff-i-c,' he says, drawing out the vowels so the word becomes impossibly long and we both laugh.

#

A few days later and I'm sitting across from Buki, my first cousin and oldest friend. We're having lunch at Tanjia, a Moroccan bar and restaurant on the island. It could have been airlifted out of Manhattan. There are plush earth-toned cushions and ottomans, wooden partitions with elaborate latticework, and the odd scimitar glinting malevolently on the walls.

I would have preferred to meet somewhere on the mainland where we live, my mother's comment still ricocheting in my mind. But, as Leke would say, our suburb Ikeja is not the premier league, more like a first division club and the only time Buki ever leaves the island is to catch a flight out of the country.

'Lola darling, you look awful,' she says kissing the air around my cheek.

She looks immaculate as usual. Her caramel skin shimmers, her body poured into a slip of a dress and cinched at the waist.

'Thanks. I'm going to pretend you said I look fabulous.'

We order—a double portion of lamb tagine for me, chickpea salad for Buki—and talk about plans for Papa's birthday. The grandchildren, all sixteen of us, want to do something special for his nintieth. Buki presses me for ideas. 'What do you think he'd like, really appreciate?'

'How should I know? What do you get for a man who has everything?

'Oh come on Lola, you're the favourite grandchild. If you don't know, then what hope is there for the rest of us?

It's a refrain that always makes me uncomfortable. It's true Papa has his favourites and logic says it should be Buki. After all, she's beautiful and smart, with two adorable children. She married well and according to the latest edition of 'City People,' she's a millionaire in hard currency. Yet for all the years she has bristled at this perceived slight, I have wanted to trade places and have wished that Aunty Folake and Uncle Bola were my own parents.

'Really, I'll go with whatever you decide. Just tell me how much I need to contribute.'

I can tell by the set of her lips it's an unsatisfactory answer. I'm about to change the subject but she beats me to it.

'So, your mum called me a few days ago. Said she had a proposition for me.'

I am mortified. 'God, I thought she only ever tried that with me. What did you say?'

'I told her all my money was tied up but that we could talk at Papa's over the weekend. I think the prospect of wheeling and dealing in front of everyone put her off. She's priceless.'

We both laugh but mine is tinged with shame. My mother is the family joke. The youngest of Papa's six children, she got pregnant at seventeen and left me to be brought up by my grandparents while she finished her education in England. Trouble is she liked the high life and spent the next twenty years, flitting from one continent to another, sometimes with me, more often without. Somehow, she never found herself destitute; our family supported her.

Buki beckons to the waitress with the slightest flick of a French manicured hand and orders champagne.

'What's the occasion?' I ask.

'Let's just say I've been relieved of a burden.'

'Cryptic. Well seeing as we're celebrating,' I say, sitting on my hands, doing my best impression of a giddy schoolgirl, 'I had my 20 week scan this morning. Still don't know the sex but everything's going well.'

'That's great, Lola.' She has always been my confidant, the one I turn to for solace but there is something empty in her smile. I don't know what I expected her to say but I'd hoped for something witty or extraordinary, anything that would echo my exhilaration. After a pause she adds, 'You know it's not always what it's cracked up to be.'

'Buki,' I whisper, for I cannot bear the thought that I should be asking her, of all people this question. 'Can't you just be happy for me?'

'I'm sorry Lola. That wasn't a very nice thing to say. Of course I'm happy for you. It's wonderful news.'

She reaches out, squeezes my hand and I will myself to be blithe and carefree.

#

Leke does not believe in handouts—says what's the point in having ambition if he doesn't achieve things for himself. So when we got married, he refused my grandfather's offer of help and paid two years' rent in advance for a house that has seen better days. He comes from a good family, so Papa didn't take offence. I didn't mind either. I liked this new way of thinking, that we didn't have to be perfect and it didn't matter who knew. The downside is that he spends too much time away, pitching for jobs and deals in the capital, but things will have to change when baby comes. In the meantime, he's back for Papa's birthday and I'm in high spirits. There's still no sign of the fabled pregnancy glow but I do the best I can with my make-up, and wear a white maxi-dress, one of the last items in my pre-pregnancy wardrobe that fits. Around eleven, we're in the car and cruising along Third Mainland Bridge on route to the island.

Papa's house in Ikoyi is not immediately visible when you drive through the wrought iron gates and curve along the gravel path. First, you make your way past the flamboyant trees and their scarlet blossoms, past the lush emerald verges that dip and rise to meet hibiscus hedges, the snake plants that coil around clusters of deep violet salvia and golden costus, the red hot cat's tails dripping like tongues across verdant foliage. Finally the house emerges, a luminous white villa with pillars and porticos, the centrepiece within acres of a Gauguin-like setting.

We are among the last to arrive. It's just immediate family but as there are more than fifty of us, it's still an event and judging by the spread and liveried staff, expenses haven't been spared. Leke knows these gatherings always make me a little apprehensive and holds my hand. He says it's all in my head but, though they'd never say it, sometimes I think that as much as they love me, I am a permanent reminder of disgrace, a single blot on the otherwise spotless public record of our family.

Most of them I haven't seen for months and almost immediately my hands are prised away from Leke's and I am passed between aunts and uncles, jostled by shrieking nephews and nieces. Congratulations spill off their tongues like wine and I am drunk from their goodwill. Finally I find my grandparents, seated on the cane chairs in the shade of the verandah, their faces as brindled and creased as the bark of the flamboyants that we drove past, and I marvel at the genetic fortitude that has allowed them to amass one hundred and seventy-five years between them. I kun le,[1] both knees on the ground in supplication for they are of a generation that believe in the old ways of showing respect. Papa lays a hand on my head, the other on the swell of my belly and with a voice wizened with age, says a prayer, invoking the spirits of our ancestors and the heavenly father to protect me. Mama tags 'Amin,[2] Amen' at the end of each sentence. Finally, he pats the empty seat beside him.

'Omo mi, my child,' he says.

The formalities are over. The party gets into swing.

I look around to see if there's anyone I've missed. I wave at Leke who is tussling with some of the kids, practicing for impending fatherhood. Then my mother comes into view with a heaped plate and Mr. Afolabi in tow. This is a new development and I can't figure out whether it's just another ploy by a woman, who at the age of fifty still feels the need to aggravate her father or whether it's a sign of real affection between them. I wander over. I'm surprised by how good she looks, plump and jaunty, and genuinely pleased to see me. She grasps my arm and pulls me toward her.

---

[1] to kneel down, a formal respectful greeting by women to elders
[2] Amen in Yoruba

'Have you heard?'

Some things never change. Next to melodrama there's nothing she loves more than gossip.

'Heard what?'

'About Buki.'

'No I haven't heard anything about Buki.'

'Well,' she says, and if she weren't holding a plate of food, she'd be rubbing her hands together with glee. 'Apparently Buki is pregnant, with twins.'

'You don't mean it?'

'Yes o,' she says, pausing for dramatic effect. 'But she aborted them.'

I laugh, a little too hard, because of course it's a ludicrous suggestion. 'I can't believe that. Why would she? Buki has everything.'

'Exactly! That's what I thought myself but it's true. Aunty Folake told me herself.'

Now I scan the vicinity for my cousin, head darting this way and that, moving as fast as my new waddling gait will allow me, which isn't terribly fast at all. I find her inside the marble hall, hands hovering above canapés as if she were making the most important decision in the world.

'Tell me it's not true, Buki. Tell me you weren't pregnant.'

'Ssshh. What's the matter with you, do you want everybody to hear,' she hisses, pulling me into a quiet corner. 'Anyway who told you?

'So it's true then. You really did have an abortion.'

'Yes.'

'But why?' I ask, incredulous.

'Because I don't want another baby. It's as simple as that. My life is exactly the way I want it.'

'But Buki, twins, how could you, after everything I've been through.'

'Don't look at me like that. This is why I didn't want to tell you, because I knew you'd be hypersensitive.'

She puts an arm on my shoulder and from behind thick and lustrous lashes, gives me a look reserved for those who are too slow to understand the glaringly obvious.

'Look, I'm not going to apologise for doing what's best for me. It's done now and I just want to forget about it.'

I reclaim possession of my shoulder and stare at her perfectly arched eyebrows, her plumped and glossy lips, her brittle pulchritude. Then I shrug and walk away because what else can I do. It's none of my business. I have no right to feel the sting of betrayal.

#

The photographer arrives at three o'clock, lighting a fire beneath us and everyone is full of energy. He carries one of those bulky old fashioned-looking cameras that's actually a digital. There is a commotion because Buki and the photographer give conflicting directions but soon all the branches of the family have their shots taken, first with Mama and Papa and then alone. My mother signals for us to take our turn but I lean into Leke and pretend not to notice. The final group photo and it's a struggle to fit us all into the picture. The photographer sounds hoarse, barking orders, arranging and rearranging our positions and with each ebb and flow of our bodies, my mother gets further and further away until she is on the very fringes; one step away from exclusion. And even though I am front and centre, I can't help but feel removed from them all.

After we finish, my niece Kumbi tugs at my dress and when I bend down to give her a hug I see two red spots on my skirt, deep and red as jewels, bright as the sunset that will soon be looming in the sky overhead. I stay on my knees, grateful that at least the pain is sharp but fleeting.

#

My mother is waiting at home when we arrive hours later; Francis has let her in. The doctors say all is still well with baby, just a mild case of placenta previa but now I have no choice but to slow down. Leke was due to catch the first flight out to Abuja but he's making frantic phone calls, trying to postpone appointments. I can hear my mother and poor Francis bickering in the kitchen.

'But dat is the way *my* Madam likes it,' he keeps saying.

Normally I would intervene. This is a woman who changes househelp as carelessly as she would a pair of shoes. I'm not sure what the fuss is about and at the moment, I don't care.

I half-recline on the sofa, stroking my belly, when she walks in with a self-satisfied look on her face. I must look terrible and am grateful she is able to restrain herself from passing comment. She hands me a brown envelope.

'The money,' she says, very matter of fact. It really has been a day of surprises, and it seems there's more to come.

'Come I want to show you something,' she says, pulling my arm. I snap. 'Mummy, what don't you understand about what I've just said? I'm going to be on bed rest for the next few weeks.'

Maybe she doesn't hear me because she trots out of the room and I shake my head, because there is only fifty thousand in the crumpled envelope. She returns, dragging a baby cot behind her, and with the white sheets, embroidered bumpers and mosquito net billowing from a small flowered canopy, it looks like a misshapen bride. I'm touched but dismayed.

'Mummy, I don't want this. Leke and I deliberately haven't bought any baby stuff because we don't want to jinx anything.'

I can tell by the droop of her shoulders that she's disappointed, maybe even hurt, and I want to say who asked you to buy this for me with my own money.

'Why all this talk of jinx and bad luck?'

I ignore her question and answer one of my own. 'I'm going to ask Francis to sleep here for the next few weeks while Leke is in Abuja.'

'Lola, bami soro,' she says. 'Talk to me.'

But I can't. I can barely stand to look at her, let alone speak. A sickening weariness creeps up my legs and the deafening chorus of generators on the street drills into my skull. Somehow, even though we are indoors, my nostrils are assailed by the acrid smell of diesel fumes and I rise to get a glass of water, quickly, before anyone can stop me. Turning away from the fridge, I come face to face with a cockroach, its tawny armour gleaming beneath our fluorescent lights, its antenna swaying brazenly as it sizes me up. Suddenly the room tilts as if in slow motion, a scream slices through the air and a hand flings a glass at the scampering insect. When I recognise the voice and shaking hands, it's all I can do not to cry, except the tears I've been holding back fall anyway.

Now I am pulled into an embrace and it is not Leke but my mother, rocking me from side to side, stroking my hair and I can smell her sweat and a lingering musky scent and realise I can't remember the last time she held me in her arms and I sob harder, holding her tight.

'I'll stay. I'll stay and look after you,' she says, and I'm so tired that to make another decision will spit my head open. I look at my husband and our eyes meet in mutual understanding—it's up to me.

'Why do you want to do this?' I whisper.

She looks at me, bewildered, as if it's the most ridiculous question in the world.

'Because you're my daughter.'

'What about Mr. Afolabi?'

'I don't see a ring on my finger,' she says with an earthy laugh and for once, it makes me smile.

I don't know if I believe her. I don't know if we'll survive more than a few days cooped up together in this house but it feels good to surrender, to cast battle lines aside. I close my eyes and let her words carry me away.

33. THE FIXER

by Joel Willans

It's Monday afternoon and it's raining. Another grey day in a long line of grey days that seem to have been queuing up for weeks. I'm wondering whether to sneak off to my work den for a quick cup of coffee when, outside the entrance to Victoria Flats, I see a yellow skip piled high with a mishmash of household junk. I run over, have a quick look around and get stuck in. It's not until I've pushed aside some soggy books and a pair of ripped lampshades that I see a lovely, burnished Birchwood dining chair. It's Edwardian with a graceful design, delicately carved legs and workmanship that makes my hairs stand on end. I run my fingers over the varnish and smile.

'You're a real beauty, aren't you,' I whisper, picking it up and placing it on the pavement. Just as I'm thinking how to get it to the den without any of the residents spotting me, I hear footsteps.

'What do you think you're doing, son?'

Vernon. I curse under my breath and face him. His shirtsleeves are rolled up showing off tattoos he's assured me were once rainbow-coloured dragons breathing the words, 'Vernon Lives for Loving'. Now, they're blue-grey smudges on old, white skin.

'Messing around with rubbish again are we, Robbie?' The rolled up cigarette hanging from his mouth jigs around with his words. He nods at the chair. 'You carry on acting like this people are going to start talking. Ain't like you're short of junk is it?'

I kick a stone into the gutter. 'It's only going to be thrown away.'

'I don't care if it'll be shot into orbit. You don't go through other people's stuff in work time. Understand me?'

I bite my lip and feel the blushing coming on. I breathe deep to try and stop it, but the heat feels like a slap on the cheek. I'm reminded of Lola, of the day she called me her passion fruit. Said she liked it when I got so hot. I lost it; started bawling about how she didn't have to suffer through school with it. After her comment, I went to doctors, hypnotists, therapists, acupuncturists, even a herbalist who called herself a white witch, I visited them all. Nothing changed. Nada, zip. My cherry face still holds me to ransom.

'Hello, anyone there? Did you hear me, sonny boy?' I nod and take another deep breath. 'Thank the Lord. Now, Mrs. Albright in number fifty-seven has a blocked sink. If it's not too much trouble, I'd like you to sort it out.'

The skip will probably be picked up at five, which gives me just over an hour to come back for the chair. I jog into the courtyard and make for Rosemary House. It's a six-story block of flats, not a house, but it is greenish like the herb. I once pointed out to Lola how the blue balconies that run parallel to each other look like the vertebrae on a giant's spine. She laughed and told me I had a poet's eye and I should write things like that down. So I did, every single observation in a pocket-sized pad I got from the Co-op. I gave it to her on our first anniversary, along with a dozen red roses and a book on antique restoration. She read the pad slowly from cover to cover, then told me how much she loved me. What I'd give to hear her say that again.

Just as I walk in the hallway, the sun makes an appearance and turns the air into a cauldron of swirling dust motes. I like the sound of that, so I chant, 'a cauldron of swirling dust motes' over and over again as I run up the stairs. Once Lola's back, I'll start a new pad and I'll make that my very first entry. Mrs. Albright's flat is on the top floor. By the time I bang on her door, my chanting has turned to gasping. I wonder if she thinks I'm some heavy breather, because it takes a while before the locks clunk open and a small face with a big bush of bluey-grey hair appears.

'Took your time, Robert,' she says. 'All those stairs, I suppose. Thank those fine fellows at the council. Never listen. Not once. I telephone all the time. Reverse the charges of course. Still keep me stuck up here, with a lift that doesn't work. Do you know how many stairs I have to climb up?'

'One hundred and twenty six.'

'You're sharper than you look, dear. Now let's see if you can use that brain of yours to fix my blessed sink.'

I get to work as fast as I can. The sink is blocked solid and it takes longer than normal for the plunger to do the job, but eventually the drain gurgles and spews stinky black water.

'All done.'

'That was quick. You'll make someone a very good husband one day,' Mrs. Albright says looking me up and down as if measuring me for my wedding suit.

'That's what I thought, but Lola says I'm too intense. She says I come on too strong all the time.'

'Nothing wrong with a bit of fire in the belly, but mind it doesn't burn you out. Take my Frank, bless him, he couldn't even put a bulb in, but such a passionate fool. Every Friday for thirty-six years he got me a present. Even when he got his dickie heart and Dr. Wallis told him to stay in bed, off he'd trot, up and down those damn stairs. Did for him in the end. Found him dead on the fourth floor landing, holding my last present.' She walks over to the mantelpiece and picks up a porcelain basset hound. 'I keep him here in pride of place.'

'I'm getting Lola a chair. She loves chairs. She says they are an amazing marriage of function and beauty. She is searching for the perfect form.'

'A practical present from a practical man. She could do a lot worse. Now, let me get you a tea and a chocolate biccy as a thank you.'

'Sorry, I haven't got time now. I've got a really important job to do before five.'

'If you want to get to my age you should learn to slow down,' she says, giving my hand a little squeeze.

I nod and say goodbye. Once on the landing, I check outside. Vernon's van is still parked beside the skip. I need to kill some time before he leaves, so I amble down the stairs thinking of Mrs. Albright's husband and trying to work out how many Fridays there are in thirty-six years. By the time I get to the ground floor, I reckon there are one thousand, eight hundred and seventy-two, which is a hell of a lot of presents.

Rather than risk going outside, I carry on walking down into the cellar until I reach my den. It smells of mould and varnish. I look at the rows of chairs lined up and try to imagine how much room you'd need for nearly two thousand; probably the whole courtyard. I imagine the look on Vernon's face at such a sight, and sit down in an old cherry wood Windsor sack-back rocker. 'Shame Lola never got to see you.'

After enjoying the silence for a while, I pull a bag from the shelf. I keep Lola's old black bobble hat inside, so I have a little something of her at work.

The day she bought it was so chilly that each time she spoke, her words came out with little puffs of breath. When I told her she looked like my gran, she giggled and smacked me with her handbag. That was three months, two weeks, and four days ago. Not so long, I suppose, but it feels as if time is moving through glue. I bury my face in the hat to breathe her, but it doesn't smell of Lola, it smells of dust. Pulling it low over my face, I put on my battered sheepskin jacket hoping that if Vernon's still there he won't notice it's me.

The sky is watery dark. I count twelve streetlamps standing like guards, their fizzy light making the skip shine. I amble towards it with my head down, listening out for Vernon's voice. Lola's chair has been dumped on top of the pile. I move at a trot and fast as I can, yank it free.

'What on earth are you doing messing in there for?' Mrs. Albright emerges from the courtyard and waddles closer. 'Is that you, Robert? Blimey, I hope this isn't the chair you plan on giving your lady friend.'

'What's wrong with it?'

'You can't use that old thing to woo a lady.'

'I know what Lola likes.'

She tugs my sleeve. 'No woman would want that in her parlour. Why don't you get her something new?'

I feel Mr. Cherry Face arriving and want to tell her to leave me alone and get out of my way. I want to tell her that I know better than anyone what Lola likes, because I love her. End of story. I want to tell her that she should know that. She should know better than to try and stop me. But I don't. I say nothing. I just walk away, hugging the chair. Only when I get to the end of the street, do I look over my shoulder. Mrs. Albright is still there, but now she is nothing more than a shadow in the twilight.

It takes me nearly half an hour to walk home. Every time I hear a car, I think it's Vernon. By the time I arrive, I'm sticky with sweat. It's a real relief to get indoors, even if it does smell of last night's kebab, paint stripper, and unwashed socks. I make my way through the brushes and pots of varnish scattered on the living room floor, and place the chair in the centre of the room.

'I bet her husband would've understood,' I say to myself. 'I bet he'd have done the same.'

This chair is the one. I just know it. I feel so pleased that I hug myself. I know it's only me hugging me, but it still feels good. I carry on, squeezing harder and harder. Then I close my eyes and imagine it's her. That's when the doorbell goes. It's so long since I've heard that sound that I stay frozen for a few seconds. It crosses my mind that it might even be Lola. Maybe my feelings for her have become a living force that's pierced the walls, zigzagged down the street, flashed across town, and kissed her hello. I dream a bit longer, and then tell myself not to be so stupid. Smoothing down my hair, just in case, I run to the door. My hand trembles when I open it.

'Evening, son. Expecting someone else?' Vernon says.

I shrug.

'Knocked off early today, did we?'

I shrug again.

'I just got a call from a concerned resident.'

'Who?'

'Mrs. bloody Albright, that's who. She said you'd been acting a bit funny and wanted to make sure you were all right. Mentioned something about a chair.' He looks over my shoulder. 'What if she had phoned them suits at head office? They'd have taken your overalls and tools back. Then they'd have had the storeroom cleared. Dumped all the stuff you've got stashed down there without a second thought.'

'I don't care. I'm doing it for Lola.'

Vernon shakes his head. 'You'll get banged away if you keep this up. You should forget about her and forget about chairs, I'll tell you that for nothing.

'I can't.'

'Then you're more of a fool than you look.' He crosses his arms. 'This is last time I'm covering for you. You hear?'

I look at my feet and nod.

'Good. Now I'm off home. Don't be late tomorrow.'

Once he has driven away, I close the door and get my toolbox. Sitting cross-legged on the floor, I sandpaper off the scratched varnish on the smooth curve of the chair leg. I carry on until my arm throbs, then I re-varnish the legs in slow careful strokes until the colour seeps back into wood. Once they're all done, I march into the kitchen and pick up the phone. I take a deep breath and dial her number. There are nineteen rings before anyone answers.

'Hello.'

'Lola, it's me. It's Robbie.'

'Why do you keep doing this?'

'What?'

'Don't play dumb with me. You know what.'

I feel the blushes blistering my cheeks. 'I've got a dining chair for you. I think it's Edwardian. Birch with a cherry veneer. It had a couple of scratches, but I've fixed them up for you. You'll love it. I know you will.'

'How many chairs have you got me in the last three months?'

I bite my nail. 'Eleven.'

'And how many times have I come over to see them?'

'I've tried so hard to find one you'd like and you don't even come and look. Please Lola, the least you can do is see it for yourself.'

A click and the phone starts purring.

'Lola?'

I stare at the receiver, willing her voice to come back. But when willing doesn't work, I go back into the living room and sit on chair number twelve. It feels good, solid and comfortable, smooth yet sturdy. I sit there for a long time, eyes closed, thinking. I think I'll keep this chair in the house.

Mind made up, I start calculating how many chairs I'd find Lola in the thirty-six years. Not that I'm going to search that long. Course not. One more, that's all. It's got to be worth a try, hasn't it? Lucky number thirteen might just be the one she can't resist. It might just be Lola's chair.

34. SOFÍA THE BEAUTIFUL

by Mary Farquharson

'There was a break in protocol today when the President of the United States interrupted an outdoor press conference to introduce journalists to a White House mascot. As a bald eagle flew over their heads, the President said, "There goes Alberta, symbol of the freedom and excellence of the American nation." As he spoke, his pet eagle flew south over ...'

Ramón switched off the TV. He'd been looking for news about the border but there were only English language programmes at this time of the afternoon so he picked up his beer and walked over to the window. The earth around his house was scorched dry but in a few weeks, with the first rains, grass would explode through the cracks and the land would turn electric green. How could anyone leave this place for long? Everything was known but nothing was predictable. Even the twin volcanoes in the distance were temperamental, a pair of superstars that appeared and then disappeared behind their curtains of cloud.

Ramón picked up a photo from the table by the window, a portrait of his daughter taken on the day she graduated from high school. She could have gone to university, could have studied medicine or become a teacher. But, instead, Sofía had followed her boyfriend to California, as if she was just another 'wet-back' or whatever she'd be called over there. Ramón had tried to discourage her, but she wouldn't listen.

Who listens? Nobody does. Not even him. His friends and family had told him to forget about his daughter but it wasn't that simple. They failed to distract him with beer and parties and the bass notes that tumble from the tuba. He buried himself inside his own head and only left the house to tend to his bees because they were his livelihood and, at this moment, his passion.

He needed to paint the new hives and then take them over to a sheltered ridge on the foothills of Popocatepetl, where his bees could live as far away as possible from thieves and insecticides. Outside on his patio, he found a paintbrush amongst the jumble of glass jars and half-read National Geographic magazines, and began to work.

After a couple of days, when the hives were finished, he stacked them in his pick-up and drove out towards Popocatepetl at first light. The volcano was crowned in swirls of its own white smoke. As he approached the lower slopes, Ramón parked the truck, put on his protective clothing, and unpacked the new hives. He worked carefully with the colonies of bees, checking that the existing hives had a healthy queen in place and there was no sign of infection inside the tiny hexagonal cells. In search of the mated queen, Ramón listened out for the little tooting noise that would identify her as she flew with her colony. It reminded him of one those small plastic trumpets Sofía had brought back from parties when she was little. Where was his daughter? Was that idiot boyfriend treating her well enough? Why didn't she call?

It was five in the afternoon, the softest hour of the day, when Ramón finished with the hives and turned back towards his truck. He untied the helmet and stripped off his over-suit. Although tired, he was satisfied with his day's work. The bees had danced around the hives, oblivious to his thoughts about the migra[1] and the dangers for a girl on the other side of the border.

Before he opened his truck, Ramón looked back at the volcano. In the distance, he saw a bird gliding in the evening sky. This wasn't a buzzard or a hawk; it was an enormous, freewheeling animal, purposeful and grand. Ramón leant against the truck to watch the spectacle: two massive wings pounded the air, sweeping up and thrusting forward, riding between the hills on a current of air.

As the bird flew closer, Ramón could make out the white breast feathers and tail, the baggy black pants and a smooth, perfectly coiffed white head. Unbelievable. An American eagle never came this far south. He might be the first person in the village to have seen one with his own eyes.

There was something so knowing, so superior about this bird that swept right past him, closer than he would have imagined. It rose on a gust of air and beat its outstretched wings to gain more height, then turned, planed, dived and rolled, calculating distances, measuring him carefully, enjoying the game. Ramón was captivated. They were alone and they were courting.

---

[1] The US immigration officers who patrol the border

He found himself walking frantically across the ridge, past the hives, trying to keep up with the massive bird. With its white tail-feathers stretched out like an open fan and its head perfectly aligned with the wings, the eagle flew past him and out of sight, into the approaching night.

Ramón began to run, like a man possessed. Then, for a moment, he stopped and told himself, let it go, let it go, but he found he was still running behind the bird when it turned on a gust and heaved downwards, almost within his reach. He could feel the air dispersed by the enormous wings, and he stretched out his arms, but the bird had already soared upwards, revelling in the open sky.

With his leather working gloves in one hand, Ramón climbed over a pile of loose boulders and squinted into the setting sun. He saw nothing so he walked in the opposite direction and then looked back across the ridge. The bird was gone. Feeling abandoned, he'd begun to walk back towards the truck when he saw something dark and solid in the last light. It was the eagle crouching on a rock and feasting on the remains of a young goat. He took a few more steps, amazed that the pleasure of fresh raw meat was more compelling than the fear of an approaching stranger.

He was now a metre or so from the bird and he watched as it held the corpse in its powerful talons and pulled off strips of flesh that hung briefly from its polished beak and then disappeared. Although it was picking at its prey, with its head bowed down, Ramón knew it was also watching him. As he put on his gloves and moved closer, the eagle dug its claws deeper into the meat and then raised its head. When Ramón stopped moving, the bird returned to its feast. It must be a female, he judged, admiring her heavy wings and ample white chest.

Why she didn't fly away from him was a mystery. He stretched out a cautious hand and held it still, a few inches away from her head. The bird raised herself onto the points of her hard and wrinkled claws and flapped her wings very slightly. 'Yes, you are beautiful,' he said. Ramón moved his right hand closer and then, very gently covered her head with his left hand; this angered her and she flapped her wings but when her eyes were free, she settled, permitting him to hold her very gently against his chest, the cage in which his astonished heart was beating like a drum.

He took the bird past the hives, across the dry stubble and towards the pick-up with the equipment piled in the open back. The eagle was calm and that was what mattered most. In the twilight, with a splash of red and the darkened hills behind, he chose to leave his truck and walk along the empty road. Slightly hunched, he embraced the bird as if it was a sleeping child.

An hour later, with the bird held firmly against his chest, Ramón reached the outskirts of the village. He passed the house where the brass band was rehearsing and saw his cousin, Pedro, standing under a street lamp, smoking a cigarette and laughing with the clarinet player. They shouted to him but Ramón walked on quickly, without stopping to explain. He turned off the road and walked past the zapote trees to an opening where his house stood alone, on the northern edge of village.

The patio was a jumble of magazines, empty bottles, and carpentry tools. Moving his chessboard from the table, he tied a long rope to the bird's leg. He watched her shuffle in the middle of the table, surveying her new surroundings like a disapproving guest. She was a masterpiece; the black rings in the amber eyes caught him and engaged him until he had to look away. She was quiet but not humbled; he had taken her, but she wasn't his.

He heard someone approaching, and when he turned his head, saw that it was his cousin. Ramón didn't say anything to him. Pedro drew up a chair and they watched the bird in silence. Then, as Pedro's hand moved towards the eagle, Ramón said, 'Don't touch her!' under his breath.

'But look at this,' Pedro said, pointing at a small ring on her skinny leg, just above the claw. On the ring was a tag with some sort of electronic chip and a US phone number stamped into the plastic.

'Hey, primo,[2] I don't believe this. Look at her, will you. She's not a wild eagle; she's almost tame. Someone with a lot of money will be wanting her back. Puta madre,[3] I think we've won the Lottery.'

'Forget it,' Ramón said quietly. 'This bird stays here.' To silence Pedro's protest, Ramón asked him to go and fetch his truck. 'I left it by the new hives. Take one of the guys from the band; here's the key.'

'But, Ramón ...'

'Look, Pedro, I know you need money right now, but this isn't some sort of a business. I never dreamed of having an eagle, here, in my house. It's a miracle, something I will tell to my grandchildren.'

---

[2] cousin
[3] whore mother

'But don't you want to share ...?'

'Yes, okay, but not tonight. Tomorrow. We'll have a party. You can tell the band. I'll buy the beer.'

Ramón was happy to be left alone with the bird. He found some salted beef in the kitchen and served himself a taco with cream and chili sauce, and then handed strips of the dark meat to the eagle, who took them willingly. They ate together, watching each other. With her wings down, she reminded him of an oversized priest with large, effeminate hips and the delicate movements of a thief.

The next night, when Ramón heard the band coming down the path, he felt a rush of excitement. He looked across at the eagle who was sitting calmly on top of the coil of rope. 'This party's for you,' he said.

Someone put a carton of beer on the ground and Ramón switched on a CD player. The small patio became a place of laughter, drinking and music, with the bird stalking back and forth across the table, upset by the noise and pulling slightly at her rope. Nobody touched her; they approached quietly, sweating and panting, and they crouched down on one side of the table to marvel at her, speaking in hushed voices, then moving away to laugh and dance again.

One of the trumpeters, who'd studied in a Seminary, led a mock baptism service.

'What shall we call her?'

Ramón's reply came quickly. 'Sofía, like my daughter,' he said. 'Sofía the beautiful,' and he stroked the bird's head very gently.

When he looked up, he noticed that Pedro—on the edge of the crowd—was talking to the tuba player and pointing nervously at the bird. The two men came to the table. 'Ramón,' the tuba-player said, 'this is serious. You don't know what you've got there, that animal belongs to the President of the United States. No, listen, it's true, I swear it. Pedro called the number on the tag ...'

'*What?*'

'Yes, a few hours ago, but he was too scared to tell you. We've got to go; they're coming to get her.'

'Pedro, I told you ...'

'It's not Pedro's fault. He's doing you a favour. Look, she's already got a name. She's not Sofía, she's called Alberta and she comes from the White House. They want her back. You know what that means?'

'Vale madres,'[4] Ramón shouted at his friend. The dancing stopped and the musicians gathered around the table. No one spoke.

'What you staring at?' Ramón yelled at one of the clarinet players.

'Come on, let's go,' a trumpeter said and several musicians picked up their instruments.

'We can't leave you here,' the tuba player said, 'look at the state of you.' Ramón muttered to himself. 'Listen, Ramón, you don't have to be so angry all the time. I know it hurts that your daughter's gone. We all understand that. But she can look after herself. Stop worrying. You're taking it too badly. Come on. We're your friends.'

'You go. I'm staying with the bird. Why should I hand her over? To a gringo? No way, not even if he is the President.'

Pedro looked worried. 'Primo, don't go crazy on me, not now.'

As Pedro spoke, Ramón noticed that a couple of the other musicians were pulling the tuba player to one side. Several others joined the conversation. He heard a murmur of approval and then the voice of the tuba player: 'To hell. We'll stay here with you Ramón; we'll show them who we are, okay?'

Someone patted Ramón on the back and handed him a beer. The party returned to life. The trumpeter told a story about his wife and daughter who'd come home safely from California. Someone went for another carton of beer. There was no need to talk any more about Sofía; they were in this together and the party kicked night into day. It was dawn when a jeep came slowly down the path, towards the house.

Two American agents climbed out of the car and a Mexican official followed close behind. They pushed through the gate onto the patio—a pair of men in clean white shirts and ties like the Mormons who'd been run from the village the year before—and then the older one shouted out, 'We've come for the President's bird.' Twenty men stared back at him and the Mexican official translated into the angry silence.

When the agents saw the bird tied to the table, the guest of honour in a drunken circle, one of them gasped and moved towards it, but his companion held him back. The Mexican official identified Ramón and told him to follow them into the house so they could speak in private.

---

[4] Slang equivalent of 'who the hell cares'

After a few minutes, Ramón returned to the party. He sat down near the bird and stared blankly at his bottle of beer. Pedro put an arm round his shoulder: 'Sorry, cousin, I did it 'cos I thought it was right.'

Ramón laughed softly. 'Sure,' he said, under his breath. He gestured to the US agents standing behind him. 'Get them out of my house. Pedro, take them to the hostel, will you?' The party was over; the musicians walked unsteadily towards the gate and Ramón was left alone with the bird.

'Come on, cousin,' Pedro said when he'd returned from the small hotel. 'It's not the end of the world. Look at it another way. Everybody believes that an eagle is beautiful, so you fall in love with her, as if she was a movie star or that English princess who died in a car crash. But an eagle is just a carrion-eating bird that doesn't fly as well as the buzzards that we see every time we go to the municipal dump. If she was a buzzard, you wouldn't be so sad to lose her, would you?'

When the foreigners returned a few hours later, the bird was already enclosed in a large wooden crate and they could hear her stomping angrily inside the makeshift cage. The senior agent checked the signal from the electronic sensor and his colleague peered through the small holes in the side of the box.

'All I can see is feathers,' he said, 'want me to open up?'

'No time. Let's get out of here.'

Ramón stood by the crate with his arms folded. He didn't offer to help when the agents lifted it into the jeep and closed the doors.

He watched until the car had disappeared and then went back into his house. He would clear up the mess from the party later on. He lay down on his bed with a magazine and went to sleep. In the afternoon, he took a drive and then returned home and switched on the evening news, flicking from one channel to the next until he saw images of the crate and the two officials who'd been in his house that morning. He watched the shuffling and heard angry shouting. The TV camera was unsteady; someone was trying to block its vision. He heard the reporter's agitated voice: 'Latest reports from Washington reveal that attempts to rescue Alberta, the President's pet eagle, have failed. FBI agents sent to Mexico to bring Alberta home, were fooled by kidnappers who attached the electronic sensor from the presidential mascot to the leg of a common vulture and then packed it up in a crate and sent it to the White House.'

Ramón was satisfied and, walking outside, looked up into the evening sky. In the distance, flying towards the shadow of the volcano, was a large bird. It circled once and then disappeared from sight. 'Adiós Sofía,' he said under his breath. He picked up a few of the empty bottles and walked back into his house.

AUTHORS' BIOGRAPHIES

JOHN BOLLAND—The Doe

John Bolland writes novels, short fiction, and occasional poetry. He graduated with distinction from Glasgow University's MLitt. Creative Writing course in 2005. He has supported his family and his writing by working in the offshore oil & gas industry in the UK and overseas. He has completed three full-length novels to date—*A Murder of Crows* (2003), *The Dark Numbers* (2006) and *Bass* (2008). He is currently working on two parallel novel-length projects *More Tales from the Vampire Coast*—a novel in English set in Paisley in the South West of Scotland between 1967 and the present—and *Line of Sight*—a novel in Scots set on the North East coast of Scotland in the near future.

In 2007, his short story, *A Good Place to Get,* was runner-up in the V.S. Pritchett Memorial Prize for short fiction, and in 2008, he won third prize in the annual Fish Short Story Competition with his story *Scottische.* John is also an enthusiastic painter and saxophonist and is a director of Top Left Corner, a creative social enterprise that brings people together in Assynt in the North West of Scotland to create written and other artworks. John continues to work in change management and consultancy roles in the global energy industry on a part-time basis.

The Doe has not been published before.

INDIRA CHANDRASEKHAR—Rock Fall and Adoration

When Indira visited London in the 1990s she was confused by the accents, not only because the cadence was different from the ones she was used to in India, where she grew up, the US, where she had worked as a scientific researcher after her Ph.D., and Switzerland where she then lived and was learning to speak German and French. It was because, she later recognised, she was listening to familiar sounds, hearing English that was spoken around her as a toddler before her parents moved back to India. When she herself returned to India, after seventeen years away, Indira switched from research in Biophysics to writing fiction. She is the founder editor of Out of Print (www. outofprintmagazine.co.in), a platform for short fiction from the S. Asian subcontinent and occasionally says something on her blog (www.indi-cs-blog. blogspot.com) where her published work and writing achievements are listed.

Neither *Rock Fall* nor *Adoration* has been published before.

ANDY CHARMAN—The World's End

Andy was born in Dorset, England, where he lived until 1989. His career as a business analyst has taken him into many different cultures and countries. He worked in Amsterdam in Holland for several years and now divides his time between homes in Logroño, Spain, and Guildford in England. He is an executive coach and a Neuro-Linguistic Programming practitioner and, as an independent consultant, has business interests in a financial software company, a design consultancy, and a technical writing agency. His stories have been published in The Battered Suitcase and Every Day Fiction and have been shortlisted or longlisted in competitions by Ballista, Cadenza, and the Global Short Story. He is writing a thriller novel based in Poole in Dorset.

His story, *The World's End*, has not been published previously but was longlisted in Cadenza Magazine Short Story Competition 2008.

TARA CONKLIN—Signs of Our Redemption

Tara, an American by birth but an expat at heart, currently lives in Seattle, WA (USA) where she writes and looks after her two young children. A lawyer by training, Tara previously worked for a corporate law firm in New York and London. She's also been an events planner in Moscow, a casino dealer in Costa Rica, and an English teacher in Madrid. Having just finished her first novel, she is now moving commas around as she looks for a literary agent. Tara's short stories have been shortlisted for the 2010 Bridport Prize and the 2010 Bristol Short Story Prize.

Signs of Our Redemption was previously published in the Bristol Short Story Prize Anthology Volume 3 (2010).

EMMANUELLA DEKONOR—Rabbit Cake

Emmanuella is a Ghanaian-Londoner who has been writing poems since she was six years old. In 1992, she was shortlisted in a Virago poetry competition for her poem *My Sister*. More recently, her short story, *The Small House on Phuduhudo Road*, was published in the Mechanics' Institute Review 7. Emmanuella writes a blog called Kenkey and Fish, (www.kenkeyandfish. blogspot.com), and was recently awarded an M.A. in Creative Writing at Birkbeck that she passed with merit.

Rabbit Cake has not been published before.

MARY FARQUHARSON—Sofía the Beautiful

Mary is an English writer who has lived in Mexico since 1987. Before moving to Mexico, she worked as a journalist in Venezuela and then returned to London to work in a small agency bringing bands from Africa, Latin America, and South Asia to British stages. She helped set up the record company that would later produce 'Buena Vista Social Club.' In Mexico, she worked for several years as a freelance journalist and TV researcher. In 1991, she met her husband, Mexican musicologist Eduardo Llerenas and they set up a label called Discos Corasón. In 2006, Mary joined a writing group and has been writing short stories since then. She still produces records of traditional music and organises the occasional concert. She is currently working on a short story collection, written in both Spanish and English.

An earlier version of Mary's story, *Sofía the Beautiful*, entitled *The Eagle*, was longlisted for the Bristol Short Story Prize in 2010.

VANESSA GEBBIE—Breakdown

Vanessa's family is from the Welsh valleys, and she has now lived in southern England for far too long. She is author of two collections of short stories: *Words from a Glass Bubble* and *Storm Warning* (Salt Modern Fiction 2008 and 2010). She is also contributing editor of *Short Circuit: A Guide to the Art of the Short Story* (Salt 2009). She teaches writing, edits a specialist magazine called Tom's Voice, (www.tomsvoicemagazine.com), and writes poetry. Her first novel, *The Coward's Tale*, completed thanks to an Arts' Council Grant for the Arts funded by the Heritage Lottery Fund, will be published in 2011 by Bloomsbury. Her website is www.vanessagebbie.com.

Breakdown was first published in Foto8—the photojournalism magazine.

SARAH HILARY—The Wedding Fair and LoveFM

Sarah was the winner of the Sense Creative Writing Award 2010 for her story, *A Shanty for Sawdust and Cotton* and the Fish Criminally Short Histories

Prize 2008 for her story, *Fall River, August 1892*. A column about the wartime experiences of her mother, who was a child internee of the Japanese, was published in Foto8 Magazine and subsequently in the Bristol Review of Books. Her short fiction can be found in Smokelong Quarterly, The Fish Anthology 2008, The Best of Every Day Fiction I and II, and in the Crime Writers' Association anthology, *MO: Crimes of Practice*. She was nominated for a Pushcart Prize in 2009 for her story, *Flood Plain*. In 2010, she was shortlisted and Highly Commended in the Seán Ó Faoláin contest. She is currently working on a crime novel.

Her story, *The Wedding Fair*, has not been published previously. *LoveFM* was published online in Zygote in my Coffee.

LIESL JOBSON—Boston Brown Bread and Soda Lakes

South African writer and photographer, Liesl Jobson, is the author of *100 Papers*, a collection of prose poems and flash fiction, and *View from an Escalator*, a volume of poetry. She won the 2006 Ernst van Heerden Award for Creative Writing for her collection, *100 Papers*, was shortlisted in 2010 for the Sean O'Faolain Short Story Competition for *On the Night South Africa is Effectively Eliminated from the World Cup*, the Thomas Pringle Short Story Award for *Help*, and the PEN/Studzinski Short Story Competition for *It Isn't Pretty*. She edits Poetry International South Africa, and is a senior correspondent for Books LIVE.

Boston Brown Bread was published in *Diner*, Volume 6, 2006. *Soda Lakes* has not been published previously and is included in Liesl's short story collection, *The Edge of the Pot*, forthcoming from Jacana in 2012.

OONAH JOSLIN—Missy's Summer

Oonah was born in Ballymena, Northern Ireland. She took a degree in French and Education. Her teaching career spanned twenty-eight years in Wales and north-east England, mostly in Special Needs. Early retirement has given her the opportunity to pursue her writing and lifelong love of poetry. Since joining Writewords in 2006, she has won three consecutive micro-horror prizes, 2007–2009, and was honouree in the Binnacle Ultra Shorts Competition 2009 for her poem, *First Love*. Her Novella, *A Genie in a Jam*, was serialised in Bewildering Stories in 2010. Oonah was a judge in the first poetry competition held by The Shine Journal and in the 2010 Micro-horror Hallowe'en Competition. She has been editor of Every Day

Poets, (www.everydaypoets.com), for two years since its inception. She has also contributed articles to Flash Chronicles. A full list of her online work can be accessed in *The Vaults* at www.oovj.wordpress.com 'Parallel Oonahverse'. She also blogs at Oonahverse www.oonahs.blogspot.com.

Missy's Summer was originally published in Every Day Fiction in 2008.

TRILBY KENT—Fallout and Stealing Their Churches behind Them
Trilby's first novel for children, *Medina Hill*, was published by Tundra Books in Canada and the U.S. in October 2009. A second, *Stones for My Father*, will appear in 2011. Her first novel for adults, *Smoke Portrait*, will be published in the U.K. by Alma Books in 2011. Trilby has lived in Toronto, Boston, Miami, Brussels, and London. Her mother is South African and Trilby has explored the role played by the Dutch in Africa in both her writing for children and adults. A graduate of Oxford University and the LSE, she has worked as a rare books specialist at a leading auction house and as a freelance journalist contributing investigative, arts and feature writing to the Canadian national press and publications in America and Europe. She has contributed essays and interviews to such literary journals as *The London Magazine* and *Slightly Foxed*. In July 2010, she was shortlisted for the Guardian's International Development Journalism Competition. Her short fiction has appeared in journals such as *Litro (A Fine Woman)*. *Her short story, The Dancing Telemetrist,* was shortlisted for the 2009 Fish International Short Story Prize.

Fallout was published in The African American Review, Volume 4, and *Stealing Their Churches behind Them* first appeared in the Spring 2008 issue of Mslexia, and was reprinted for Broadsheet Stories in September 2009.

JULI KLASS—Manic
Juli grew up in South Africa and now lives in Cambridge. She's been a career woman, a stay at home mother and an entrepreneur. Through all of those phases she has written; her main interest is in the people who fall outside the workings of everyday society, those displaced and misplaced identities. She uses poetry and short fiction as vehicles for expression and is working on a novel set in apartheid South Africa.

Manic has not been published before.

SARAH LEIPCIGER—Passport and Some Game

Sarah is a Canadian living in London. She has been the Writer in Residence at a young offenders' prison since 2003 and is currently writing a novel. She has written several short stories that have appeared in Canadian literary journals including Prairie Fire, subTerrain Magazine and THIS Magazine. One of her stories, *In Kampuchea*, was shortlisted in the Fish Short Story Prize 2009/10.

Passport was first published in Room Magazine Vol. 30.3, 2007. *Some Game* was longlisted in the Fish Short Story Prize 2009/10 and shortlisted in the Bridport Prize 2010, but has not been published before.

CLAYTON LISTER—The Undercurrent

Clayton is a Londoner whose sole remaining connection with the city is Arsenal Football Club. He has recently moved from Oxfordshire to Northumberland, and lives with his partner and daughter. Most of his working life has been in social care, supporting people with learning disabilities. He has completed an MA in Creative Writing at the University of East Anglia and is currently trying to interest publishers in a collection of short stories—of which *The Undercurrent* is one—and his novel, *Tom Thumb's Chunky Blues*. The latter is about a rather ill-planned adventure that two men with learning disabilities go on from their homes in the Home Counties to Newcastle.

The Undercurrent was highly commended in the HISSAC 2008 short story competition and published in Scribble No. 46.

REBECCA LLOYD—The River and Raptor

Rebecca is a novelist and short story writer. Her short stories have been published in Canada, USA, New Zealand, and the UK. Her adult novel, *Under the Exquisite Gaze*, was shortlisted in the Dundee International Book Prize 2010. She was a semi-finalist in the Hudson Prize 2010 for her short story collection *Don't Drink the Water*. Her first children's novel, *Halfling*, was published by Walker Books in January 2011. She teaches creative writing on Writewords and hosts the short story group.

The River won the Bristol Short Story Prize 2008 and was published in the anthology that followed. *Raptor* has not been published previously.

KATIE MAYES—There's Nothing I can Do

Katie Mayes is a new writer based in Brighton, England. After working in accounting for over ten years, she decided on a career change. In 2008, she enrolled on an 'Introduction to Writing Fiction' course at her local Adult Education centre. She is now halfway through a degree in English and Creative Writing at the University of Chichester. She is currently fine-tuning three short stories for which she hopes to find a publisher this year. She blogs at www. katie-mayes.blogspot.com.

There is Nothing I can Do is her first published short story.

SHOLA OLOWU-ASANTE—Big Sister and City People

Shola was born in Nigeria but lives in Edinburgh with her husband and two children. She is a freelance broadcast journalist but is hoping to reinvent herself as a writer of fiction. In 2010, her story, *Dinner for Three*, won the Anietie Isong Special Prize for the best Nigerian story in the Commonwealth Short Story Competition. This story was broadcast on Radio Netherlands Worldwide in December 2010. Her flash fiction story, *Branded*, was published in The Linnet's Wings in Autumn 2010, and her short story, *The Bedroom Window*, was published in The African Writer in August 2010.

Big Sister and *City People* have not been published before.

TOM REMER WILLIAMS—You're Dead

Tom was born in Swindon, in the UK. He grew up in Kansas and once worked as a primary school teacher in Belize. He studied Philosophy at UCL, and spent five years working in literary agencies in London. He now lives in Amsterdam with his wife, Otto, and works as an editor and copywriter. He recently co-wrote the memoirs of a Dutch polar explorer. Tom has given readings at The Poetry Café and Foyles Book Shop in London, and has been published in Tales of the Decongested and online at The Pygmy Giant.

You're Dead was originally published in Pen Pusher 7, and was also recorded and broadcast by BBC Radio 4 as part of their 'Ones to Watch' series.

CAROLINE ROBINSON—Matilda and the Missing

Caroline lives in a caravan on a croft in the Scottish Highlands whilst building her home with her partner. She has been published twice in Binnacle, the Anthology of Maine University. She was winner in the micro-horror Halloween Competition October 2009 for her story *Samhain*, and shortlisted for her story *Boho's Hobby* in the Fish Criminally Short Short Histories Award 2007. She can be found at www.wildwritingfromtheedge.blogspot.com.

Matilda and the Missing has not been published before.

LISA MARIE TRUMP—Places to Go and People to Meet

Lisa Marie Trump is an English born writer who has lived all over the UK from Shetland to Cornwall and most places in between. Her arts career has been predominantly in the theatre industry—having worked for sixteen years as a costume designer—and having written plays and topical comedy sketches, as well as poetry, short stories and journalistic articles Like her designing, her writing reflects her love for the theatrical, and often juxtaposes humour and darkness through complex exploration of character. Literary highlights include *Cedar of Lebanon* (sonnet) written for HRH Prince Charles in a poetry compilation gift celebrating his sixty-fifth birthday (2009), *Still Life with Mango*, finalist at Lost Theatre's one act play competition, London (2005), *The Treason Show* at The Kommedia, Brighton (2000–2004), *Art Against War* and *Bodyworlds* (articles) published in Human Journey magazine (2003), *Frankenstein*, a play produced by Dream Productions Theatre Company (2001), and *Telling Tales Too* (co-writer, touring children's show) produced by Dream Productions Theatre Company (2000).

Places to Go and People to Meet was originally published in Chimera Magazine and performed at the Poetry Cafe in Soho, London.

STEPHEN TYSON—White Horses and Hollows

Stephen lives and works in Cumbria as a bookseller. He was also born in the county of Cumbria, though the small town he grew up in and still lives in was at that time in Lancashire. He has just completed a two-year creative writing course with the Open University where he gained a distinction. His story, *A New Life*, was published in Thirteen Magazine, vol.1 Issue 7. *All the Things we Said* was published in The Gentle Reader, Issue 33, 2005. Two of his stories, *Other Lives* and *Old Sloop* were published in The Quarterly Ephemera, vol. 1, Number 2.

White Horses and *Hollows* have not been published before.

JENNIFER WALMSLEY—Mother's not Home

Jennifer was born and brought up in Wales. She is married with three children and two grandchildren. She attended creative writing classes at the University of Glamorgan and started writing at the age of forty. Her stories have been published in My Weekly and the Welsh literary magazine, Cambrensis. She has had flash fiction published in Micro Horror, Bewildering Stories, Pygmy Giant, The Shine Journal, Static Movement Backhand Stories, and Long short stories. She has recently started writing poetry and has had a Haiku poem in Every Day Poets, as well as poems in Shine and Pygmy Giant.

Jennifer's story, *Mother's Not Home*, was first published in Bewildering Stories in 2008.

DEE WEAVER—Hunter's Quarry

Dee is Northumbrian but now living in Yorkshire, which is about as far south as she wants to be. Now retired, her eclectic career path has spanned animal nursing, the Civil Service, interior design. For the last twenty years, she has been a member of an ethical wholefood distribution company. Her current passions, apart from reading and writing, are English history, rock music, Formula 1, traditional needlecrafts, Paganism, and the occult. In the summer of 2001, she started learning the craft of novel writing. Drawing on her varied experiences, the result is *The Winter House*, a paranormal romance set in North West England. She has written five novels, none of which have as yet been published, although her novel, *Driving Force*, came second in the National Association of Writers' Groups Competition 2003, a national competition for new novelists.

Her story, *Hunter's Quarry*, is one of a series of short stories, three of which have won or been placed in regional competitions.

JOEL WILLIANS—All for just Fifty Baht and The Fixer

Since leaving the English county of Suffolk, Joel has lived in London, Vancouver, Helsinki and an Andean village in the Peruvian departmento of Apurímac. Currently, he runs his own communications agency and lives in a converted hospital in the Finnish countryside. His stories have been broadcast on BBC radio and published in nearly twenty anthologies. His work has also appeared in a wide variety of British magazines, including Pen Pusher, Brand, Southword, Riptide, and Route. In the last couple of years, he's achieved recognition in many competitions including the Bristol Prize and Flatmancrooked Prize for Excellent Writing. In 2008, he was nominated for a Pushcart Prize and won the Yeovil Prize and Global Short Story Award. In 2010, his short story collection, *Buy ma biscuits or kiss ma fish*, was shortlisted for the Scott Prize for Short Fiction. He is currently seeking representation for his first novel.

All for just Fifty Baht was first published in issue 14 of Southword. *The Fixer* was first published in the Momaya Annual Review 2008.

FEHMIDA ZAKEER—Shuttered Landscape

Fehmida lives in the southern city of Chennai in India where she works sometimes as a freelance journalist and other times as an Instructional Designer. Her articles have been published in various Indian and International publications including Azizah, Herbs for Health, Good Housekeeping, Better Homes and Garden, Prevention, and Child. Fehmida's stories and poems have been published in various online journals. *Basic Instincts* was published in Out of Print, (2010), *Repossession* was published in The Linnet's Wings, (2009), and *Candlelight Beginnings* was published in The Shine Journal, (2009). Her work has also appeared in Bewildering Stories, Ink Sweat and Tears, Muse India and Everyday Poets. Her story, *Auspicious Numbers*, had an honourable mention in the Binnacle competition 2010. Her story *Twilight Sojourn* was included in the Asian Writer anthology Happy Birthday to Me (2010).

Shuttered Landscape was shortlisted in the Open Spaces (India) 2010 competition and appears on the Open Spaces website.

www.ingramcontent.com/pod-product-compliance
Lightning Source LLC
Jackson TN
JSHW020019141224
75386JS00025B/599